A KINGDOM KEEPERS NOVEL

THE RETURN

BOOK TWO

LEGACY OF SECRETS

ALSO BY RIDLEY PEARSON

🐾

WITH DAVE BARRY

For a complete listing of Ridley's published books
visit www.ridleypearson.com

A KINGDOM KEEPERS NOVEL

THE RETURN

BOOK TWO

LEGACY OF SECRETS

RIDLEY PEARSON

DISNEP · HYPERION

Los Angeles   New York

First Hardcover Edition, March 2016
First Paperback Edition, March 2017
10 9 8 7 6 5 4 3 2
FAC-026988-18005
Printed in the United States of America

This book is set in 11.25 point Caslon
Designed by Joann Hill

Library of Congress Control Number for Hardcover Edition: 2015038743

ISBN 978-1-4847-3414-8

Visit www.DisneyBooks.com
www.kingdomkeepers.com
www.ridleypearson.com
www.kingdomkeepersinsider.com

SUSTAINABLE FORESTRY INITIATIVE   Certified Sourcing
www.sfiprogram.org
SFI-00993

THIS LABEL APPLIES TO TEXT STOCK

DEDICATION

To Becky Cline, Director, Disney Archive;
Kevin Kern, Disney Archivist;
and to all those who keep the past so alive
for the rest of us.

ACKNOWLEDGMENTS

Special thanks to: Amy Berkower, Dan Conaway, Jessica Kim, Los Angeles Public Library, Joanna Fabicon, Wendy Lefkon, Jeanne Mosure, Brooke Muschott, Chris Ostrander, Nick Perkins, Tim Retzlaff, Lisa Rutherford, Matthew Snyder, Laurel and David Walters, Jennifer Wood, Nancy Zastrow, and Mary Ann Zissimos.

TABLE OF CONTENTS

A KINGDOM KEEPERS NOVEL

THE RETURN

BOOK TWO

LEGACY OF SECRETS

1

OPENING THE DOOR

FINN WHITMAN HELD THE DOOR for Charlene. A gymnast and high school captain of three sports, Charlene now had her telltale sun-streaked blond hair in tight curls, her eyelashes clumped with mascara, her full figure crammed into an aqua-blue-and-white summer dress with a crinoline skirt, white bobby socks, and black flats. Her girl-next-door face was caked in makeup.

Girls in high school had hated Charlene for her looks. But those who actually spoke to her, who took the time to get to know her, liked her. What would those same kids think now? she wondered. High school was three months in her past; the world beyond the door was a full sixty years in the past—1955. She laced her transparent fingers in front of her like a bridesmaid to keep her hands from shaking.

Her four friends about to follow her through this same door were time travelers—just like her. They'd been part of her life since seventh grade. That was when she'd auditioned and been picked to be one of the human models for computer-generated holograms that would serve as personal guides through Disney World theme parks.

Finn addressed the remaining three teens. "We don't know what form the Overtakers will take, or if they even exist in 1955, so stay alert."

"And remember," said Philby, the redheaded boy at the back of the line, "our holograms aren't even holograms. They're two-dimensional, low-res projections that will barely fool anyone. So keep moving and don't stop to have conversations. The more movement, the less we appear two-dimensional. The brain will trick the eye—or maybe it's the opposite, but you get the point. No stopping. This is dangerous ground, people."

The five Kingdom Keepers had little opportunity to contemplate the strange set of circumstances that had delivered them to this door. Their collective focus was instead on several things, all at once. 1) They were currently in 1955, a time they knew little about; 2) their mission was to locate and steal a fountain pen owned by Walt Disney; 3) the creative legend, Disney himself, was alive on July 17, 1955, and therefore somewhere in Disneyland, just beyond that door.

As it turned out, so were seven thousand news reporters from around the world, a camera team from ABC TV, hundreds—perhaps thousands—of Disney Cast Members, politicians, VIP dignitaries, and guests.

Anaheim, California, had never seen anything like this. Today would change the course of history for the small orange-growing agricultural community. The Kingdom Keepers, being from the twenty-first century, knew all this. They were alone in this knowledge, as they prepared to crash the grand opening. If they failed to retrieve Walt's fountain pen, and find a way to ensure its discovery (by them!) nearly six decades hence, then years of battling the Disney villains, including the death of two close friends, would all have been for nothing.

"You'll have about twenty minutes," Wayne said, joining them at the door. "Mr. Disney's naps are very short, and he has a terribly busy day today."

Wayne was a few years older than they were—nineteen or twenty. They knew him better as a man in his eighties; a mentor; their advisor and confidant. Time travel was tricky.

"Napping?" Willa asked. Though Willa lacked the striking looks of Charlene, and the confident brashness of Philby—she was dark-haired, a little wide in the face, and reserved by nature—she had the brains of a wizard, the mind of a mathematician, and the calm of a lab scientist. "We're going to pick his pocket while he's napping?"

"It's the best opportunity you'll have," Wayne said. "Mr. Disney keeps his pen in the inside pocket of his sport coat. He won't sleep in the coat, so unless one of you is an expert at pocket picking . . ."

"We've got this," Finn said. "No worries." He had every worry, but wasn't about to put them on display for all to see.

"That's way too cheerful, Witless." Terry Maybeck seldom withheld his opinions. He claimed that, as an African American kid interested in art, he'd always felt sidelined, bullied, or otherwise ignored. His parents had either abandoned him or died; he didn't talk about it. He'd been raised by a bighearted aunt who ran a pottery shop. She claimed that Terry had been a head taller than any other kid in his class since the third grade, and had been spoiled by all the attention his teachers gave him, and because of this, had never been shy about sharing his thoughts.

"Thanks for that, Maybeck," Finn said. "Charlene . . . let's go!"

Once they were out in the park, everything looked and sounded so different from what they knew. The five holograms moved through a Cast Member entrance leading from backstage into Town Square.

"What's weird," Maybeck said, "is how completely different something can look."

"I hear you," said Philby.

Sapling trees surrounded Town Square. Grass sod had been laid, but it looked more like green carpet.

Flowers had been planted in neatly organized rows in front of stubby bushes. Only a few of the flowers held blossoms, which contributed to the naked look of the place. The park had the feeling of a model of Disneyland, not the real thing. Even the people were strange, in their white shirts, white dresses, and fancy shoes—the hair-sprayed hairdos of the women, the men's greased haircuts; everything about everyone was so intentional and perfectly in place that it looked more like a wax museum display than a day in Disneyland.

"Listen to them! They speak so differently," Charlene whispered to the others. "What's with all the 'gee whiz' and 'gosh'?"

"Don't look now, but it's 1955. 'Heck!' and 'Darn it!' are the closest they get to swearing. And look, they behave so differently!" Willa said. "Did you see that man tip his hat to that woman? So formal and polite."

A pair of burly men dragging television cables into place each gave Maybeck an unpleasant look.

"I have a feeling," Finn said, "that they probably believe differently as well!"

Disneyland had more of a weekend carnival feel than that of a theme park.

"This is way cool, by the way!" Maybeck said, ignoring the men. "We get to see the original Disneyland!"

"See?" Professor Philby repeated, questioning him.

7

Philby, always playing the academic. "Maybeck, we're not just seeing it, we're living it."

* * *

The five Keepers had once helped to restore the Disney magic in Disney World by using Walt's pen to draw on an old blueprint of the park. That transformation had reversed the darker magic of the Disney villains—the Overtakers—and had launched a long string of successful battles against their dark forces. Their purpose here in 1955 was to find the correct pen and make sure it would be in the Disney Hollywood Studios attraction One Man's Dream, so that they could find it again fifty-odd years later, in the future.

As the moment approached, the five began moving in eerie resemblance to a well-rehearsed team of bank robbers or street thieves. Outside of the Disneyland firehouse, alongside the Emporium, while the four teens stood side by side, a fifth, Finn, moved through a solid gate. Finn, whose boyish charm had matured into an intriguing forbearance. He had wildly expressive, almost hooded eyes, a mane of brown hair, and square shoulders that added up to a kind of Knight of the Round Table look of nobility. Now he found himself in backstage Disneyland.

It was nothing like the backstage Disneyland of the

future. Carpenters, artists, craftsmen, and people from the television broadcast were so busy they were talking, walking, and banging into each other all at the same time. It looked like the world's busiest airport on the busiest day of the year. There were other inconsistencies: the sawhorses were wood, not plastic; the workers wore suspenders and heavy leather boots—not a running shoe to be seen. Not a single sports cap, either. These guys wore tams and berets.

Everyone smoked; cigarettes dangled from lips, were pinched between fingers. Unlit cigarettes were tucked behind ears, along with yellow pencils. There was not a bottle of bottled water in sight, nor aluminum cans. Finn saw some Coke bottles—greenish glass—a few glass milk bottles, and metal lunch boxes in the shape of small barns. Finn moved toward a carport that held four shiny new trucks. As he did, his DHI projection sparkled and flared like a flickering TV signal during foul weather. Once at the carport, his image stabilized.

Next through the wall was Willa, followed by Charlene and Maybeck. At last, Philby's flickering projection came backward through the closed gate like a ghost.

"No matter how many times I see that it still looks so strange," Maybeck said.

"I hear you," said Charlene, equally awed by the

metaphysical element of the projected holograms in action.

The five quickly split up, taking positions relevant to the scaling of the gray-painted staircase, which rose nearly two stories to an unassuming set of casement windows and a nondescript door. Charlene moved down the backstage lane and took up a guard position. Maybeck stood sentry at the bottom of the staircase, prepared to buy his friends time. Willa, Finn, and Philby moved their ghostlike projections through the metal chain strung across the staircase as a barrier. They climbed the stairs quickly, with as much confidence as they could muster. Moments later, they slipped through the exterior back door that led into Walt Disney's family apartment.

Each Kingdom Keeper had learned over the years to discipline his or her thoughts and to control his or her emotions. Everything they believed, everything they felt, affected the quality and abilities of their projections. Fear instilled limits; no fear opened up possibility. Entering Walt Disney's apartment uninvited while he was supposed to be napping felt criminal to each of the three. It took every ounce of confidence and patience they'd learned over the past few years to keep their composure.

Philby, the most analytical of the five, showed little

outward reaction. Willa, who in high school had excelled past Philby in some academics, was less courageous. She looked ready to melt into the plush carpeting underfoot. Finn wanted to project confidence while not seeming pushy. He found himself the unofficial leader of the Keepers, but was occasionally challenged by Philby for that role.

The three communicated by hand signal. With everyone "talking" at once, it looked as if they were trying to flap their wings to fly.

When Willa slapped her hand over her mouth and stifled a squeal, Finn spun to see a fully dressed man asleep on the short red couch, his dress shoes indenting the armrest. Finn stared in awe. He'd seen so many videos, photographs, posters, and statues of Walter Elias Disney that seeing him in the flesh seemed so otherworldly he couldn't move.

Walt Disney snorted and began snoring softly.

Willa relaxed her hand. Philby placed his projected arm around her, and she leaned her head against his projected shoulder. Finn stuck his projected finger down his projected throat, indicating how he felt about the touching moment between the two. Philby stuck out his tongue and then laughed silently.

Finn took in the many items and pieces of furniture in the apartment, noting the differences between the real apartment and the restored version sixty years hence. Foremost was the brass fireman's pole mounted through a hole in the floor. The artwork on the walls was different as well: more photographs, fewer paintings. A suit valet stood by the end of the couch that wasn't there in the present.

As planned, Philby and Willa searched the closet. Finn inspected the suit valet and Walt Disney's sport coat, which hung there. The valet tray held U.S.-minted dimes, quarters, nickels, and pennies unlike any Finn had ever seen. The dollars clasped inside a silver money clip looked fake—in small letters they read "Silver Certificate." Finn reached to look inside the suit jacket, but his hologram hand passed through the fabric.

The easiest way for him to achieve the materiality that would lend his projection human substance was to allow fear into his thoughts. But that was risky—once mortal, he couldn't move through walls. Worse, weapons or fists wouldn't pass through him—they would injure him. Equally important: once fear sank its talons in and took hold, not only was it sometimes impossible for Finn to find his all clear projection again, but any harm that came to him in this condition would linger.

Leaders, Finn thought, didn't sit around thinking and stewing. Leaders led. He allowed himself to think about trespassing and attempting to steal something from one of his personal heroes. If caught, he'd be mortified. If caught, then fifty-odd years into the future, there would be no pen to save the Magic Kingdom. The Disney villains known as the Overtakers would face one less obstacle in their objective to crush the Disney magic.

Finn's body tingled. He knew the feeling well: he was losing all clear. He was going mortal. More human than projected light. Allowing it to grow stronger—warmer—he waited for the pins and needles to excite his fingertips. At that point, he fingered the fabric of Walt Disney's sport jacket, and the jacket came open.

A knock came from somewhere behind him. Finn froze, the fountain pen within reach.

The sleeping giant stopped snoring and startled awake.

* * *

Willa and Philby, in the midst of conducting a blind search of the few clothes hanging up in the dark closet, heard a knock. They paused. A second knock. "Maid service!" Another knock.

Philby stepped toward the closet door, but Willa held him back. Anxiety stole most of the all clear from her projection. She placed her ear against the cool door, catching the voices mid-conversation.

"I'm telling you, if Mr. H says there's something here, then there's something here."

"And we're going to steal it?" said the other, her voice edged with uncertainty. Both voices were female; both sounded young. "Golly, Gina! Doesn't that seem wrong?"

Mr. H. . . . Hollingsworth? Willa wondered. She knew the name somehow. Her study of Disney history? Hadn't a man going by that name been fired from Disney and ended up suing the man and the company for unlawful dismissal? Were these women working for the same man?

Trying to focus wasn't easy. As with the others, Willa had a great deal on her mind. How college was likely to separate her from Philby, whom she liked a lot. How the best years of her life seemed destined to come to an end. How friendship was like some kind of puzzle: just when you thought you understood it, there turned out to be deeper, undiscovered levels.

Willa had kept her excitement to herself when Finn proposed this final effort to recover Walt's pen. Secretly, she'd been brimming with joy. This would keep the five of them together, even if it was just for a few moments longer. Her thrill at being in Disneyland on Opening Day was like sunshine wanting to burst from behind a cloud. Everything was clean and fresh, like a brand-new house whose front lawn hadn't grown in yet. She wanted to dance her way down Main Street.

One of the women spoke. "Remember: anything unusual. A wand, in particular."

Willa heard the instructions, but her mind was back on the name: Hollingsworth. What could a man sixty years in the future have to do with Opening Day at Disneyland?

"You hear that?" Willa whispered to Philby.

"His snoring stop? You betcha I did!"

Willa wanted to correct him, to explain what she'd heard the maid say. But he was right: Walt's snoring had stopped. Finn!

"Right," she said, trying to remain calm. "We'd better get out of here."

* * *

Finn had just taken hold of the suit coat's lapel when the napping Walt Disney rose up on one arm. He looked in the direction of the knocking.

At that moment, Willa and Philby stepped through the closet door and into the narrow hallway behind Finn.

With Walt distracted, Finn focused and directed his prickling fingers to the valet's tray table. His first effort to pick up one of the pennies failed. But he pushed, gathered his full concentration, and managed to make himself solidly physical enough to manipulate matter. In an instant, Finn had flung the coin toward the small table at the window looking out onto Town Square, which held a replica gas lamp. The coin clinked as it landed.

The groggy man whipped his head toward the sound.

Finn peeled open the sports coat, snatched a fountain pen, which had been clipped inside the chest pocket, and headed for the back door, a step behind Willa and Philby, who moved, ghostlike, through the solid wood. Finn clutched the pen tightly in his hand. As a material object, it wouldn't pass through the door like his projection. He was reaching for the dead-bolt lock when an eerily familiar voice called out, "Hello?" It was a voice Finn knew from DVDs and YouTube. It was as powerful to him as the Wizard was to Dorothy.

It was Walt Disney.

Finn dove for the fireman's pole. He slid down the brass pipe and landed on a hissing cushion shaped like a doughnut. Except for a single silhouetted figure standing in the open bay door, the firehouse stood empty.

Finn tried to catch his breath. The air was hot and smelled of sawdust and pine. Being a projection, Finn didn't actually breathe, but to him he felt he did. If you asked Finn Whitman, he sweated, breathed, ached, and itched, just like his human, solid self. And he maintained that illusion. By agreement, the Keepers kept their projections secret. There would be far too many questions to answer if found out. Now he just needed to get past this man without incident.

"And just where did you come from?" the man's thin, almost cartoony voice asked. It had no place in one so tall and formidable. Finn wanted a better angle, a chance to see the man's face.

Finn had to think quickly. "I run errands for Mr. Disney. I'm an errand runner."

"Is that so?"

"I like taking the pole. Makes me feel like a fireman." Even without seeing the man clearly, Finn could tell he didn't believe him. He could think of several reasons why that might be the case—first and foremost, Finn was a lousy liar. But another possibility was that the man had expected someone else to come down the pole.

Finn heard the muted sound of feet coming quickly down the stairs. The silhouette heard them as well. The stairs led to Walt's apartment, but Willa and Philby—who wouldn't make clunky sounds—should have already made it down.

"Mr. Hollingsworth!" the voice of a young woman

17

called. The man spun. Finn saw his face in profile: a Roman nose and cleft chin, wide eyes—brown?—and big ears. Plain looking, not handsome, Finn thought.

The name meant something to Finn—he'd heard it from Philby, maybe.

Hollingsworth shot a final look in Finn's direction. Though he remained silent, something shouted to Finn: "Watch yourself!" Then Hollingsworth turned and caught up to the two young women, both of whom were dressed in maid uniforms. The three vanished into the overwhelmingly thick crowd.

Feeling threatened and afraid, Finn ran for backstage. He couldn't get there fast enough.

It would be the last Finn ever saw of the two girls.

2

LOST CAUSE

THEY MET IN THE SHADE of a pair of orange trees
beyond the Shooting Gallery, near the Pack Mules ride.
Their projections were caught by the dappled sunlight
cast down by the overarching limbs and leaves, making the teens into virtual checkerboards. Wayne sat in
a crouch, up on his knees like a runner on the blocks.
He checked around for eavesdroppers, and then hastily
unrolled a blueprint that showed the construction plans
for Main Street USA.

"Here you go!" Wayne said. He spoke nervously,
his voice hushed, even though no one nearby appeared
interested. "You're saying the pen will change this,
right?"

"Strengthen it," Finn said. "I know it sounds ridiculous, but we've seen it . . . in the future. I just touched
the pen to the paper and it was magic! Magic happened!"

"Gee whiz!"

Finn uncapped Walt's pen, glad to have at least
some control over his projection. "You'll see! Watch
this!" he said excitedly. The other Keepers joined them,
surrounding the blueprint. Finn touched the fountain

pen's bulbed nib to one of the darker lines on the plans. He pulled the pen's lever, spilling a drop and making sure the ink flowed. The blob of ink just sat there. "That's weird."

"Maybe that page doesn't need any magic," Charlene hypothesized. "Or maybe it only responds to certain people. Like Jess for instance."

"Who's Jess?" Wayne asked. "Golly! Are there more of you?"

"Jessica is a friend of ours," Philby said. "There are two others, her friends, Amanda and Mattie. Special girls. You'd like them. Jess has a particular artistic skill. If she drew something with that pen, we'd know if it's the right one."

"No offense," Wayne said to Willa and Charlene, "but I'm not sweet on any girls. I like my job too much to get all distracted."

Everyone laughed, including Finn, who considered Amanda more than a friend. He thought of her all the time; he talked to her inside his head. He missed her. Was there a word for how he felt?

The smile fell from his face amid the laughter. He hurt inside.

Philby spoke. "This pen is identical in appearance to the pen we came looking for. It has Walt Disney's name engraved on the side, just like the one we're after. It's black with a silver ring on the cap. That fits. All I can say for sure is that it looks exactly like the pen we need."

"But it can't be the right one if it doesn't do anything," Finn argued. "Nothing happened."

"So maybe he has more than one pen," Maybeck suggested. Since he was the only real artist in the group, his opinion carried weight. "If I had a special pencil, I sure wouldn't carry it around with me all day. I'd keep it near where I draw. I'd keep it safe so there was no chance of ever losing it. Whether it was magic or superstition, Walt Disney must have believed in his pen."

"He's still alive at this point, let's not forget," Wayne interjected. "I don't like you talking about him that way."

"Right. Sorry. He believes in this pen," Maybeck said. "So why risk it?"

"Terry's right," Wayne said. "If the pen is as important as you all say, Mr. Disney won't make it easy to find. He's a careful man. He probably has several of these monogrammed pens. But the one you're looking for, the powerful pen, is clearly different, maybe enchanted. And if it's special, then it's probably old. Oswald the Rabbit, Mr. Disney's first animated character, came early, right after the war. Did you happen to know Mr. Disney trained to drive and repair ambulances in the Great War? He didn't ship out until after peace was declared, but he served six months in France."

"So . . . what?" Maybeck said bluntly. "What does that have to do with anything?"

"Gypsies!" Wayne said. "Mr. Disney has a great love of magic. I've always wondered where that came from. And I have a theory." He stopped, awaiting their interest.

"Okay," Maybeck said impatiently. "Let's hear it."

"I've often thought a European witch or conjurer had something to do with Mr. Disney's love of magic. Maybe one enchanted him. Once he came home from the war, everything started going great for him."

"That's . . . an interesting theory," Willa said, kindly. She considered mentioning what she'd heard in Walt's apartment, but decided to tread carefully. The fact that the two girls were looking for a wand—Mickey's wand?—interested her. "Does anyone think we should be looking for Mickey's wand instead of Walt's pen?"

"Mickey doesn't have a wand," Wayne said. "A tail, but no wand!"

"He does in *Fantasia*," Philby said, reminding him.

"You mean his conductor's baton?" Wayne said. "True enough. I hadn't thought of that one."

Maybeck turned to Wayne. "Where does Walt do the most drawing? His favorite place?"

"He always seems to have a pen or pencil in hand.

But a pen like that?" Wayne shook his head. "If I were him, I'd want to be able to use it when I needed it, but keep it safe, too, put it someplace where I wouldn't lose it."

"But someplace easy to get at," Maybeck said, "if he still uses it, that is."

"There is something else to consider," Wayne said. "He'd have to make sure that Lillian, his wife, would be able to find the pen if anything happened to him. Mr. Disney travels a lot. Airplanes. Trains. He's a practical man. He'd want either Lillian or Roy, his brother and business partner, to be able to find it. Maybe both."

"Which leaves us where, exactly?" Finn asked.

"We're toast." Maybeck shook his head.

"Toast?" Wayne asked.

"An expression," Willa said. "We have a lot of strange expressions. It means we're cooked—we're in trouble."

"Ah! Well, I like toast," Wayne said. "Buttered, with cinnamon." He licked his lips. "Gee whiz, that made me hungry!" He looked out at five dumbfounded expressions. "What I'm trying to say is that I doubt very much if Mr. Disney would leave any mention of such a special pen in any kind of will or note or legal thingamajig. No lawyers or stuff like that. Gosh, the person he'd trust the most to get the pen to Lillian would be

Roy. Mr. Disney trusts Roy with everything. Rumor is Disneyland wouldn't have been built if it weren't for Roy believing in Walt. His own board of directors didn't want Mr. Disney to build this place."

"Where's Roy's office?" Charlene asked.

"At the studio in Burbank," Wayne answered.

"I don't mean to be Mr. Negative," Philby said, "but given that our projections seem to barely work inside the park, I don't see how the five of us are going to get to Burbank to search an office."

"He also has a day office above the Story Book Shop on Main Street USA. And I can drive. I could go to Burbank and snoop around for you."

"We can't ask you to do that, Wayne," Finn said immediately. Then he caught himself. "It's super-duper nice of you to offer," he added, trying to sound like young Wayne, "but if you got caught, if you lost your job . . . well, let's just say it's incredibly important you keep this job for a very long time. It's probably more important than the pen."

Wayne whistled as the five others nodded. "Golly, that's a nice thing to say, Finn."

"It's the truth," Philby told him. "We need to protect you, Wayne. If anyone's going to snoop around, it's got to be the five of us. You have to keep doing your job like always."

"We could look in Roy's office here," Charlene said.

"Walt does all his real work at the studios," Willa said. "I don't know about Roy."

"Roy, too," Wayne said. "Though his office here is more convenient in a lot of ways, I'm sure."

"Walt might keep it here," Maybeck said, "to help with construction plans. It must have taken more than a little magic to get something like this started."

"You can say that again," said Wayne. "Just look around, would ya?"

They did, and Willa saw a Disneyland so different from the one she knew that it made her catch her breath. It was, in many ways, like looking into the eyes of a baby. All the sparkle and promise of great things to come. Sure, the flowers and trees needed time to grow. There were great gaps between attractions that new ideas would fill. But the streamers and flags made it so American and wonderful. And authentic. The signs were hand-painted wood. The music was from real bands, not recordings. Disneyland on opening day looked a little like an Old West town with carnival attractions, raw and ready for the years of growth that lay ahead.

"All this, despite the problems," Wayne said, innocently enough.

"Problems? What problems?" Philby asked. All the

Keepers leaned in slightly toward Wayne, collectively aware of what problems in the parks often implied.

"The stuff Mr. Linkletter didn't tell the people watching TV."

"Such as?" Willa inquired.

"Well, for one thing, in case you didn't notice, the place was packed. You want to know why? Mr. Disney invited seven thousand members of the press from all around the world. That's what today's opening was supposed to be: reporters, radio people."

"And?" Charlene said.

"Are you kidding? There were over twenty thousand guests today. Twenty, not seven! No one was prepared. Food service, you name it."

"How'd that happen?" Philby asked.

"I heard it was counterfeit tickets. Fourteen thousand counterfeit tickets. The public outnumbered the press two to one. It was a nightmare."

"It seemed all right to me," Willa said.

"Well, that's good, isn't it? That's the way Mr. Disney wants it. But it could have gone very badly. Very, very badly. And think of the reviews we'd get if it had."

The five kids looked back and forth between them. Finn spoke for the group. "So the counterfeiting could have sabotaged the park, made it look bad, hurt its reputation."

"It could, still. We haven't read the reviews yet. And there's tomorrow to think about. Opening Day for the public, and a VIP reception at the Golden Horseshoe. That had better be Fat City."

The idea of a world without CNN and Twitter and Instagram, without instant news and constant feedback, took some getting used to. "But it was on live TV. The biggest live show ever telecast," Philby said.

"The newspapers come out in the morning. Mr. Disney may get copies later tonight. I have no idea. My fingers are crossed for good reviews."

"You said 'problems.'" Willa's voice was barely above a whisper. "Plural. We know of some of them, but can you refresh our memories, please?"

"Well, gee whiz! There was the drinking fountains!" Wayne shook his head. "The water union went on strike late last night. They cut our water supply in half. At 7:30 in the morning, Mr. Disney had to choose between water in the toilets or water in the water fountains. He picked the toilets, thank goodness. Think of the reviews we'd get with no working toilets! And then there's the asphalt."

"The asphalt," Charlene said.

"We hit a whole bunch of delays. A lot of the asphalt wasn't laid until late Friday, and we've had very hot days. Did any of you happen to see the women getting their high heels stuck in the asphalt? Thank goodness most all of the reporters are men or we'd really be in trouble."

"You mentioned delays. What other kinds?" Philby asked. He saw in the faces of the other Keepers the same concern he felt: sabotage. Someone had tried to ruin opening day for the press—it couldn't all be put down to coincidence and bad luck.

"I'll clue you in: the company kept telling us they couldn't deliver the asphalt."

"So, to recap," Finn said, catching Philby's eye, "someone counterfeited and gave away fourteen thousand tickets; the water union just happened to go on strike the night before the park opened; and the asphalt company had repeated 'delays'? Is that about it?"

"Can anyone spell 'Overtakers'?" Maybeck asked.

"I beg your pardon?" Wayne said.

"I think," Willa said, "that it's time I share something." Her calm tone won everyone's attention. "When Philby and I were stuck in Walt's closet, I heard two maids mention that they were searching for a wand."

"A wand?" Wayne asked. "That's an oddball thing to say."

"Mickey's wand," Maybeck muttered. "Like you said earlier."

"They were following orders, these two," Willa

said. "The OTs, or a force like them, are already here. They're after the magic. They want to control it."

"A man named Hollingsworth met up with them." Finn felt unreasonably small, like the air around him was suddenly heavier.

"Hollingsworth?" Wayne said. "That can't be right. He was fired by Mr. Disney. He's been nothing but trouble for the company."

"Guys," Willa said, "Disneyland opened today for the first time. That means as of today, the Disney villains are no longer just movie characters or fairy tales. Today—"

"—They're for real," Philby finished her sentence as his projection went pale.

"They have purpose," Willa said ominously. "They have a place, a way to get organized. And I'm afraid that whoever—whatever—is behind them is just getting started."

3

OLD FRIENDS

W<small>RAPPED IN THE SHADOWY DARKNESS</small> inside an Indian Encampment teepee, Philby kept examining his own hand. "Here's what I find interesting," he said.

"No one asked," said an irritable Maybeck.

"Because no one has thought of it but me."

The teepee was one of a cluster in an Indian village visible from the Mark Twain Riverboat cruise ride. Surrounded by spare bushes and trees that had been transplanted only a month before, the setting lacked the lush, dense feel of its duplicate in present-day Disney World's Magic Kingdom. All five Keepers were hunkered down inside the center teepee nearest the campfire circle, a place young Wayne felt they could safely spend the night. Finn and, later, Willa had tried to explain to Wayne that DHIs didn't sleep, but regardless of their nighttime habits Wayne wanted the five somewhere they wouldn't be found. The problem was, the Keepers had a history in the teepees, and not a pleasant one.

"Please!" Maybeck said. "We all appreciate what you bring to the table, Philby. But why you feel the need to keep reminding us of your brilliance is beyond me. We all bring stuff; every one of us."

"Think about it," Philby said, as if not hearing Maybeck's rebuke. "Look at your hands."

On cue, the rest of the Keepers held their glowing hands in front of their faces.

"So?" Maybeck said.

"Anyone remember our little visit from Maleficent last time we were in the teepees? What happened? What saved us?"

"DHI shadow," Willa responded, like a pupil in the front row.

"Which is?" asked the professor.

"The blocking of, or radio interference with, the hologram projection system."

"Yet?" Philby said, moving his hands in front of his body, mimicking the others.

"Oh my gosh!" Willa said. "It's 1955. We have maybe one-tenth the projection technology, hence the two dimensions, not three. The kind of washed-out colors and low resolution. But here we are, inside a teepee, where the most sophisticated technology available could not reach, and yet our hands and everything about us look perfect."

"Voila!" said Philby. "Care to hazard a guess?"

Willa shut her eyes and considered. "It's the transmission. Wayne must have us on television radio waves, not hologram projectors." Philby nodded. "He's created his own little TV station." Another nod. "Which means we won't get caught in DHI shadow, because it's not optical, it's radio."

"Correct. And we need to test how far his transmission reaches," Philby said. "At some point our images will start to break up and disintegrate."

"That could actually help us!" Charlene said. "If someone's after us and we run past that line, we could dissolve and become invisible."

"Nice," said Maybeck. "I volunteer to test it."

"It'll work best with two. One in front, one a ways behind to observe."

"That would be me," Charlene said. "Better at night, as in now, when there are fewer people around."

"But we glow at night," Maybeck said.

"All the better," she said. "If someone sees us, maybe they'll think we're part of the show. They're still working like crazy out there."

"Not once you're out of the park, they won't, so be careful," Finn said. He'd never been comfortable around all the tech talk. Action, though—action he could do. "But one hour. No longer. Half hour out, half hour back. We'll expect you at a few minutes past midnight."

To his surprise, Maybeck did not object. When the

two were gone, Finn lay down on the coarse dirt. Philby and Willa followed his lead.

"It's weird to feel tired, isn't it?" Finn said, yawning widely. "When crossed-over, I mean."

"This whole radio wave transmission is weird, if you ask me," Philby said. "Two dimensions—it's so limiting. And don't get me started on our resolution."

"I won't," Finn said. Willa laughed. "I actually feel as if I could nod out."

"Me too," Willa said.

Finn closed his eyes and tried to rest, which basically never worked for him. It was like trying to grow taller. He rolled over and lay flat on his back, looking up at the teepee's tapering cone, at the small patch of black sky at the very top. Low clouds slid past in hypnotizing patterns. Time slipped. He felt as calm as he ever had while a projection. His back felt cool on the soil, which was new to him as well. He sighed long and slow, welcoming a wave of disorientation.

A sudden pain stabbed in his chest, sharp and hot. It felt as if a stake had been driven through his heart. Finn couldn't move. Couldn't sit up. Couldn't call out. Was he dreaming of being a vampire? But the pain was so intense. It stunned him. He couldn't breathe. Straining to sit, he realized he was paralyzed. He managed to rotate his wrist. 12:15 a.m. He felt a kiss on his cheek, long and slow and . . . definitely Amanda, he thought.

He sat up suddenly. Philby and Willa were . . . sleeping. Unless Philby snored when deeply relaxed.

He stood and left the teepee. Maybeck and Charlene would be back at any minute. Finn shook his head to clear the cobwebs. Squatted by the campfire and looked out at the tranquil river; moved down to the shore's edge and saw his reflection in the dark water. In the distance, he heard the workers, toiling to ready the park for its opening in the morning.

Idly, Finn reached down and poked his reflection. Watched the perfect circles ripple across his face. He lifted his finger. A droplet of water fell from his fingertip, producing another, smaller set of concentric waves. There was something wonderful and odd about the moment. He thought back to the gentle kiss on the cheek—his absolute certainty it had been Amanda. A wonderful dream. The best. He missed her something fierce, the kind of missing where your chest hurts and your throat chokes just thinking of her.

He wondered what he'd done—leading the Keepers across Disneyland at night, jumping onto King Arthur Carrousel and crossing the boundaries of time. He shivered at the thought that he and his friends might have no way to return to their real lives.

Wait! he thought. Water, dripping? He touched the

water's surface. Splashed with his fingertips. "Philby . . ." he called softly. He reached down to his side, made a fist around some of the sand and dirt, and let it trickle from his grip. He touched his chin, his nose. He rubbed his hand into the dirt. And then he laughed, running all the way to the teepee.

Finn shook Philby, who reached out and slapped Finn's arm away. "Get lost! I'm trying to sleep."

"Yeah, I know," Finn said.

"So stop shaking me. Let go!"

"You were snoring. You were sleeping." Finn delivered this matter-of-factly.

"Take special note of the past tense. I would like to continue that process, if you don't mind."

"My hand's wet," Finn said. He touched Philby's face. In spite of his appreciation for all things technical, Philby had developed into a thickly muscled kid with rust-colored hair, freckles, and more strength than he'd learned how to control. He shoved Finn off him. Finn practically flew across the teepee, spraying sand as he landed. Philby sat up, angry. Finn, playing with the sand, began to chuckle like a kid in a sandbox.

"What is wrong with you?" Philby said.

"You know, for all your brains, sometimes you just don't get it. Allow me to make it a puzzler: what's wrong with me is what's right with me. And you, for

35

that matter! You were asleep. You just pushed me!"

Philby, caught off guard by a challenge from Finn, held his tongue in concentration. He mumbled, "What's wrong with me is what's right with me."

Willa groaned and came awake on her own. She sat up.

Philby touched his own face, clapped his hands. He stared at Finn in wonderment. "You shook me awake," he said. "I shoved you. We're mortal. No projection!"

"Fifty dollars to the boy with the red hair!"

Blinking, Willa spat out her words. "What? Are you . . . Can you possibly . . ." She ran her hands down her sides. "W . . . h . . . a . . . t?"

"You were sleeping," Finn told her. "So was Philby. I think I was dreaming. Then I went out and saw my reflection in the river. I wasn't glowing. No blue line. When I touched the water, it rippled. The surface rippled! Now Philby shoves me across the teepee?"

"If we're mortal . . ." Willa said. "Why? How? What changed?"

"It got later," Philby said. "I think that's the most obvious explanation. At some point a few hours after closing, the park shut down, right? That would include the power to Wayne's little TV studio. My guess is he's not transmitting our projections anymore."

"Then shouldn't we just disappear?" Willa said. "Sleeping Beauty Syndrome?"

"One would think," a confused Philby said. He clapped his hands again just to make sure. "One thing about time travel? I don't think it plays by the rules."

"Now there's a surprise," Finn said.

"If there're rules, then Einstein's the umpire," said Willa. Philby laughed.

"Got that right." He was still marveling at his own mortal body. "Note to self: this changes everything."

"Guys! Make room!" Maybeck and Charlene leaped through the teepee's raised open door and splashed face-first onto the sand. The two scrambled to hands and knees and physically pushed the three others to the very back of the tent enclosure. Willa made an attempt to speak, but Maybeck clapped his hand over her mouth while nodding frantically. He pinched his side to indicate his physical self.

Charlene whispered, "Pigs. Shh!"

As the five Keepers huddled at the back of the teepee, the sound of wet snorting drew closer and intensified. Shadows appeared outside on the sand: two big animals, their snouts to the ground. The menace they represented was clear. While one sniffed and snorted around the campfire ring, the other meandered to the waterline, where Finn had been sitting. DHI projections didn't leave smells behind, he thought. Mortal kids were another story. Willa squeaked, either a stifled sneeze or a burst of terror. The pig at the fire ring snapped its head in their direction, looking at the teepee.

It looked like one of the Three Little Pigs, but there was nothing little about it; the thing had enormous triangular ears, black button eyes, and a frozen piggish grin. It took Finn a moment to recognize that odd smile as part of the character costume. This was no ordinary pig. It sniffed and grunted and moved its ugly cloven hooves closer to the teepee. Finn and the others pressed their backs—their human backs—against the canvas. With intentional flair, Finn reached out his open palms and scooped some of the sandy dirt into his hands. The others saw this and did the same. Maleficent had used sand against the Keepers inside the Magic Kingdom teepees, to her advantage; Finn thought it was about time to repay the favor—if there even were Overtakers in the kingdom yet.

But if there weren't, who were the pigs? And why did they appear to be hunting?

The closer the thing came, the more apparent its exaggerated size—a "walk around" character from the park, now pork on all fours. What sealed the deal for Finn was the line of drool dripping from its snout. No matter how much it resembled a cute costume, the pig was very much alive. The disgusting way it snorted and sniffed confirmed its intentions. It was not looking for someone to pet it.

As the pig stumbled into the teepee, the Keepers all threw their handfuls of dirt at once. It emitted a shrill, ear-piercing scream and, in trying to back up, sat down onto its haunches and tipped over. Another of the same agonized screams deafened the kids. The pig tried to rise to all fours—but rolled instead.

"Blood," Finn said, seeing a line of red on its hind-quarters.

The teepee entrance now framed the face of a humungous wolf. It looked at the kids hungrily, kicked the suffering pig out of its way, and lifted its hairy paw to claw out its entry. But just as that paw was about to land, the wolf spun, having been struck by the other pig at a full charge. The pig and the wolf engaged in a dogfight, spinning, tumbling, biting. The wounded pig joined in—far Bigger and Badder than any nursery story could depict.

Maybeck was the first to hurry out of the teepee and start kicking the wolf. Charlene and Finn followed, though Finn wondered what kind of fool inserted himself into such a fight. Maybeck yanked the wolf's hind leg. The animal snapped back at him, and Charlene caught the wolf in the face with an acrobatic and well-placed kick. The high-pitched pig screams, mixing with the wolf's guttural growls, enhanced the terror. Finn grabbed for the other hind leg. Maybeck bravely took hold again, and together the two boys dragged the snarling wolf backward on its belly. It fought back, but Charlene caught it with the toe of her shoe. As the wolf separated from the pigs, the swine took off into the woods. The boys and Charlene counted to three, Maybeck having already called out, "The river!"

On three, Finn and Maybeck released the wolf. The boys and Charlene sprinted for the water and dived in. Willa and Philby fled the teepee and climbed a nearby tree. The wolf ran to the water's edge, but wasn't about to wade in. As the kids popped to the surface and looked back, they saw the wolf slink into the underbrush and vanish.

Treading water, Maybeck said, "And here I was hoping I'd enjoy the original Disneyland."

Finn swam to shore, marveling at the ease of having his human body back. "You know what this means?" he said to Philby as Philby dropped out of the tree.

"You're going to need to hang your clothes dry?" Philby quipped.

"Yes," Finn said. "But first, if we're not projections any longer, we can go to Burbank and Roy's office— tonight."

"If the power's shut off," Willa said, "then Wayne will be heading home. As in: right now."

4

PRESSURE POINTS

JOE GARLINGTON'S DESK converted from a sitting desk to a standing desk with the push of a button. Currently, he was standing, a colored pencil in hand, a Kanga hat cocked on his head, reading glasses pushed down his nose past tired eyes. He wore shorts and red Hoka running shoes. He looked up at Amanda as she entered. She was carrying an old blue can, like something that had once contained protein powder.

"Miss Lockhart. I told Nancy just now I couldn't see anyone. I'm busy here." He gestured to his drawing. Amanda just stood there, waiting for his full attention. "Are you going to speak? Do we have something to discuss? Please don't argue your suspension. Honestly, that won't help your case."

When Amanda didn't so much as flinch, Joe hollered for Nancy to close his office door. It shut. He occupied a corner office on a studio lot side street with a view of the commissary. "Look," he said once they were alone, "I appreciate everything you did in Orlando to help your friends. We got them here safely in large part because of you and Jessica."

"And Mattie Weaver."

"Maybe. I'll give you that. But it does not give you a Get Out of Jail Free card, Amanda. I'm sorry."

"You're going to reinstate me to the Disney School of Imagineering, Mr. Garlington. I'm going to room with Jess, just like before. You, or the dreaded Tobias Langford, are going to establish an independent project for me. Name it whatever you like so long as I can work, well, independently. Tim Walters and Emily Fredrickson and Jess will be on my team. I need access to Ms. Kline's staff at the Archives."

Joe trained his unsympathetic eyes onto her like blinding headlights. "Careful, Ms. Lockhart. You and Jessica, and Ms. Weaver, are valued members of the Disney team. Currently, you—and you alone—are serving a suspension for meddling with your . . . powers? . . . unusual abilities? . . . in the parks and being close-mouthed about your involvement."

"You mean like this?" Amanda leaned her head forward slightly and focused on Joe's work area. A moment later, the corners of the papers curled up as if caught by a wind. She made a small swiping gesture with her hand. The papers moved, creating a space on his desk that she filled with the can. "You're going to reinstate me because I know what this means and you don't. Because you and I both saw a video of Tia Dalma appearing in

Walt Disney's apartment near his music box. Seeing her scared you as much as it did me, and please don't lie about that."

"Tia Dalma is a powerful villain."

"A powerful Overtaker, you mean."

"The Kingdom Keepers silenced the Overtakers. You were there. We both know that's done."

"Maleficent. Chernabog. Not Tia Dalma."

"One villain does not an army make."

Amanda tapped the can. As she did, she caught sight of herself in the mirror on the office wall. It gave anyone who faced it Mickey Mouse ears. Amanda saw a face some called darkly tanned; others knew it to be her natural skin color. She could tan standing next to a lightbulb. She had long dark hair and slightly hooded eyes that suggested an Asian mother or father, neither of whom she knew or would ever meet again. She saw what she'd done to Joe's desk with just her thoughts and the wave of a hand, and for the millionth time, she wondered how she'd become the freak she was and if her "unique ability"—she was so tired of the euphemisms— would ever leave her.

"You saw the photograph," she said. "It was from this can. Opening Day, Disneyland, 1955. We both know it wasn't manipulated. It's real." She opened the can for him. "A white glove, faded now, because women wore white gloves back then. A game of jacks with a rotting rubber ball, because that was a game played back then. By burying all this as a time capsule, Finn was letting us know what happened to them. Where they were. Are," she corrected herself. "Now, factor in Tia Dalma being in Walt's apartment, near the music box. Are you paying attention?"

"Do not address me like that, young lady. You will find my bite is much worse than my bark. Your suspension is a result of actions committed during your enrollment at DSI. You used your . . . gift, your telekinesis, to damage Disney proper—"

"I saved my friends from the Queen of Hearts and her insane army of cards!"

"In public!" Joe shouted. "At night, when the park was operational and guests were in attendance! You could have been, probably should have been, expelled! There is time left on your suspension. Reinstatement now wouldn't even be seen as a slap on the hand."

"No one knows about this," Amanda protested, tapping the can. "Besides, hardly anyone knows why I was suspended. They certainly don't know about my . . . strength."

She'd decided on this term for her unusual ability. Jess's strength was dreaming things about to happen. Mattie could read your thoughts by touching your skin.

To Amanda, these weren't gifts or abilities, powers or spells. They were strengths that when practiced and/or worked on became more potent.

"Don't kid yourself, Amanda. You and Jess are the curiosity of everyone in those dorms. You and Tim in the basement? Don't think we don't know! Everything you've done is already the stuff of myth. Believe it. Our company thrives on myth. Being attacked by robots? A secret archive? You've set us back years. Why do you think Mr. Langford has his nose so out of joint?"

"We both know why the Keepers are not waking up. They've managed to time travel. How? I have no idea. But you and the Imagineers haven't helped them any."

"That's a difficult proposition, given their current status."

"Which is?"

"Confidential."

Amanda found herself intrigued. "How do you know their status?"

"Same answer: that's confidential information."

"You're not going to help us." She hadn't wanted to cry in front of Joe. If she did, he would think of her as "a little girl." Nonetheless, pools formed in her eyes and she fought to avoid blinking and sending them skidding down her cheeks.

No. He would take her less seriously. Just because

a girl has the capacity to show emotions, Amanda thought, we're condemned as weak. When we should be seen as socially sensitive.

"We have no evidence, Amanda," Joe said gently. She didn't want his sympathy, his fatherly tone of voice. She found it patronizing. "Only theory."

"I need your help. They need your help and you're going to do as I ask," she said, holding back the tears.

"No, I'm not."

"Yes, you are. And you want to know why?"

"I certainly do," he said skeptically.

"Amery Hollingsworth."

She might as well have punched him. Joe blinked. It was a name she could not possibly know without also knowing much, much more. "How could you possibly—"

"Now, please," Amanda said, interrupting, "do what you have to do. But we are going to help the Keepers to return."

5

THE MAYFAIR

Wayne drove a 1950 Ford half-ton pickup truck that had spent too much time at the beach. Its two-tone paint job was unintentional; rust and forest green. The leaf springs didn't merely cry whenever the truck bounced, which proved to be a nearly continual motion. They screamed.

The two girls rode in the cab with Wayne, the three boys behind, in the open truck bed, with its wooden rails and the curving black rubber of the spare tire, mounted to the side behind the driver. The ride out of Anaheim took them past dark orchards of sweet-smelling orange trees, the brightly lit Broadway shopping center, with its vast, empty parking lot, and its neighboring Ralph's supermarket. The roads were mostly randomly lit four-lane undivided highways, though they traveled briefly on a new six-lane freeway, its opposing traffic separated by chain link fence.

The car designs were big and bulky, with the occasional finned Cadillac parked at a motel, like the Arches along La Habra's Euclid Avenue. The towns were hodgepodge conglomerations of architecture, from

47

simple boxes to attempts at modern, and everywhere the black lumps of vegetation and the night cry of cicadas. Sand and dust and so many electric wires strung from telephone poles. The smells of tar, motor oil, and asphalt clouded the air. It seemed like construction was under way everywhere, on buildings, roads, reservoirs, and all of it in a kind of milky haze created by pitch-black roadways and man-made illumination reflecting off the swiftly moving clouds as they left the ocean and fled into the mountainous east.

Once over the hills, Glendale's central avenue was mostly empty, a set of trolley tracks splitting it in two, the nearly uniform awnings reaching like stunted wings from stores named Webb's and Penny's.

"I feel like I'm in one of those black-and-white movies my grandparents watch," muttered Philby.

"I think we are," said Finn.

"Hey," Maybeck shouted over the constant rumble of passing cars, "how many teal-green Dodge four-doors could there be on this road after midnight?"

"What are you talking about?" Philby asked.

"I've seen the same car, off and on, practically since Anaheim. It passed us maybe twenty minutes ago. Then I saw it at a Shell station getting gas. Pretty sure it was the same car. Green, with a black roof. It passed us again maybe a minute ago."

"Coming up on a red light," Finn said, looking around the pickup's cab.

"So, check it out. A Dodge four-door. Couldn't read the model," Maybeck said.

"What's it matter?" Philby asked. "There are five million people living in Los Angeles at the moment."

"I don't like coincidences," Maybeck said. "Let's get the license plate."

"What for? It's just a car."

"It's a car headed from Anaheim north on the same exact roads we're taking. It's passed us twice, and while I admit that no one looked over, there are kids in that car. Kids our age, maybe a little older. In a very nice, very new car."

"Five million people," Philby repeated. "And a lot of them are rich. They have kids, no doubt. Who spend the day in Disneyland, and then drive home."

"After midnight?" Maybeck questioned.

"It can't hurt to get the license plate," Finn said, and knocked on the cab's back window, startling the girls. He mimed that he needed a pen. Maybeck looked over appreciatively, while Philby shook his head. He disapproved.

Finn walked a delicate line between his friends. They saw him as the leader of the Keepers, which meant he had to express his opinions, sometimes boldly.

He respected each of the others, but he also saw their weaknesses, as they no doubt saw his: Philby's arrogance; Charlene's vanity; Willa's reservation; Maybeck's overconfidence. His own insecurity. He couldn't make enemies. He had to not only listen, but hear; not only speak, but say something. In every expression of his, every word counted.

To lose the trust of the other four Keepers would put Philby at the helm. By no means a disaster, but Philby's soaring intellect often made him his own worst enemy; he dismissed others as not worthy of consideration. For the Keepers to be effective, they absolutely had to operate as a team. Individual efforts had failed miserably in the past.

The girls silently spoke to Wayne and searched the glove box. Then Charlene leaned out the window and passed a ballpoint pen to Finn. A moment later, the entire procedure was repeated: Charlene handed him a nearly blank page torn from the owner's manual.

They stopped at a stop sign. They could see the roof of the Dodge, but not its license plate. A few blocks later, they picked up a partial plate number at a traffic light: 3A 13.

"It's a Dodge Mayfair," Maybeck proclaimed.

The Dodge sped away from the light. Wayne's old truck lagged behind, and the boys lost sight of the car.

They passed near the Burbank Airport, which looked like any other street of low two-story buildings, its special status announced only by an American flag and a conning tower that looked like it belonged on the corner of a prison wall.

For the remainder of the drive, the presence of the Dodge kept nagging at Finn's mind. Philby was right: the boys might have been some of those with counterfeit tickets to the park's press opening; they might have had dinner or visited friends and then headed north later at night. All that could be explained, at least to some degree of satisfaction for Finn.

But what he'd noticed, and had deliberately not mentioned for fear of sounding paranoid, was that the two boys he'd seen—at a distance and only in profile—had both been wearing short-sleeved white shirts. Cast Members at the press day opening had also been wearing short-sleeved white shirts. But Cast Members turned in their costumes at the end of the day. So, if these boys were friends, all of whom worked at the new park and commuted from their homes north of the area, why hadn't they turned in their costumes? He tried to explain this to himself repeatedly and had just come to the decision to share the conundrum with Philby and Maybeck when the truck rolled to a stop.

"Keep down!" Wayne called softly out the driver's window. "We're here."

OF VILLAINS AND VANDALS

Having directed the five Keepers to climb the fence behind the Property and Drapery warehouse, Wayne slowed his pickup truck to a crawl, but did not completely stop. The two girls slipped out of the cab, climbing the chain link immediately. Philby and Finn stepped over the truck's tailgate to the back bumper and hit the ground running. Maybeck, who always had to be different, leaped onto the fence from the bed of the truck, shaking it so badly he nearly caused the two girls to fall. Higher than all the others, he was up and over and down the other side well before the rest of the Keepers.

The paper towel map Wayne had drawn for the girls had the Keepers coming around the warehouse, clearing the Set Lighting building, and heading straight forward, through what turned out to be a dark, narrow alley between the Operations Center and Cutting. At the end of the alley, they waited in shadow before crossing Minnie Avenue one at a time. They regrouped in the landscaping around the Animation Building. On the map, the long structure resembled two Hs connected by a hyphen. The map showed an X in the lower left leg of the topmost *H*. Office 2-E 6, belonging to Roy Disney, Walt's brother and partner.

"There's security at the studio," Wayne had warned from behind the wheel.

"Now you tell us?" Charlene had complained.

"My advice is to stay out of sight. If you were dressed as park Cast Members or had the correct identification I wouldn't think twice about it. The clip-on badges I gave you all will look good from a distance. They're the right color. They identify you as guests, and are typically given to actors or actresses on set. Some nights there's a lot of activity here, so you don't need to act like you have cooties or something. Gosh, no. It's perfectly possible a bunch of kids would be in the studio this time of night. But I wouldn't go getting too cozy, either. With a good look, those passes won't fool security."

Charlene reminded the others not to panic if spotted. Nearly in the same breath, she instructed them to keep their distance from all adults. "No one's going to follow us into a bathroom stall. If we do hit panic mode, we head straight to the restrooms."

Inside, it was deathly quiet. The lights were at half power, giving the space a dim and spooky feel. As keeper of the map, Willa pointed ahead to what turned out to be an exceptionally long hallway lined with Disney art. As a group, they turned to the right.

Charlene pointed out the restrooms and nearly won a laugh from the others.

They reached a stairway and ascended to the second floor. Charlene automatically took up a position as guard. The others took an immediate left, which deposited them in a narrower hallway, right by the office marked as number six, its small business card–sized placard reading ROY O. DISNEY.

The door was locked. "If we were still projections," Willa said, "we could walk right through."

Maybeck unpinned the ID card Wayne had provided from his own suit coat. It was constructed of thick card stock, with a safety pin glued to the back. "Too bad no one in 1955 has figured out how useful plastic is. I'd have rather had a laminate."

He placed Willa's hand on the doorknob as he wrestled the edge of his ID card into the jamb between the knob and the molding. "One thing about these old locks . . ." he said, wiggling and pushing the bent card. Each time he nodded at Willa, she pulled on the door—but to no avail. Maybeck worked the card some more. With a good shove, most of the card disappeared into the jamb; Maybeck nodded, Willa tugged. The door came open.

"I'm glad you're on our side," Philby said. Without instruction, he placed his back to the wall by the door. He would stand guard, just as Charlene had.

Willa, Maybeck, and Finn entered the office. "No lights," Willa whispered.

"It's not going to be out in the open if it's super important," Maybeck said.

"You never know," Willa said.

"Willa, you take the desktop, the coffee tables, and counters. Maybeck, the shelves and cabinets. I'll take any drawers and the closet over there."

No one countermanded Finn's directive. They knew that in situations such as these, time was their biggest enemy. The sooner they were out of this office and off studio property, the better. A finely tuned team, they worked fluidly, their actions complementing one another's. Willa began inspecting awards and papers and books on the desk while Finn opened and searched drawers. Maybeck was on his knees, digging around the inside of a cabinet below a set of bookshelves. They had no time to waste.

WALTER E. DISNEY

At the top of the stairs in the dim hallway, a few strands of Charlene's fine blond hair lifted and fell. The occurrence was enough to flash heat up her spine and direct her attention to the stairwell. At first she thought it might be her imagination—in situations like these her imagination went a little crazy—but after several seconds of concentration, she knew she was hearing the brush of clothing from down on the first floor. More than one person; possibly three or more, heading toward her, not away.

She took two steps, caught Philby's eye, and made a walking motion with her fingers. She pointed down, indicating the floor below. Philby nodded and leaned his head into the office. Then he pulled the door closed and moved farther down the narrow hall, into shadow. Charlene found restrooms down the hall. She eased open the door marked "Minnies," prepared to slip inside.

Focusing her hearing was not like training her vision on something, but she listened carefully all the same, and eventually picked up the sound of rustling cloth. She moved into the restroom, her hand on the inside handle, keeping the door open an inch. Spotting a small louvered vent in the base of the door, she let the door shut and kneeled, putting her ear to the slats. Again, it required all of her concentration to isolate the faint sound of people coming up the stairs—but coming up they were.

"Which way?" she heard a boy's voice whisper faintly.

A different boy answered. "He said it's called Public Relations. This hall, halfway down. They're the ones doing the VIP thing."

"This gives me the gosh-darn heebie-jeebies," said a third boy. "Let's get these stupid plans and blow this clambake. Hey, what's a 'logistic,' anyway?"

"It's the . . . How the heck should I know?" said the voice of the first boy. "'Sides which, he said 'logistics,' not 'logistic,' for your info."

"As if that matters," said the third.

Their voices faded as they passed. Charlene pressed her ear to the slats, then leaned back with a shiver of disgust. It was a bathroom, after all.

"Shut up, will youse?" The second boy again, barely audible now. "It's the schedule for tomorrow, okay? He wants the schedule none of the guests ever see. Now mind your own beeswax and just stick to the plan."

"Do we have a plan?"

"I said, shut your trap!"

"Shh!"

After a minute or two of silence, Charlene ventured a peek. Seeing no one, she hurried back to the narrow hallway, where she joined Philby. The short hallway formed a T at the end by a suite of offices marked WALTER E. DISNEY. A different sort of shiver crept down Charlene's spine.

"For the record," she whispered warmly into Philby's ear, "this is way cool."

"For the record," Philby said, "I recognized one of those kids."

"Just now?"

He nodded. "Yeah. From the Dodge we played tag with on the way up here. That kid was riding shotgun. Did you see their clothes? Their ID badges?"

Charlene shook her head.

"Cast Members from Disneyland."

"Those guys? But they're . . . I think they're trying to steal the schedule for tomorrow's opening. What kind of Cast Member would do that?"

"The fake kind," Philby said, his face twisted with concern. "I'm going to tell the others. You hang tight."

6

ANSWER ME, PLEASE

WILLA WORKED HER WAY ACROSS the top of
Roy's desk, feeling hurried and under pressure. Despite
the expression "hiding things in plain sight," she didn't
believe for a moment that Roy would leave Walt's pen
lying around. A housecleaner, a visitor—just about anyone could accidentally walk off with it. If it wouldn't
be found lying around, that meant Finn had assigned
himself and Maybeck the choice jobs of drawers and
cabinets.

Let the girl have the meaningless task, she thought;
if it makes her feel important, it'll keep her off our cases.

She shook her head, reprimanding herself. This was
no time to complain; the Keepers worked well as a team,
which meant that sometimes you got the funky jobs. She
inspected each and every object on Roy's desk, looking for
ways a pen might be concealed. The three framed photos
offered her nothing. Nor the star-filled hemisphere of
polished, clear glass that served as a paperweight. The
two pens in plain sight were in a little stand, which held
them like rabbit ears at the top of a leather blotter.

Next was a group of a half-dozen awards, several of

them gold statuettes on a wooden stand. She picked up each one, studying them from all sides, including the bottom, looking for clever Walt Disney hiding places.

"Guys!" she called out, holding a heavy Academy Award in her hand. The gold-plated statuette was of a rigid man, his arms crossed. Finn and Maybeck joined her. She pointed to a small cork in the award's stand. "Look," she said, hoisting a second, similar award. Only the first had the cork in the bottom.

"That doesn't look big enough for a pen," said Finn, "but it does look like it was added."

"Do either of you feel like a criminal digging around in Roy Disney's stuff? Roy Disney, as in *the* Roy Disney. Criminal, as in definitely breaking the law."

Maybeck picked at the cork and caught its edge. "We can argue about how we shouldn't have done this later." He pulled the cork free. No pen fell out.

"Okay," Willa said. "No pen. We plug it back up and mind our own business."

Maybeck shook his head. Using a long, tapered pen from the desk stand, he poked into the drilled hole. What looked like a tightly rolled dollar bill fell out onto the desk, along with a few flakes of sawdust.

The three kids stared at the money. Maybeck put his eye to the hole. "Empty."

"What do you suppose . . . ?" Finn unrolled what

he now saw was half of a twenty-dollar bill. It had been torn neatly down the center. Its orange serial number was printed beneath an orange wreath. Gray engraved words identified it as a Gold Certificate. The back of the bill was printed in vivid green ink.

"Bizarre," Finn said. "Maybeck, can you memorize that serial number?" The best artist in the group, Maybeck also enjoyed something of a photographic memory.

He took a long moment to do so, then nodded. "Got it."

"Some kind of code. A partnership. Someone else has the other half," Willa theorized.

"But why, and who, and is Roy hiding it or leaving it for someone?" Finn said.

"Nothing written on it," Willa observed.

"And nothing left inside," Maybeck said, checking again.

"We've got to put it back," Finn said.

"Because? You don't actually expect he checks it very often, do you?" Maybeck sounded as if he'd already decided to keep it.

"We put it back," Finn declared. "Maybeck, you're sure you have the number?"

"Got it."

"Back to work," Willa said, sighing. The boys

moved off, and she studied the other awards and oddities on the big desk.

The other trophies and pieces of art were gifts from business groups; their engravings mentioned Roy, not the Disney company. One, smaller than the others, caught her eye. It was a brass or copper coin embedded in thick glass, a fortune-teller's face on one side, "To Absent Friends" stamped into the metal on the reverse. There was no plaque. Another award or trophy showed a glass ballerina rising out of a glass pond, her back arched, her face aimed heavenward. On the shelves, Willa found a hole-in-one golfing award, a curled ballet shoe, a framed ticket to the Bolshoi Ballet, and another to the Opera House in Paris. No pen, and very few items that could hide one.

The boys fared no better. Finn found a half-dozen pens in the desk drawers, including a new fountain pen still in the box. It had no engraving on its side and its mechanics were perfectly clean, suggesting it had yet to see ink.

"Strange," Willa said, "how you can form a picture of someone based only on his stuff. He golfs. He likes ballet. Opera. He's been generous to the city and the businesspeople."

"He was a heck of a businessman," Maybeck said.

"Is, you mean," Finn corrected.

"Yeah . . . still hard to get used to that."

The door popped open. "Security coming." It was Philby. "To the bathrooms. Now!"

Finn, Willa, and Maybeck tidied up and hurried out of the office. In the hallway, they saw a shadow looming, projected at the top of the stairs.

"Stalls. Standing on the seats," Philby whispered. "Leave the doors partially open. Charlie's already in."

The boys took three of the four toilet stalls. Finn climbed onto the fixture and leaned against the cool metal barrier, the stall door between him and the line of sinks and mirror.

"Hello?" a man's low voice called out. "Security check." He switched off the light. The restroom went darkroom black. Finn released a pent-up breath. He heard knocking. The Minnies' room. The guard announced himself. Then, nothing. He'd moved on.

"What . . . now?" Maybeck whispered. "Or are we going to stand here all night?"

The lights came on. "Hello?" A man's voice. "I heard you talking just now, whoever you are. Unless you were talking to yourself, then there are two of you. Maybe more. Now, I don't know why you're not answering, and maybe it's none of my business. But we're closing up Animation in fifteen minutes and I'm making the rounds so as no one comes crying that they need more time, and no one calls telling us we locked them inside. Hello? Can you answer me, please?" He paused. "I'm not trying to interrupt nothing. I'll just wait outside then. We can talk about this in a minute."

"You sure it wasn't us you heard?" Charlene's voice.

Finn couldn't see what happened next, but it sounded as if the guard said, "Girls?" The door thumped shut on its springs.

"Go!" Philby said.

The three boys each stole a look out of their stalls: no guard. They rushed to the door. Philby swung it open and stuck his head out. "He's going the way we came. The girls bailed us out."

The three boys dashed into the hall and faced in the opposite direction. "This is the way the boys went," Philby whispered.

"What boys?" Finn asked, confused.

"Don't look now," Philby said, pointing, "but I think we're about to find out."

Three boys emerged from an office down the hallway. They were all dressed identically, in khakis and short-sleeved white shirts. They looked at the Keepers; the Keepers looked back. A brass badge was pinned to all three of their shirts: a Disneyland Cast Member number badge.

The race began.

7

THOSE GUYS

FOR ONCE, FINN REALIZED, it was not the Keepers being chased, but the Keepers doing the chasing. More confusing still: Why were the Cast Members the ones fleeing? It had to have something to do with the papers one of the boys was holding, he thought. The papers, and the office they'd come out of.

The boys were fast and hard to keep up with, much less catch. They bounded down the stairs, followed a second later by the three Keepers. But it was a long second and a great distance. By the time the Keepers threw open the glass door to the outside, the boys had turned and were waiting for them. The paperwork was nowhere to be seen—shoved up a shirt or discarded in the bushes.

All six boys were winded and labored for air. They stood ten yards apart, saying nothing with their voices and everything with their eyes. Decision time. Clearly neither group knew exactly what to do.

"Numbers," Philby half-whispered to Maybeck. "Pins."

Maybeck nodded, face screwed up and focused. He'd already started memorizing.

Philby called out to the boys. Finn realized it was in an effort to turn them so that their badges could be read more easily. "Who are you?"

"We're not the ones trespassing," said a boy with no eyebrows. He might have been wearing a wig. His face indicated a moment of consideration; he was debating his options. "S ... E ... C ... U ... R ... I ... T ... Y!"

The Keepers took off, entering the same narrow alley they'd followed to get in. The girls were visible in silhouette at the far end, waiting. They took off the moment they saw the boys.

"Did you get them?" Philby said as he ran alongside Maybeck. He sounded surprisingly calm.

"Two. I got two."

"Excellent," said the professor.

"Who were those guys?" Finn asked, at a full run to keep up.

"Trouble," Philby answered. "Those guys are trouble."

8

HALF ABSENT

"Now I know how Cinderella felt," said
Charlene.

It made sense. She was arguably the closest thing
the Keepers had to a Cinderella.

The group had fallen asleep with beating hearts and
awakened as two-dimensional projections once more.
Having returned from the harrowing night in the studios, they had elected to spend the night in the Opera
House in Town Square, rather than risk wild pig and
wolf attacks in the teepees. The Opera House wasn't
actually an opera house, but a warehouse full of lumber.
The air held the sweet scent of pine and redwood, like
camping at the edge of a lake.

"Wayne and I will try to figure out how any of this
is possible," Philby said.

"I wouldn't try too hard," said Willa, coming awake
on a bed made of bags of peat moss. "When the base-
line of a theory happens to be time travel, it isn't likely
to make much sense. I think it's way smarter if we just
accept and learn to work with the fact that we're going
to turn mortal about two hours after the park closes each

night. As weird as it is, as nonsensical, that's what seems to be the case. Better to take advantage of it."

"I want to find those three guys and debrief them," said Maybeck, referring to the Cast Members—presumably fake—they'd seen the night before.

"They were after today's schedule that includes the big shindig tonight at the Golden Horseshoe," Charlene said. "Opening Day for the public. It's going to be huge. Their poking around can't be good."

Finn sat up on the drop cloth he'd laid atop a pile of sawdust and called the Keepers into a tighter circle. They needed to keep their voices down. "Maybeck, Charlene, and I will search Roy's office on Main Street for the pen. Philby and Willa, you figure out Wayne's transmission and work out a way to return us."

Philby stared down Finn. "We have to remember, it's always been me, manually taking control of the Imagineers' DHI server in order to return us. It's totally different now. One: I've never done it from a phone, always from a laptop with more power. Two: our phones don't happen to work in 1955, and the personal computer won't be invented for thirty years."

"Philby, you and Wayne and I will figure this out," Willa insisted, somewhat weakly. "We need to see how Wayne managed to project us in the first place and work from there. Don't worry, guys. We're going to find Walt's pen and get it back where it belongs."

Finn felt he belonged in the future—his future. He missed Amanda. They had the ability to solve huge problems together. With half of the equation absent, the chance of any such solutions lessened. He could picture her face, her smile, her laugh. He missed her laugh most of all.

9

THE LOOKOUT

REACHING ROY'S OFFICE in the park required Finn, Charlene, and Maybeck to travel backstage from the Opera House woodshop to a set of stairs leading up above the Main Street Cinema. Maybeck and his choice of a business suit and hat stood out backstage, particularly as the only African Americans in the park seemed to be workers or Cast Members dressed as Indians.

Finn, in coat and tie, and Charlene, who wore a pretty cream dress, looked like Opening Day guests, but hardly had the right appearance to be backstage Cast Members. For these reasons, and the fact that they were two-dimensional projections, the three stayed away from each other. Out ahead of the other two, Finn led the way. Using the construction chaos in an area that would one day be a parking lot, he kept to the walls at the back of the Main Street shops. Maybeck followed, and, a few seconds later, Charlene.

They'd agreed on a common story to tell if questioned: they'd wandered backstage by accident, but, finding themselves there, were hoping for a bird's-eye view of Main Street and the castle.

Finn reached the fourth door—the one Wayne had told them to use—and ducked inside. Backstage lacked the paint and polish of the working park; it was all rough wood, with a few bare bulbs lighting the way. He waited for Maybeck and Charlene to catch up.

"All good?" he whispered. But he could answer for himself. All was not good. There was some kind of interference in this building; their projections were sparking and fuzzy.

Charlene held out her long arm and waved her thin fingers. "Kind of wonky, if you ask me."

"We should hurry," Maybeck said. "If we get caught when we're this unstable . . ." He didn't need to finish his thought.

Finn took off up the stairs, keeping an eye on his own hands and arms. The higher he climbed, the more his image deteriorated. Not good, he thought. The stairs led to a hallway, which ran a short distance in both directions. It was no more charming than the stairwell. The doors were unmarked. Finn stepped his projection through the first and looked around—it was clearly tool storage. He walked back through the door and rejoined the others.

"Nothing," he said. "Tools."

Charlene leaned only the head and shoulders of her projection through the next locked door. When she stepped fully inside, Finn and Maybeck followed, their projections crisp and sharp once again.

The room was a spare office, carpeted with a simple desk and chair, a telephone, and a desk lamp. Attached to the side of the desk was a crank-driven pencil sharpener. Several Disneyland posters were thumbtacked to the wall. The room's two small windows looked out beneath an awning onto Main Street's Crystal Arcade.

"This has to be it," Maybeck said. He gestured at the view. "It looks across at a window marked 'Elias Disney: Contractor.' Walt and Roy's father. How cool is that?"

Together, the three searched the desk. They found a rubber-banded bundle of #2 yellow pencils, opera glasses, a paper punch, a stapler, some paper clips, a leather-bound checkbook, and several cardboard-covered ledger books with pages and pages of carefully written numbers. They found letters, blank stationery, an address book, and postage stamps. In the lower desk drawer, Roy Disney had a stash of yellow-and-red bags of Fritos and two bags of potato chips.

"Junk food," Maybeck said. "I'm liking Roy."

"No pen," Charlene said disappointedly. "I mean there are three pens, but they're all Reynolds Rockets, all ballpoints. No fountain pens."

"This is getting frustrating," Maybeck said.

"'Getting'?" Charlene raised an eyebrow. "What planet are you on?"

"Not sure," Maybeck said. The three laughed together.

A sharp knock on the office door startled them.

"Mr. Disney? You in there?"

A man's gruff, low voice. The Keepers hurried to stand behind the door should it swing open, their backs against the plaster wall.

Another knock.

"Sir?"

The doorknob rattled, but the door was locked. All three expected to hear a key being inserted and the doorknob turning. If they timed it right, they could simply step their projections through the wall.

But thankfully, it didn't happen. There was a protracted silence; it seemed the man had moved on. Charlene tried to elbow Finn, but her elbow went through his image's side. Still, she won his attention and pointed straight ahead.

At first, Finn saw only the office window. Why would Charlene point it out? he wondered. Then his vision shifted, and he looked through instead of at the glass. Across the street, inside a set of bay windows that carried the name ELIAS DISNEY at the center, there was movement.

Charlene, the first to venture forward, led the way past Roy's desk, keeping to one side of the windows. "Oh my gosh!" she said. "I think it's them."

The boys rushed to her side, also avoiding being seen through the window.

"Sure looks like it!" Maybeck said. "Or, if it isn't . . . Nah, I'm not so sure it is."

"Do you recognize the second from the left?" Charlene asked.

"Maybe," Maybeck said. "It's hard from this distance."

"Who's that they're talking to?" Finn asked, squinting.

"Can't see. It's a guy in a business suit? He's got a hat like yours," Charlene said to Maybeck, who moved quickly back to the desk.

"Look," Charlene said. She reached down for a small, gummed notepad on the windowsill. Someone had been standing at this window, taking notes. Her projected fingers passed through it, unable to grab hold.

The note was a series of numbers—4, 157, 323, 54, 204—and the initials SR.

"Check it out," Maybeck said. He'd gotten the opera glasses from the desk drawer. Lifting the small binoculars to his eyes, he muttered a string of curses.

"What?" Charlene asked.

"The numbers on the pad are badge numbers.

Badges 162 and 51 are over there now. Roy was keeping track of who was meeting in that office."

"So the other numbers are other Cast Members?" Charlene inquired, bending low as she crossed back to Roy's desk. "That makes sense!" She concentrated and was able to pick up a sharpened pencil.

"There's another . . ." Maybeck said. "Eighty."

"Eight-zero," Charlene said as she wrote it down.

"Correct. If the guy would turn his head . . . but he's in the dark and his back is to us."

"SR," Finn said. "Roy wrote down the initials . . . of what?"

"Hang on!" Maybeck muttered. "I think they've spotted us."

One of the Cast Members in the center window was pointing directly at them. Maybeck was already setting down the binoculars when Finn saw the adult in the room also turn, his face cast in half shadow. The man pulled the curtains. Finn tried to imprint the image of his face, an attempt clouded by two of the boys taking off at a run.

"I think . . ." Finn said, watching the same two boys explode out of the recessed doorway of a bookstore to the right of the arcade and sprint across Main Street, ". . . we gotta get out of here! Come on!"

Finn ran smack into the door as he tried to pass

through it. "Fear," he said, twisting the doorknob, his stomach in knots. As early DHIs, the Keepers had had to deal with fear limiting their projections. Now it was happening again. Maybeck passed through. Charlene waited for Finn to get the door open, and they both slipped out into the hall.

"They're coming," Maybeck whispered from the top of the stairs.

"Tool room," Finn said.

Maybeck—able to keep his cool—passed through the door, unlocked it, and admitted Finn and Charlene. He got the door closed just as the two boys bounded up the stairs, panting.

Finn held his hands apart, then, focusing, swept them through each other in wraithlike fashion. Maybeck and Charlene nodded in agreement. Charlene indicated the tools at their feet, making a motion of clubbing something. Finn shook his head. They would not be striking Cast Members with hammers. Not today.

Door by door, the Cast Members searched the rooms, saying things like, "Nothing," "Empty!" and "No one!"

Finn tried to concentrate and make his hands lose their all clear. When he tried to clap, his palms passed through one another.

"We back away the moment it opens," Maybeck said. The others nodded.

Finn heard the door to Roy's office bump shut. Theirs would be next. Timing was everything. He had no desire for the Cast Members to see three ghosts step through walls—that would start too many rumors. Nor did he want them to have a chance to see and possibly remember their faces. Finn concentrated and picked up the sound of the boys' shoes on the hallway's plywood floor.

As those same footsteps slowed, Finn held out his hand, so that Maybeck and Charlene could see him count down with his fingers: three, two, one. They stepped back and through the wall in unison just as the door swung open.

All would have been fine had the Cast Members not left a sentry in the hallway. But one boy entered the tool room, and one remained behind.

He turned. "Got 'em!"

He likely hadn't seen them step through the wall, but he might wonder later how they'd miraculously shown up only a few feet away. The three Keepers ran for the stairs.

"No sides!" Maybeck called to his friends. He didn't want the Cast Members to see the side view of their two-dimensional projections: a thin blue line. He took the stairs two at a time. Finn, Charlene, and the Cast Members followed a yard or two behind. At the bottom,

Maybeck didn't hesitate for a second: he headed straight through the wall instead of taking the door leading backstage. Finn and Charlene followed suit, finding themselves in a darkened theater where Disney cartoons played on multiple screens.

"Look, Mommy! They came out of the picture!" said a young boy in shorts with suspenders.

"Don't point, Jimmy! It's impolite." Thankfully, the mother had missed their entrance. Still, she stared, perhaps wondering why the three kids had glowing blue outlines. The Keepers sidestepped out of the theater-in-the-round trying not to reveal their lack of depth.

Getting across Main Street proved trickier. They waited for a horse-drawn trolley to use as a screen, Finn thinking all the while that somewhere behind them were two very confused Cast Members who had to be wondering how three people their own ages had managed to vanish into thin air.

10

TINKERS

In the second-floor conference room in Disney Studios' Frank G. Wells building, eight grown-ups and a young woman sat around a blond-wood oval table. Refreshments and drinks awaited on a side table. A projector screen displayed art images of the current project under discussion: a virtual maze to be installed in Disneyland, which would match the one discovered in Cinderella's Castle in Walt Disney World.

Jess, who considered herself as close to being Amanda's sister as a nonrelative could get, thought back to Escher's Keep, a confounding assortment of Hogwarts-like misleading stairways, virtual floors, and trapdoors that, if climbed correctly, led the climber to what had been planned as Walt Disney's private apartment atop the Castle. Still, as a newcomer to the Imagineers' "Tink Tank," an elite think tank comprising the company's most brilliant creative minds, Jess, one of only two teens in attendance, kept her mouth shut. She wasn't sure if she was supposed to have seen Escher's Keep in person, much less climbed it with Wayne.

A knock on the locked conference room door stopped the conversation. When the chairman accessed a small security device, Jess gasped at the face on its video screen: Tim Walters. This had to be some kind of joke! She knew Tim from the dorm at the Disney School of Imagineering, where she and Amanda were in residence. He couldn't possibly be a member of the Tink Tank without her knowing. But obviously he was. So more to the point: How long had he been in the Tink Tank, and had he had anything to do with her invitation to join?

Tim was admitted and the door secured behind him. As he took a seat across and down the table, he looked straight at Jess from his six-foot-five towering height.

For Jess, this changed everything, though she wasn't sure exactly how. She had been searching for a way to find out more about a new version of DHI that would likely put her friends, the Kingdom Keepers, into the history books and out of service. She'd heard about the version 2.8 DHIs at an earlier Tink Tank meeting and had been terrified ever since. If the Keepers were retired from service, who would protect the parks?

"I wonder if," Jess said to those at the table, "when the virtual maze is installed, DHIs wouldn't make the perfect guides? A hologram can step on but not trigger a trapdoor, for instance, or walk through a mirrored hallway, causing all sorts of illusions."

"I like that," the man she took to be a film director said. Exact identities of Tink Tank members were not part of introductions. Members simply went by their first names. Jess thought there was at least one Disney animator, an architect or engineer, and a college professor in addition to the film director in the room. But she had many others to figure out. "When we roll out the new line, it wouldn't be a horrible idea to add a couple DHIs dedicated to just the maze. Thoughts?"

Several attendees nodded. Tim glared at Jess, as if trying to tell her something. His countenance bothered and distracted her. She wanted to ignore him, but found it nearly impossible.

"When would that be?" Jess asked, trying to sound innocent. "Would the timing work?"

"We can leave that kind of detail to the Imagineers," said today's chairperson, a woman who was likely an Imagineer herself. "Let's make a note of it. Good thinking, Jessica."

Tim's eyes were like lasers, trying to melt her face like a candle held up to wax. Jess managed to look away. Now she understood: he was jealous!

After fifteen minutes of discussion about partnering with a British aviation company to create a working replica of the *Millennium Falcon*, which would offer flights out of John Wayne Airport in Anaheim, the board members took a ten-minute refreshment break. The Tink Tankers paired off and clustered in small groups to socialize or discuss proposals "off-line." Jess headed straight for Tim, who seemed to want to avoid her.

"Look what the cat dragged in," Jess said.

"Let me give you the four-one-one: I've been a Tinker—that's what we call ourselves—for six months. Yes, I was asked to keep an eye on you and Amanda, but not like spying, not in a bad way. More like an evaluation, a tryout, you could say. Yes, I recommended you and not Amanda to the Tinkers, and if you ever tell her that, I'll never speak to you again. Sadly, I had no influence whatsoever. By the time I made my suggestion, they'd already decided to invite you. No, that had nothing do with our friendship." He shook his head, deep in thought. "Joe knows some of what we've done, I suppose. . . . I haven't told anyone personally."

Jess, unable to speak, toed the carpet.

"Look," he said, "I'm going to pull rank on you. I'm older. I've been in DSI longer, and I've been a Tinker longer. In here, you learn things you can't tell anyone about, and it drives you a little nuts. You learn to get good at saying nothing when you hear a rumor you know all about, but after a while you become pretty isolated and introverted. You want to watch that with Amanda. Don't let it mess up you two. I've lost some friends I wish I could get back." He smiled suddenly. "Now, praise the Disney gods! I have someone I can talk to!"

In that moment, Jess saw Tim in a whole new light. He was a Tinker, helping to shape Disney for years to come. He'd had to work through having a chip on his shoulder. What she'd taken to be arrogance was likely a defense mechanism, a way to protect himself and keep from spouting out details about top-secret programs. His intelligence was for real—unless he had some gift like hers that he had yet to mention. She measured him differently; appreciated him more.

"You broke the rules," she said softly. "You and Amanda. I'm not like that."

"I think I figured that out."

"There's more we need from the basement," she said. Amanda and Tim had previously snuck into the dormitory's restricted area in search of the DSI's secret archives. "It's not like you two can go down there again."

"No." They had nearly been caught by a pair of robots under the direction of an old maintenance man, had been questioned by Imagineering School authorities, and had come so close to being expelled that only quick thinking and luck had saved them. Tim had apparently learned his lesson.

He turned her, so she was speaking toward the wall. Jess got the message, and lowered her voice. "I need your support on this," was all she'd tell him. He tried to provoke more from her, but Jess was whisperingly stubborn.

"We're friends, right?" she asked.

"Well, yeah," he said begrudgingly. Tim was not a boy easily led down the road of sentimentality.

"Then let me be blunt." As if another option was on the table. "Being so tall has some advantages, I'm sure. It's kind of hard not to pay attention from down here, not to be intimidated by you, not to place more trust in you as a leader."

Tim's face contorted, expressing concern, but Jess kept talking.

"But being tall and a boy does not make you right more often than me. Being smarter does. And if you're smart, you'll help me out on this, because then I'll help you out on stuff you want to propose."

"I never considered doing otherwise."

"Oh." She looked almost hurt.

"But not because of any of your psychobabble. Because you're a friend, Jess. That's all: I like you. I won't support stupid stuff you propose, and you shouldn't do that for me either. But I have yet to hear anything stupid come out of your mouth. That's why. Not for any other reason."

"Seriously?" Was her face as red as it felt?

"Would you like me to pretend I'm in awe of your and Amanda's . . . talents?" he said, finding the word after a moment of thought. "I'm not. Well, maybe a little, but I'm not gaga or anything. I've worked with the people in this room for almost a year. Maybe they can't move a chair without touching it the way Amanda can, or freakishly draw stuff that hasn't happened yet, but that doesn't make their talents any less awesome."

Jess didn't like being called freakish. She was about to object when she realized that Tim had probably suffered through the same descriptions, but for even longer. She had a hunch that being six feet tall in sixth grade had seemed cool to everyone but the person who was six feet tall.

"It's about what that kid Nick told us," she said.

He nodded. "I figured."

"Seriously?"

"You ask that a lot," he said. "You can assume I'm serious unless I make you laugh."

She laughed.

"There." He wasn't only six foot five; his smile was big as well, his teeth blindingly white and perfect. It was the fact that all this came in a kind of goofy package that made Jess feel things for Tim she'd have rather not. "Break's over," he said, indicating the conference table.

"Do you trust all these people?" she asked.

Tim looked around carefully. "Well, I did until you asked me that. Now I'm going to have to think about it."

Back at the table, business chugged along. Tinkers raised issues or projects or problems. When a lull occurred, Jess spoke up. "I've got a question."

"Yes, Jessica?"

"I've heard at least one file was confiscated from that storage area," she said. "Can that be confirmed?"

Shock registered in the eyes of the other Tinkers. "I can confirm that," said the chairwoman.

"Since I'm basically at the level of an intern on this board, I thought I could volunteer to inventory the collection, to reveal what else might have been taken."

"That's a big job," the chairwoman said. Her voice indicated at least passing interest. "But that's quite an idea."

"When will you possibly find time for such a project?" asked a middle-aged woman with dark hair whose identity had stumped Jess so far. The woman's apparent knowledge of DSI caused Jess to wonder if she wasn't connected to the program.

"There are nights," Tim said. "I could help her. Since we're both board members, I'm assuming the information wouldn't be considered off-limits and," he added, continuing before anyone could correct him, "it might be good to get the archiving up-to-date and into a database of some kind. Unless, of course, that's already been handled."

"No, I don't believe it has," said a man with wispy gray hair, a thin, straight mustache, and drooping eyes. He reminded Jess of an old dog. "I like this idea," he declared, nodding to the chairwoman.

"If it hasn't been done, Arthur, it would be of value. . . ." the chairwoman said.

Jess nearly shrieked! Arthur Chancefeldt was a Disney Legend. He'd written several best-selling histories of the company and had been a force behind forming the Disney Archives.

"Of course it would!" the old dog proclaimed.

"We could bring in others," Jess suggested. "To help lighten the load, so long as Tim and I oversaw the work."

"I don't recommend that," the man said sternly. "Few outside this group know of the vault's existence, much less its content. That material was tucked away for a reason."

"It was too sensitive for Cast Members, too important to destroy," Jess said, theorizing, freezing the air and everyone in the room along with it. The effect was so profound and immediate that it startled her. She drew the scorn of Tim. But she had their attention now, and she felt the urge to push forward. "A schism. A challenge to authority—to the company itself. Damaging information, or at least potentially damaging. I can see I must be close! If we're all sworn to secrecy, then why not tell me?"

"And me!" Tim said. "Accidents in the park? Lawsuits against the company? What can be that damaging?"

"Suffice it to say," said the chairwoman, "that this is a committee that deals with the present and the future, not the past. There are others who handle such things, not us."

"But the completeness of the archive," said Chancefeldt, nodding his support of the chairwoman, "is very much our concern. The absolute secrecy and security of the documents therein must be ensured."

The chairwoman's disapproving face implied he'd gone too far. "Never mind all that," she said. "Those in favor of Jess's proposal?" A number of hands went up. "Opposed?" Two hands: one, from the movie director, who struck Jess as the type who enjoyed voting against the others; the second from a bone-thin woman with an artist's flair to her appearance. Her lack of mass made it difficult to determine her age; she might have been in her late twenties or early sixties. Her dark eyes conveyed a deep-seated warning to Jess, less threat than caution. It was almost as if she were trying to say, *I've been there and you do not want to go.*

What it all meant, Jess wasn't sure. But it colored her moment of triumph—she and Tim were approved to inventory the secret archives!—and left her feeling like a child on her own for the first time, watching her parents turn the lock behind them and wondering about being in the house at night, all alone.

11

MAD TEA PARTY

"I'VE HAD AN IDEA. Follow me."

So much as a projection could startle, Finn did. The voice belonged to Wayne, who even as a teenager could be as cryptic as the man he'd turn out to be later in life. And just like that much-vaunted Imagineer, this younger version of Wayne took off before allowing Finn, Maybeck, or Charlene any chance to respond—a "my way or the highway" man, not disposed to democracy.

The three followed him, Maybeck checking behind for the boys they'd encountered at Roy's Main Street office.

"Although, it's good to be cautious," Wayne said, leading them through a mercantile shop. It was stocked with toys and items the teens viewed as antiques. The Mickey Mouse stuffed animals looked nothing like the Mickey they knew; the postcards and trinkets they'd seen only on eBay, selling for hundreds of dollars. A few of the T-shirts and sweatshirts were the same as in present time; Disney had come out with a line of "retro" clothing that attempted to duplicate these same relics.

"Mr. Disney knows me, you see," Wayne said. He

spoke over his shoulder, as if expecting the Keepers to be hanging on his every word—which they were. "I know for a fact he and Mrs. Disney plan to ride the various attractions today, just as they did yesterday. I happen to know their schedule as well," he added proudly. "They are riding the Mad Tea Party in a few minutes with their children. Mrs. Disney does not like taking her purse on the more active rides."

"What's that supposed to mean?" Maybeck asked, dodging a rack of black-and-white postcards.

"It means," said Finn, "that Wayne intends to hold Mrs. Disney's purse for her."

"Because," said Charlene, "women carry what's important to them in their purses."

"We're going to pinch Mrs. Disney's purse?" Maybeck said. "And you think somehow that won't attract attention?"

"We're going to inspect it," Wayne said. "More specifically, you three are. As you pointed out, I can't afford to lose my job. And you'll have to have it back to me before the ride ends."

"This should be interesting," said Charlene.

Wayne nodded vigorously. "The way you three look, by golly! You'll have to remain at arm's length so that you can't be identified or asked questions. And most of all, be very, very careful."

12

SNATCHERS

"WE NEED TO LOSE ALL CLEAR," Finn said. "We won't be able to hold the purse, much less search it, if we're pure projection."

"Well, you're an idiot!" Maybeck said aggressively.

"That's it!" Finn said. "I definitely felt something. More."

The three Keepers stood across from the Mad Tea Party. A large crowd had approached, partially surrounding two adults who were instantly recognizable as Walt and Lillian Disney. The two young women with them, both in their early twenties, were clearly either related or close family friends. It was something of a parade, the Disneys walking at a leisurely gait, the trailing crowd keeping pace.

"You're an idiot, and I'd slap you if I could!" Maybeck told Finn.

"My fingers are tingling," Finn said. It wasn't only fear that could provoke a loss of pure projection. Anger, frustration, and other negative emotions did the job, too. He turned to Charlene and wrinkled his nose. "Your hair looks stupid and that ugly dress doesn't really work at all."

"Okay, okay," she said, flexing her fingers to test them. "Keep it coming."

Maybeck tried pushing Finn, but his hand went through his friend's body. Finn, who'd always had a degree more control than the others, returned the shove and managed to connect with Maybeck, turning him violently.

"You got frustrated, not being able to hit me," Finn taunted. Maybeck pushed back. This time, he made contact. Now they were going, both boys shoving each other while speaking meanly to Charlene.

"You and Willa cry too much," Finn said, a complete lie.

"Do not!" She shoved him, and he felt it.

"Do too!" he said, egging her on. The three Keepers were well on their way to being partial holograms and capable of retrieving the handbag from Wayne, who was waving at his employer. Walt waved back, a good sign.

"Shouldn't stop," Charlene said. They kept smacking one another in the shoulders and pulling on each other's arms. From a distance, it appeared to be quite the quarrel, and when Maybeck struck Charlene so hard she stumbled back, a man crossed the path, heading toward them.

"Uh-oh," Maybeck said. "Don't look now, but we've got company."

Finn did look, and just in time. "Backs to the wall," he ordered, not wanting them exposed from the side.

"Excuse me, sir!"

The sound of Philby's voice turned the heads of his friends, as well as that of the man on the way to rescue Charlene from what appeared to be a slickly dressed assailant. The man looked in Philby's direction. And Philby disappeared.

In fact, he'd reduced himself to a thin blue line of one dimension, but given the park guests, the blue sky, and sunshine, he appeared to have vanished. The man looked bewildered. When Philby reappeared a few strides later and called out again, the enchantment was complete.

Unfortunately, Charlene's would-be rescuer wasn't the only one to have seen Philby's magic "act."

"What in tarnation was that?" The voice sounded so familiar to Finn. He took it to be Walt Disney's, but couldn't confirm it. A passerby blocked Finn's view; he heard the same voice again saying, "You see that? There!"

Philby reappeared, disappeared, and was then apparently gone for good.

"We gotta go!" Maybeck said.

But Charlene's would-be rescuer had almost reached them now. "Hey, boy!" he called out cruelly, aiming the words directly at Maybeck, who pointed his thumb at himself, shocked. "Yeah, you! What do you mean putting your hands on that girl?"

"Oops," Maybeck said under his breath to Finn and Charlene.

"You say something to me, boy? City slicker, are we?"

"He's my friend, sir," Charlene said, stepping forward. "We were just . . . horsing around."

"He tell you to say that? This boy threatening you, miss?" The man had a tattoo of an anchor on his forearm, with the letters USN beneath. United States Navy. A World War II veteran, Finn thought. Tough, and willing to show it.

"No, sir, he really is my friend."

The man was still far enough away not to pick up on their low-resolution pixelation, but if he drew any closer . . . Charlene laced her very solid hand with Maybeck's and squeezed. This man's threats had pushed all three Keepers well out of their projections and into something more mortal.

"I don't mean no trouble, sir," Maybeck said, sounding nothing like himself and more like the stereotypical black man from an old, old movie. Finn blinked at him in surprise. "We here to have a good time, me and my friends."

"Well, maybe you should have it without the lady for right now, boy. What do you say to that? What do you say you let her go and you just walk free and clear of here? Maybe out of this here park altogether."

"Now, now!" A lady's voice. It belonged to Mrs. Disney, Finn realized. She was without her purse—there was Wayne behind her, wiggling it for the three of them to see. Walt had been engulfed by his fans. "That's not how we treat our fellow guests in Disneyland, sir. And I should know. My husband created this park."

The aggressive man pivoted toward Mrs. Disney, already lifting his hat from his head. He bowed and uttered a string of apologies in rapid succession. It gave the Keepers the perfect excuse to move, their backs kept to the wall, slipping away from the problem. As they got out of Mrs. Disney's peripheral vision, they angled themselves and caught up to Wayne, who'd stepped into the path. Charlene took the purse. Miraculously, it stayed in place instead of crashing to the ground.

Mrs. Disney could be heard behind them. She was polite but firm with the man, who sounded ever so humbled. A reprimand from a celebrity had reduced him to a gushing sycophant.

The three teens rounded a hot dog cart; Charlene set the purse on a bench.

"You two check it out," Finn said, "while I keep watch."

Finn wanted to search the purse and find Walt's

pen; he felt certain it would be there, that Wayne's theory was solid. But one of the qualities he'd learned as a leader was the willingness to take crummy assignments. If he took all the fun and glory, resentment from the others would pile up quickly. It was something Philby had yet to learn, and it separated his and Finn's styles of leadership.

Mrs. Disney returned to her husband, just in time for the Disneys to board the Mad Tea Party. There was a massive push by other park patrons to line up and join them on the ride. Thankfully, as far as Finn was concerned, it kept all the attention there, and away from anything else. He checked over his shoulder, repeatedly wanting to shout, *Get on with it!*

Within seconds, he could tell there'd been no immediate discovery. Maybeck and Charlene dug around desperately in the small purse. Charlene stood, the purse in hand, obviously ready to return it. Maybeck had the slumped shoulders of the defeated; after a second, he squared up and reached for the purse. Finn divided his attention between the events at the Mad Tea Party and his friends, arguing behind him. He heard Maybeck say, "One of the coins!" Charlene relented, surrendering the purse. Maybeck unsnapped it and put his head so close the brim of his hat struck the purse and dislodged.

"Oh no!" he heard Maybeck say as his hand passed through the bag instead of stopping inside it. Finn understood what was happening. His own fingers had begun to tingle the moment they'd found a safe hiding place behind the cart. Maybeck tried again. His projected hand waved through the bag.

The Mad Tea Party was slowing down, the ride ending! Wayne looked frantically at Finn.

"Switch!" Finn called, and Maybeck reacted instantly, taking his place.

"There's a coin with the others," Maybeck told him, "a little smaller than a quarter, a little thicker than a nickel. You're a pigheaded piece of dog poo, by the way."

Finn felt his hands grow more solid. "Thanks." He joined Charlene, who had also returned to all clear, her fear rising as their time ticked down. Together, they dug into the purse. Seconds passed, and Charlene's hand went spongy against the bench.

"Will we be able to carry it back to Wayne?" she whispered.

"You have a zit the size of a raisin next to your nose," Finn said, attempting to jolt her.

"Oh! That's better!" Charlene proclaimed.

"Your hair, besides looking pathetic, hasn't been washed in three days."

Her hand smacked the bench. "That did it! Though I may never forgive you for the 'pathetic' comment."

Finn had the interior coin purse open. He saw a torn half of a twenty-dollar bill. He grabbed for it, and failed to pick it up. It was too light, too thin.

"They're getting off," Maybeck said. "Hurry!"

"Got it!" Finn announced, taking hold of the coin that fit Maybeck's description. It looked familiar, though he couldn't place it. It wasn't American currency.

"I have no idea if my pocket will work," Finn said. "These projections are so unstable."

"We've got to hide it. We can't have it falling out of your pants somewhere."

"We could give it to Wayne," Finn said.

"Too tricky. It'll be hard enough for me to pass him the purse," Charlene whispered.

"Hurry!" Maybeck hissed.

"Go!" Finn told Charlene, who scooped up the purse mumbling, "Pathetic?" and headed toward Wayne.

Disneyland's 1950s grounds were so different, so sparse. Finn was afraid the hot dog cart might be rolled away at any moment. Maybeck had an artist's eye; Finn turned to him and explained their predicament.

"There!" Maybeck said, pointing behind them. "That boat."

The boys took off in the direction of the replica

pirate ship under construction, a square-rigger painted black and gold. It was permanently docked and set up as a restaurant. The gangplank boardwalk leading to the door in the hull had rope railings fixed to stanchions every eight feet. Maybeck reached the second of the posts and told Finn to remember it. "Tuck the coin between the rope and wood. We'll come back for it after midnight, when we're solid and handling it won't be so risky."

It was a brilliant solution. The coin all but disappeared.

"Let's gather up the group," Finn said, smiling.

* * *

"Does anyone else think meeting here is really weird?" Willa said, poised on the edge of a futuristic bathtub.

"Actually," Maybeck said snidely, "I was just thinking they got this one incredibly right. This is basically what bathrooms have become."

"I meant that we're meeting in a bathroom in the first place!" Willa said.

"It's a display bathroom," Charlene said. "I mean, that's a glass wall over there. It's like a fishbowl."

"It's not somewhere anyone's going to look," Wayne said. "That's the point."

The futuristic bathroom of 1955 looked exactly

like a contemporary bathroom in a nice home of the 2000s: large, partially sunken tub, two sinks—his and hers—corner shower tiled in stone, and a toilet behind a wing wall, all lit by architectural lighting. The group's voices reverberated off the stone and glass, but couldn't be heard outside of the room—all part of Wayne's planning.

"The Golden Horseshoe reception starts soon," Finn said. "We know those other kids, the fake Cast Members, have something planned, but we don't know what it is."

"I still can't believe you left that twenty-dollar bill in her purse," Maybeck said to Finn.

"I tried. What's important is: Mrs. Disney and Roy each have the same coin, and they each have one-half of a twenty dollar bill, meaning Walt or someone wanted them to put those two halves together to prove their connection."

"Trouble," Philby repeated. "The Cast Members we saw are planning trouble. The question, therefore, is how to stop it without knowing what it is."

"I'm not invited to party at the Horseshoe," Wayne said, "but I think it might be possible for me to get a waiter's costume and join the catering staff. As long as I work hard, no one's going to complain. We're a team here."

"That's good," Philby said.

"At least we're dressed for a party," Charlene said, ever conscious of her appearance.

"Our projections are so limiting," Finn said, raising his wavering hand and shaking it in frustration.

"Philby and I are working on that," Wayne said. "The technology he describes from . . . where you came from . . . I think the company is going to be 'ahead of the times' for a long while if I can get even half of it to work. And no one will ever know why."

He drew laughter from everyone but Finn, who was all business.

"We can't be seen from the side, so we'll take up places around the room, our backs to the walls. We keep an eye out for any of the Cast Members we've seen, either at the studio or at Roy's apartment."

Finn nodded to Maybeck, who repeated a list of the ID tag numbers they suspected belonged to possible Overtakers. "Wayne will check out the waiters and waitresses as well."

"'Check out'?" Wayne said, having no idea what the expression meant. "Like checking a hat or coat?"

Charlene explained as best she could. Wayne nodded and told Finn to continue.

"You'll keep an eye on all of us," Finn explained to Wayne, who nodded. "We'll signal you if we see something weird—suspicious," he said, correcting himself. "From there, I guess we improvise."

"Our specialty," Maybeck said, playing with the sink hardware.

"Please don't touch that!" Wayne admonished. Too late. At that exact moment, Maybeck pulled loose a faucet handle—and fumbled to put it back into place.

"It's got to be some form of sabotage they have planned," said Willa, smiling ruefully at Maybeck. "I mean, right? They wanted the schedule of events for the day, but nothing really bad has happened yet. This is the last event. Any clue at all, Wayne?"

Wayne shook his head. "I've gone over this repeatedly," he said. "On the horrible side: someone tries to poison Mr. Disney. But I'll be in and out of the kitchen, looking for something like that. On the bright side, someone—possibly the Cast Members—is planning an innocent surprise, a congratulations to the Disneys and their friends. This has been an incredibly complicated construction, difficult and expensive. So many challenges. The man deserves a crown and a throne."

"It's not how these people work," Maybeck said ominously. All the Keepers wanted to disagree or soften the tone, but they couldn't. What Maybeck said was true.

"Right!" Finn said. "So, that's the plan. And we're

uninvited, so we'll need to come through the walls as projections. We'll do it one at a time, a few minutes apart."

"Bathroom stalls," Wayne said. "I can direct you to step through the walls of the empty bathroom stalls. No one can see you enter that way."

"What about us girls?" Charlene said.

"I'll get you close enough," Wayne said. "Two taps"—he knocked twice on the tile—"and it's safe."

"Appropriate enough, given this place," Maybeck said, still struggling to get the faucet handle back on.

13

RULES WERE RULES

TIM AND JESS GOT OFF to a late start. Absent from their Disney School of Imagineering classes because of the Tink Tank meeting in Burbank, they'd spent much of the afternoon laboring to make up classwork. Tim had been helping Emily Frederickson with the tech details of her fiber-optic clothing designs while Jess reviewed a video of a lecture on Addressing Design—"The Essential Elements of Guest Movement."

Jess had barely seen Amanda all day; so when they finally crossed paths in a hallway, they ran to the fourth-floor commissary and grabbed Starbucks. Once again, Jess had to make excuses for where she'd been. Her membership in the Tink Tank was secret, even to her best-friend-slash-sister. She felt horrible for lying, and was terrible at it, clearly raising Amanda's suspicions.

"I didn't see Tim all day either," Amanda said, nudging her friend.

"Is that right? He must be around here. Probably with Emily."

"No, I saw Emily. She hadn't seen him either."

"Is that right?" Jess said.

"Okay, now I know there's something going on. I haven't seen you make that face since Mrs. Nash almost caught us eating her frozen waffles. What's up with you two? You can tell me!"

Amanda sounded unbearably excited by the notion of romance. Jess hated to let her down. "Actually, it's not like that. I kind of wish it were . . . but it's not. It's the Hollingsworth files."

"We'll never get back down there."

"I'm in. I was asked to inventory the collection by Professor Fielding."

"Seriously? Do you think they know something?"

"If they do, they obviously don't suspect me. I'm allowed to ask one other student to help, but it has to be a boy. I'm going to choose Tim."

"This must be because of our being almost caught down there—Emily and me."

"Probably. They want an inventory to know what's missing. But I can put back the files we took so they won't be noticed."

"They? Who are they?"

"Ah . . . Professor Fielding didn't just make this up on her own, right?" Jess had nearly slipped up. She hated lying to her best friend, but rules were rules. And lies were worse! Each lie was a link in a chain that eventually bound you to them. Jess knew to keep details out of her explanations. Details came back to bite you. "Hey, it also gives me and Tim a chance to search for anything else to do with Hollingsworth. We'll see every piece of paper in that entire place."

"That'll take forever."

"We're going to help them, Mandy, I promise."

"Don't make promises you can't keep," Amanda said, her voice fragile, her eyes aimed at the floor.

* * *

An hour later, Tim and Jess rode an elevator from the dorm lobby down to the mechanical basement level, two stories underground. They were met by a sour-smelling, craggy-skinned man. A stubble of white beard on his cleft, pointed chin stretched up onto the sunken cheeks of his narrow, pinched face. He looked like someone large had sat upon him as an infant, and then put him on a rack in a dungeon and stretched him into Jack Skellington. But he had an even voice, which made him sound much younger than he looked.

"Ever been down here before?" he asked. Being that it was against DSI rules to enter the basement, and that there was no known way to even get down there, the question was either meant as a joke or was an attempt to measure the students' expressions, in light of the break-in that had recently occurred.

"No," said Tim, "but I love what you've done with the place."

The former hotel—and its vast basement—covered an entire city block of Anaheim. Down here, it was all giant rusted pipes, metal columns, concrete, and narrow rows of metal shelving that held all manner of hotel furniture, lighting, mechanical parts, carpet scraps and replacement parts. It looked like a furniture store of yesteryear. Dirk the Jerk—as the students called him—harrumphed and led them into the grid of shelving and aisles. The end caps of the stacks carried references to the contents of a particular row: LL FURN, HVAC, EL MISC.

Jess tried memorizing the route—left, left, right, left—but lost track fairly quickly. Tim followed alongside, his head tilted back, watching the ceiling. After a time, Jess realized he was using the overhead wires and pipes like a road map.

Dirk walked quickly, again belying his apparent age. Jess knew of the robots he'd modified into mechanized sentries; suddenly, Dirk made sense: a displaced Imagineer, ousted decades before.

Sweat trickled down her ribs. A third person had been on the elevator with her and Tim. Emily Fredrickson, whose foray into tech fabrics had led to the invisibility suit she currently wore, had walked off a step behind Tim. The plan called for her to immediately break away and parallel them, so as not to risk Dirk hearing or sensing her. Emily had been down in the basement before, with Amanda and Tim, wearing the same suit. She knew which direction to head.

"Did you know Wayne Kresky?" Jess asked, trying to distract herself.

Dirk stopped dead in his tracks and turned. Jess immediately thought something had failed on the suit and that he'd spotted Emily. "What's it to you?" he said.

That inquiry allowed Jess to also stop and steal a look behind Tim. Thankfully, if Emily was there, she remained invisible. Jess wasn't made for such subterfuge, for spying and lying. She wasn't comfortable having to role-play; she liked being herself, had enough on her plate contending with her random dreams and the way they often foretold the future.

"He was a friend of mine, that's all," she said, somewhat defensively.

"Was he?" Dirk considered this a moment. "Well, never mind that. He's gone, isn't he." It wasn't a question. "A good man, Wayne. A favorite of Mr. Disney's right from the start. That was a long time ago." Bitterness colored his voice.

"You were an Imagineer back then," Jess said, taking

a guess—and possibly a chance at riling him. "Probably still are."

"What one was before hardly matters. It's what one is now that counts. I'm good with keeping this old lady up and on her feet." He lifted his arms like a priest, indicating the walls around them.

"The hotel," Tim said.

"You see any other old ladies?" Dirk asked scathingly. "Look." He fixed Tim with a searing gaze. "I know them were your sneakers I seen in the dumbwaiter that night. Never no mind they gone missing from your room. You took down two of my best, and I ain't the forgiving type."

Tim and Amanda had short-circuited the two modified inventory robots with a combination of laundry soap and water. The robots had sparked and smoked and, in all likelihood, melted their motherboards. Dirk was probably still trying to repair them.

"You searched my room. How'd that work out?" Tim said defiantly. Jess winced; she'd be trying to keep him and Dirk from exchanging blows if they didn't hurry up and reach the storage room. "I'm as interested in you and this basement as Jess is. It's all new to me."

"Uh-huh. So how'd you bark your knuckles?"

Tim hesitated, incriminating himself immediately. Despite looking like a person who lived on the streets,

Dirk had mettle—and he was showing it now.

"Ah . . . moving furniture around," Tim said, almost fast enough to sound convincing. But not quite.

"And how many other DSI students in this dorm do you think walk around in size thirteen sneakers?"

"I wouldn't know."

"One, and you're him."

"And that's significant, how?"

"Size thirteen shoe prints all over the laundry room. Leading to the very spot where I seen a pair of large blue sneakers and a set of very long legs crammed into the dumbwaiter." He stared pointedly at Tim's long legs. "But I suppose that's just coincidence."

"Without being completely rude, I thought we'd established that you searched my room and found no pair of sneakers."

Dirk harrumphed again, dissatisfied and displeased.

"Is that it?" Jess said, pointing enthusiastically.

"Yes it is, missy. Quite the job the two of you are fixing to do. Necessary. Long overdue, to be sure. But not something for the faint of heart. As I understand it, you've been sworn to secrecy."

"Many times over," said Tim.

"I wasn't talking to you, Daddy Longlegs. I don't trust you, pal, and I don't believe a word you say. Neither should you, missy. A boy the likes of this one here will get you in more trouble than it's worth. Expelled if you're lucky. Arrested, more like."

Jess swallowed dryly. She'd been thinking the same thing practically from the first time she'd met Tim Walters. "Yes, sir. I'll keep that in mind."

"Practically speaking, missy, let me offer a word to the wise." Dirk stopped them in front of the reinforced wire door and chain-link, floor-to-ceiling walls that enclosed the archive. "This here is under lock and key. Plenty of secrets are at home in this place. You been sworn to keep 'em that way and," he said, addressing Tim, "that's all well and good, but it's only a piece of paper. So let me tell you this: you will be held to your word. By me, and by others, too."

He peered over Jess's shoulder as if he could see Emily standing there in her invisibility suit. The gesture reminded Jess to be wary of this man and his overly keen senses. Hopefully Emily had moved into the room and was in hiding. Jess shifted from foot to foot as Dirk continued speaking.

"Best if you check your curiosity at the door. Take your inventory by matching the file tabs with the list pasted under the lid. Nothing more. You start reading and, first, it's going to slow you down to a crawl. Second, well, there's stuff in there you ain't never going to get out of your head once you read it. As special as that may make you feel right now, it'll bore down into you like a weevil and eat you from the inside out. Take it from one who knows."

Perhaps it was the stark lighting catching his angular face just so. Maybe his eyes flashed red for a millisecond. Or maybe it was the sound of sucking between his teeth that gave Jess a sickly feeling. Whatever the cause, her gut did a couple of somersaults. How far to the nearest restroom? she thought queasily.

"We got the download already. Thanks anyway," Tim said rudely. Jess could have kicked him; it was senseless to provoke Dirk. It would achieve nothing and would only intensify his scrutiny, which they could ill afford, what with Emily only two feet behind Jess.

"An added warning, you two, though I don't know why I bother. Security down here has been beefed up, not that you two need to hear that, given your being sworn to secrecy and the rules of behavior as you been. I have some inventory machines of my own you may encounter. Just step out of the way and present your dorm room card if asked. You got that?"

This was new information to both Jess and Tim. "Dorm room card," Jess repeated.

"Got it," said Tim.

Both were wondering exactly what Emily was

supposed to do if one of the robots picked up a heat signature or used some other kind of technology to detect her.

"And listen, I don't mean to scare you," the old man said, savoring the moment. "But it would be unfair not to warn you of the ghosts and other inhabitants, holdovers from the night of the lightning and the fire, the earthquake and the terror. The bodies that were found—they did fine, even the dead ones. But those that were trapped, or crushed and mutilated—there were twenty-three souls unaccounted for that night—they got stuck in a kind of limbo, if you will. It ain't often, but it ain't never neither that they come poking their heads out all curious and cold. My robos can throw up a charge between their hands that would fry a stuffed pig in minutes. Strong enough to powder those plasma-dripping, vacant-eyed remnants. But I don't reckon it's anything either of you should mess with. They come a-haunting, the best thing you can do is scream your heads off. My robos hear that, they'll come a-running. They can take it from there."

"Ghosts," Tim snickered dismissively.

"Laugh, and the world laughs with you, sonny boy. Cry, and you cry alone."

Dirk unlocked and opened the door. Then he left them, shuffling off, caught beneath one hanging lamp, then the next, appearing and disappearing like a time lapse of the moon in the sky.

Jess let out an audible sigh, looked up high into Tim's somewhat pale face, and stepped through into the caged room. Listening carefully, she could hear Emily, right behind her.

14

THE WILD LION

DISAPPOINTMENT HUNG OVER Jess, Tim, and Emily like a cold mist. They sat in a glum row, poised on the edge of one of the two beds in the girls' dorm room, and explained their lack of a discovery to Amanda.

"All we found were these," Tim said, holding out a small group of newspaper clippings. "Filed under Legal, Concerns, Conspiracy, and Collusion. It was a lucky find; we'd have missed it, except, as you can see, someone scribbled and then highlighted Amery Hollingsworth's name with a question mark after it."

"The really weird thing," Jess said, "is that the article is dated 1959 and has to do with a wild lion discovered on the Jungle Cruise during morning run-through. There was a lion escape reported by the zoo at about the same time—the two articles are stapled together. If that lion had attacked park guests . . ."

"So the obvious question is: Did the lion escape, or was he kidnapped? And if so, why is Hollingsworth's name written onto the article?"

"And why is any of this in the archives?" Amanda asked, exasperated.

Emily spoke for the first time. She still wore her skintight invisibility suit, which was made of woven fiber-optic threads and Mylar. Her Spider-Man–like hood was pulled off, leaving her hair in a tangle.

"At the risk of sounding stupid," she said, "do you think the boy you told me about could help? Nick Perkins? Wasn't he the one who knew about the Legacy of Secrets and Hollingsworth in the first place?"

"Yeah. We met him at an ice hockey game, of all things," Jess said. "He's not a real public kid."

"If the point is to find your five friends," Emily said, "and if their disappearance is tied up with the Legacy of Secrets, then isn't Nick the person to ask?"

"Not if you're wearing that invisibility suit," Tim said. "You look like you've been dipped in something. Clothes would help."

The three girls snarled at him. "Pig," Amanda said. "The thing is, it's a good idea, Emily, but Nick kinda found us last time."

"You two never really explained this whole Legacy of Secrets thing," Emily said to Amanda and Jess. "I admit—I'm a little confused."

"Didn't we? Sorry! If we had it figured out, we could explain it," Amanda said ruefully.

"Basically," Jess said, "it comes down to some kind of plan—as yet to be determined—that explains the formation of the Overtakers. The Disney villains—"

"Wanting to run things," Tim quipped.

"I know it sounds preposterous," Amanda said, "but it's legit. The Keepers, the Overtakers, the whole thing. Two of our friends died fighting them, both incredible people. Died, as in gone. As in heartbreaking, aching loss. And here's the thing: if we can tell the Keepers about the Legacy of Secrets, about Hollingsworth maybe being behind it, if they're able to understand this before it ever happens . . . You see?"

"Are you saying those two wouldn't have to die?" There was awe in Emily's voice.

"I'm saying history and time are the same. If you mess with one, maybe you mess with the other." Amanda crossed her arms, holding herself as if cold. "And you're right, Em. To do that, we need Nick's help. But how to find him?"

"He's a sneaky guy," Tim said.

"Can't you send up the Bat Signal or something?" Emily asked playfully.

Tim took her literally. "Actually . . . maybe I can!"

15

THE GOLDEN HORSESHOE

THE COSTUMES CHOSEN by Maybeck, Charlene, and Willa before crossing over into the Disneyland of sixty years prior were formal enough to allow the three to attend the Opening Day VIP reception at the Golden Horseshoe. Philby and Finn, whose DHI projection costumes were too casual, wanted a view of the goings-on without the risk of being seen. They decided to hide out on the Mark Twain Riverboat.

Inside, the party was just getting started. It led off with a rousing performance of saloon tunes by Betty Taylor and four high-kicking dancers on a small stage, which faced out onto the mock Western saloon. A pianist, trumpet player, and drummer, all clean-cut men dressed in white shirts and ties, occupied the small orchestra space and faced the performers. Bookending the stage were four box seat compartments. Additional balcony seating, marked off by a gleaming white banister, wrapped around the room.

Overhead, the smoked glass chandeliers helped convince guests that they'd stepped into a bygone era—the irony of which was not lost on the two-dimensional visitors, who kept to the left wall beneath the balcony as Wally Boag slipped seamlessly into a comedy sketch. Dance hall girls in frilly skirts mingled.

"There," Maybeck said, cocking his head toward the front table. By wearing a hat inside he drew attention to himself—not proper etiquette in 1955, but he had no choice: it was part of his projected image.

In the direction he pointed, Walt and Lillian Disney occupied a small table. They appeared to be hosting two other guests.

"Anyone up on history?" Willa, the bookworm, asked.

"History of the U.S. women's gymnastics team," Charlene whispered, hoping to win a smile.

"Don't look now," Maybeck said, "but half the men in this place are looking over here."

"It's Charlene," Willa said. "You're too pretty, girl."

Charlene's more advanced hologram could actually blush. The two-dimensional Charlene simply smiled. "I'm the one staring, believe me. How amazing is this? We're in Disneyland—*the* Disneyland—on the second day it ever existed. We're looking at stuff people only wish they'd seen. They make up stories about these days, and yet, here we are! I want to freeze this moment!"

"The history lesson is this," Willa said. "If the couple sitting with the Disneys looks familiar, it's because I'm pretty sure the guy is Ronald Reagan, future governor of California and president of the United States. At this point, he's a big deal radio host and film actor, which explains the seating arrangement. Mind you, it may not be him, but it's pretty cool if it is."

"Thrilling," Maybeck said sarcastically. He sounded bored out of his mind.

"You can be such a killjoy!" Charlene said, glaring at him. "We are living history."

Willa was not to be browbeaten. "Not just living. We are part of history. Who gets to say that? The rest of the guests are probably business and community leaders, their husbands and wives, and some of Walt's creative team. They have a lot to celebrate. They had fifty thousand paying guests in the park today. Huge crowds! Disneyland is open and running and making money. That's got to feel good."

"Again: fascinating," Maybeck quipped. "So where are the idiots who got all up in my face? 'Cause if they aren't here, I suggest we make like shadows and follow them out. If Charlene draws any more attention, we'll be the main show."

"I wish you wouldn't tease me like that," Charlene said.

"He ain't teasing, sweetheart," Willa said, trying to sound Western. "We're drawing way too many looks."

"If nothing's happening, we should get out of here," an unusually nervous Maybeck repeated.

The crowd applauded. Waitresses dressed as saloon girls and carrying small trays slipped between tables, taking orders and delivering drinks.

"It's all so low-tech," Willa said. "You know? The attractions are like amusement park rides—a steamboat, wagon, and mule rides—only Peter Pan's Flight and a couple of others show you what's to come. And things like this . . . I get why it seems fun. No one was doing this kind of reproduction back . . . now. But it's—"

"A little dated?" Charlene said, causing them all to laugh.

An emcee came on stage, and introduced and thanked the Disneys. The applause was thunderous. Maybeck made the mistake of trying to clap, his hands passing through one another. A simple error that might have meant nothing, except for a well-dressed man with slicked back brown hair who looked like Leonardo DiCaprio. He saw the illusion occur, and his jaw dropped.

"Oh, shoot," Charlene said.

"I see him," Maybeck told her.

"He's coming over here."

"Yeah, and if we take off, we're going to disappear or look like three flags hurrying toward the door. That's nothing but trouble."

"I've got this," Charlene said, taking three quick strides

toward the handsome man and intercepting him before he reached Maybeck and Willa. Away from the wall, she'd placed her two-dimensional form into a three-dimensional space. It was a huge risk. If she could keep the man six to eight feet away, he might not notice her flat face and body. No one had seen such projections before; the human mind didn't know to see their images as incorrect. It was an advantage. But too close and there was no hiding.

"Hello, there," Charlene said. She stopped the man cold. "Or should I say, 'Howdy'?"

He bowed his head slightly. "Pleased to meet you."

"You won't go giving away our secret, will you?" she asked.

"What secret is that?" he asked.

"Mr. Disney arranged a little treat for the guests," Charlene said.

That surprised and intrigued him. "Do tell!"

"A new ghost." She waved her arm so that his hand passed through her. "Impressed?"

He took a startled step back, keeping his distance. "I've never seen anything like that!"

"Well, if you had, it wouldn't be much of a surprise now, would it?" She paused. "Enjoying the party?"

He couldn't speak. He reached out for her, but she stepped back.

"Me?" she said, as if he'd asked. "All but the smoking."

The man held a cigarette burning between his fingers. "I find it a disgusting habit. My prediction is that fifty years from now, it'll turn out to be the cause of heart disease, early death, and spiraling national health-care costs. That's just a wild guess. Still, you might want to consider it."

He looked at her curiously. "I . . . ah . . ."

"Enjoy the show."

Wisely, Charlene chose to back away rather than turn around to return to her friends. Managing a two-dimensional self made her feel like Joy in Pixar's *Inside Out*, during the abstraction chamber scene. Her friends at school talked about envying girls who were paper thin. In truth, it wasn't so great.

"Way to go," Willa said, as Charlene put her flat back against the flat wall.

"Check it out!" Maybeck said, a little too loudly. He directed their attention to the wings of the stage, where they saw two boys, arms out, preventing the emcee from entering. The emcee was not pleased; the boys were giving no quarter. "You think that's them?"

"Could be," said Willa, keenly interested and edging forward.

"Why stop the singer?" Charlene said. "Unless . . ."

"They have another show in mind," Maybeck finished for her.

124

16

THE ENTOURAGE

FIVE MINUTES EARLIER, from their perch aboard the Mark Twain Riverboat, Finn and Philby had seen four Cast Members, all boys, approach the Golden Horseshoe. Philby expressed the same reservations about the boys as Maybeck had, believing they looked similar to the ones at the studios.

Now Finn spotted a group of well-dressed adults coming quickly toward the saloon on foot. At first, he'd thought they were just people late for the party and eager to reach the building. But something about them put him on guard. There was a man at their center with two women and three men surrounding him like a security detail. Those in the detail were younger by far than the man they protected. The 1950s dresses and suits gave the whole thing a theatrical feel; it was hard for Finn to see it as anything more than a scene in a stage play or musical. Like at any second the group would burst into song and start dancing.

Finn found the displacement into a time six decades earlier as difficult an adjustment as he did his two-dimensional projection. Was he alone in this? he wondered. Willa and Charlene seemed to be enjoying wearing their fancy dresses. Philby and Maybeck were unbothered by the change. All the Keepers seemed in awe of being part of the park's beginning.

He shook his head, clearing his thoughts. Focus. This group of adults was real. So were the four guys dressed as Cast Members, who'd already disappeared inside the Golden Horseshoe.

"Listen to them talking," Finn told Philby. "It's not exactly like they're friends, but they all know each other."

"The guy in the middle's the boss."

"I can't see him perfectly from here, but the guy in the middle is Hollingsworth," Finn said. "I'm pretty sure that's the guy from the firehouse."

"Could be. The others obviously work for him. Not just the men, the women, too. See how they're paying such close attention to him? They're being overly attentive."

"You're being professorial again."

"Can't help it, I guess. It's like they're either in awe of him, or he scares them."

"You guess?" Finn said. "Okay. So a guy and some employees. And four possibly fake Cast Members leading the way. What's that spell for you?"

"Disaster," Philby said. "Whatever's about to go down, it can't be good."

17

DIVERSION

SENSING A LULL in the entertainment, the excited audience inside the Golden Horseshoe returned to its loud conversation. The saloon played host to high-pitched laughter, shouts of joy, and more laughter.

"This isn't right," Willa said. She had her eye on the Disneys' table. Lillian was leaning over to talk to her husband; Walt's attention remained on the stage. Shivering, Willa moved closer to the front of the room, Charlene and Maybeck right on her heels. "Something's bothering Mrs. Disney. Something's not going as planned." She stopped. "We all agree on our top priority?"

"Protect Walt and Lillian," Charlene said instantly.

"He's not in any immediate danger," Maybeck said. "We know he lives for a long time after this."

"But how do we know that's not because we do something to save him?" Willa said.

"Now you're just messing with me."

"No, I'm saying by being here, we change history. We have no idea how time travel works, or what effect it has. We have no idea if we can think it through and make sense of it, or if our being here can't be explained, predicted, or even theorized. Maybe time is random. Maybe it's as fixed as we think. Maybe no matter what we do, things will always work out as we know them to in the future. But what if Walt needs us? What if we're part of the solution, not part of the problem?"

On every side, dance hall waitresses wove between tables. Cigarette smoke rose from ashtrays into a gray haze.

"What are you saying?" asked a concerned Charlene. "And FYI: you sound like my school advisor, which I don't appreciate."

"I'm saying I'm scared," Willa admitted. "I have a very bad feeling about this."

"Oh, good! Me too," Charlene confessed.

"Me, three," Maybeck admitted. "But what are we supposed do about it?"

"What we've always done," Willa said. "We pay attention. And when the time comes, we use our heads."

"A diversion," Charlene said. She tried to tap Willa on the shoulder. Thankfully her fear and anxiety gave her a physical presence, so she made contact. All three took note of the change. "I never thought I'd like being scared," she said, "but it has advantages." They chuckled nervously. "I thought . . . since we may need a little help . . . you might want to look at the wall behind us."

A canvas fire hose was curled into a wheel on the wall next to a valve and a warning sign. On the floor stood a red fire extinguisher, though its 1950s form was barely recognizable as such.

"Devil child!" Maybeck joked.

"We can use it, right?" Willa said. "If we have to?"

"Oh, yeah," said Maybeck eagerly. "We can definitely do this."

18

SOUNDLESS MOMENT

FINN FELT CERTAIN NOW that the man at the center was Hollingsworth. He wanted the names of the others. "If we can get in there," he said, "maybe we can use our DHIs to lift a few drivers' licenses. It would be good to know the names of his team."

"With you," Philby said.

Finn moved first. He slipped silently down the gangway and hid behind the ticket kiosk, with its pink fringe roofline. All the while, he kept an eye on the arriving party.

Finn paused at the ticket vendor's, finding it hard to adjust to the fact that, in 1955, each ride required payment for a ticket. The idea of all-park access was still years away. But the small booth and the pale green fencing running up to it provided adequate "cover," and for this Finn was grateful.

It struck him as significant that the entourage of arriving adults did not enter through the Golden Horseshoe's main door. Instead, they moved as a group around the side, in the direction of the Davy Crockett Museum Theater—whoever Davy Crockett was, Finn thought.

A *pop-pop* sounded from the Shooting Gallery; Finn winced, marveling at the use of lead pellet ammunition. How America had changed in sixty years! Disneyland had changed a good deal as well. There was too much open space between him and the Golden Horseshoe. No carts or statues to hide behind. If he was going to keep up with the group, he would need to run for it.

Arms pumping, legs blurring, Finn raced across the fifteen yards of black asphalt between the ticket booth and the Horseshoe's porch area. He reached a line of benches and ducked behind a standing wooden barrel banded with metal straps. He edged closer to the next barrel, and the next, picking up sight of his quarry as he moved in.

"Go on," spoke one of what Finn now took to be bodyguards. "I'll catch up."

Finn had been spotted. He knew there was no use running. He took a deep breath and closed his eyes. Releasing the lungful of air, he filled his mind with an image of a dark night. Through that dark came the clickety-clack of a train, its small white light ripping open the darkness.

"You!" the heavyset man cried, his voice booming out above Finn.

Me, Finn thought, but did not say. He'd lost two friends to reach this particular place, in this particular time. He'd endured pain, fatigue, heartbreak, and anguish, all debts for which he felt he should be repaid. He'd scared his parents, had been scared himself by dragons and fairies intent on killing him. The man, whoever he was, had no right to get in his way or question his actions.

"Boy!"

"I'm not a boy. I'm not even here." Finn shot his legs out straight and rolled onto his side, offering the man standing above him only the thin blue line of his two-dimensional form. Rolling farther, he came to his feet and stepped through the man who'd come to inquire. Doing so spun the astonished man around like a pinwheel. Finn turned sideways again. Gone!

He pivoted back, fully seen. He was closer to the door now than his six-foot-tall opponent. Finn backed up, step by step. Behind him, he heard the room go instantly silent—an eerie, soundless moment that signaled the occurrence of something unexpected.

The bodyguard reached into his jacket pocket. His hand came out holding what looked like a short strap of black leather with a bulge on the end. Finn recognized it from a movie, though he didn't know its name—it was used to quietly club a person unconscious. About as fair in a fight as a pair of brass knuckles. If Finn lost his DHI even slightly, one *thwap* from that thing would have him seeing stars and carrying a lump on his head the size of a softball.

"Excuse me!" said Philby.

The man, angry and frustrated and red in the face, raked his head back over his right shoulder. Coming at him, high speed, was one of the wooden barrels, miraculously held aloft above Philby's head. Philby the nerd. Philby the geek. Philby who'd managed to lose his all clear long enough to hoist a barrel.

He hit the man's face, hard. The leather strap dropped from the man's hand; his legs gave out, and he crumpled to the wooden porch, eyes rolling inside his sockets. As he landed, his eyes closed and he moaned.

The Keepers rarely took time to celebrate even small victories. This was no exception. Finn and Philby charged inside the saloon. Silence met them—silence that was suddenly broken by a man's voice. A commanding voice, loud and abrasive. An angry voice, filled with hatred and conceit.

19

THE SPOTLIGHT

MAYBECK, CHARLENE, AND WILLA stared, dumbfounded, as a man emerged from a group of adults entering at the side of the building.

"Hey, do we know that guy?" Maybeck asked as the man in question mounted the stage a step at a time. The Cast Members in the wings continued to hold back the actors and dancers.

The man strode onto the stage and stepped into the spotlight at its center.

"You have a good eye, Terry," Willa said. "A real artist's eye."

"What's that supposed to mean?"

"He looks almost exactly like that Dapper Dan named Ezekiel! The guy who followed me and Philby around after the Disneyland battle. He claimed he wanted to help us, but he gave us both the creeps and we blew him off."

"I never met your Ezekiel," Maybeck corrected her.

"No, but Philby described him to you. That's how good your memory is, Terry, and your imagination. You have an image in your head from that description!"

"I try," Maybeck said cockily.

"Ladies and gentlemen," the man in the spotlight called in a booming voice. "Although it proved impossible to rain on today's parade, I will do you one better."

The crowd giggled nervously. Some outright laughed, assuming this sudden arrival was part of the evening's entertainment. Walt Disney was known for surprises.

But had anyone bothered to take a good look at Walt himself, as the three Keepers did, his expression would have filled the onlooker with discontent.

"I can promise you confidently that within thirty days there will be no parade." The crowd booed, not liking what it was hearing. "Walt Disney, this man right here at my feet, is a thief and swindler!" The booing grew louder. "He will find his feet held to the fire of righteousness . . ."

"Go home!" The shouts piled on top of one another. "Take your preaching someplace else." "Get on with the show!"

". . . for his creations are not only borrowed, as we all know, from the legendary Grimms' fairy tales, but stolen from the very men and women he trusts to carry his stories to all of you, to your children and families. Walt Disney is a fraud!"

A man in the crowd jumped to his feet. While his

voice sounded familiar, the Keepers could not see his face. "Now listen here! That's quite enough! Take your insults outside. We're trying to have a party."

A smattering of applause gained momentum. As the man tried to speak, the clapping fell into a deafening rhythmic unison.

"Look!" Willa shouted over the roar. Philby and Finn had entered through the side door.

That was Maybeck's cue. He pulled the entire roll of canvas hose off its spool. It fell to the floor, and Maybeck held firmly to the nozzle. "He's all washed up!" Maybeck whispered to Charlene, who manned the valve. "Hit it!"

Charlene spun the wheel, which was mounted to a wide pipe. The hose spit air noisily, drawing a good deal of attention.

Water sprung from the nozzle, limply at first; then it charged like a bolt of lightning, aiming straight and true to the stage with barely any arc. Maybeck hit the man on his first try. To the sound of raucous cheering from the crowd, Hollingsworth was knocked off his feet and driven upstage on his back by the powerful stream. He spun and slid like a piece of soap dropped in the shower, and was whisked stage left, knocking down his two young Cast Members, who'd given up trying to hold back the actors.

Everyone near the stage rose and ran away from the water. In the chaos, Philby and Finn tried to read the name tags on the speaker's posse of bodyguards and protectors. They had to learn their names.

The band struck up a song. Dancers twirled across the stage, kicking their legs high. The crowd went wild.

"Off!" Maybeck said, dropping the nozzle and turning to help Charlene shut down the hose. Some of the men from the crowd were hurrying toward them. Maybeck wanted to think they were coming to help, but what would they do when they found out the three "kids" were colorful wisps, tissue-paper thin, and invisible from the side?

"Run," Willa called out. "Side door! Now!"

By working as a squad, the Keepers had learned dozens of unwritten codes. Chief among them was to respect a call for retreat. There was no taking time to argue its merits. If any one of them called for it, every one of them moved, like it or not, agree with it or not.

Maybeck, Willa, and Charlene hurried for the side door, where, as it turned out, Finn and Philby were done picking pockets. A few wallets lay on the floor. Philby and Finn left from the same door as their three friends, hands bulging with a half-dozen licenses and other ID cards.

Cheering and applause reverberated out the door

behind them, bouncing off the walls of the Mexican Restaurant and the Shooting Gallery across the street.

A Cast Member poked his head out of the Shooting Gallery, saw the five, and barely hesitated before grabbing a small box of something and taking off after them. Exploding out of the Golden Horseshoe's side door came three more Cast Members, running at a full clip.

"We've got company!" Charlene announced. "And I am NOT all clear."

The one from the Shooting Galley was fast. He aimed at a point in front of the five Keepers, toward the paddle end of the Mark Twain Riverboat. To all five, the kid seemed to have misjudged, moving too far in front of them, his angle of intercept all wrong.

That was when he dove onto his chest, extending the box in his right hand. Maybeck was thinking he had to be some kind of tough guy to take a dive like that onto asphalt. He'd have road rash for weeks.

That was when the contents of his small box released and spilled.

"Jujubes?" Willa cried. Indeed, the tiny cylinders looked a great deal like the hard candy sold around the park.

Not Jujubes, it turned out. All five Keepers went down hard as they hit the ball bearings rolling around underfoot. Lead pellets from the shooting range. Several hundred of them. The frightened Keepers, well out of their comfort zones and their pure projections, struggled to get up but slipped on the pellets and fell down again.

The Cast Member imposters chasing them stopped short. "Good thinking, Brandon," one of them called to the kid who'd spilled the pellets.

Willa took note of the name. "Roll!" she called out.

Again, the Keepers responded in unison, without pause. Like synchronized swimmers, all five stretched their arms overhead and started rolling in the direction they'd been running. To those watching, with each revolution, and entirely independent of one another, they each disappeared and reappeared twice. The shock of such a sight gave their attackers a moment of pause.

A long moment.

Willa called out again. "Water!" The five ran for the Rivers of America and dived in. Willa knew all about the combination of water and weak projections—Ariel had once saved her in Echo Lake. The moment the Keepers entered the water and dove under the surface, their analog projections struggled, helping to camouflage them. They could feel themselves swimming underwater, could see where they were going, but couldn't see each other well at all. When they came up briefly for air, the imposter Cast Members saw only sudden splashes, like a pelican or duck had dived after a fish. But there were no birds. There were no fish. The five Keepers crossed to the nearby bank, and stuck their mouths out in order to breathe. They could hear, but only in that muted way when one's head is partially below the surface.

It was Willa who spoke first; she sounded as if she were gargling mouthwash. "What just happened?" she gurgled.

Philby said, "Amery Hollingsworth is not alone."

20

A Costume Party

"HE DOESN'T OWN A PHONE," Tim said, "so I posted on his Web site, BigEars-dot-biz." He and his team were eating breakfast together in the dorm's commissary. The four had a table to themselves, though they had to keep telling other kids that the two extra seats were taken. Jess didn't like treating people this way and was becoming more upset and distracted as the meal continued. Amanda, who knew her better than anyone, could see her sister's inner turmoil and was about to say something when she recognized the fatigue in her eyes.

"You didn't sleep well," she said, privately.

Jess winced, trying to push aside the comment.

"Oh my gosh! You've had a dream," Amanda said.

"Shh! Never mind that," Jess said, deflecting the inquiry. "You posted a message on his Web site." She looked at Tim.

"He responded with a direct message." Tim showed them an image of an orange cone. *Posted by Nick Perkins.* Below the picture was: 9AM.

"Show me. Please," Amanda said quietly to Jess.

"Leave it alone, will you? It's nothing. Let's stay focused."

"Please, Jess."

Jess withdrew a small notebook from her backpack, winning the interest of Emily and Tim as well. Its pages had worn edges; its binding was bulging and cracked. Jess opened to a drawing of people standing around the edges of a small, seated audience.

"It's a party or show of some kind," Amanda said.

"It's not the future like it usually is with me," Jess said. Her throat felt dry and raspy despite the hot tea she'd been sipping. "Or if it is, it's a costume party. The clothes were very clear to me."

Amanda and Jess locked eyes. They had elected not to tell Tim and Emily about what they thought had happened at King Arthur Carrousel. They hadn't told them about the old can they'd dug up in Finn's backyard, about the rescue they'd engineered with the help of Finn's mother and Maybeck's aunt; how they'd had to protect their friends, all caught in Sleeping Beauty Syndrome—a coma-like unconsciousness—from the reach of the Overtakers.

About how the Imagineers had taken over and flown four sleeping teens to Los Angeles, where they were currently held under private medical watch. Days now, and still in SBS. Nor had they told Tim and Emily about a photograph, taken in 1955 on Opening Day in Disneyland, which clearly showed the five costumed Keepers among those celebrating.

Normal, sane people didn't react well to the idea of time travel.

"Is that orange thing a hat?" Amanda said, redirecting the conversation to Nick's cryptic message. "Like the sorting hat or something?"

"Looks more like a road cone to me," Tim said.

"Oh my gosh," Emily said, "it is a road cone. It's Radiator Springs, the Cozy Cone Motel. Snack shacks built to look like road cones. Brilliant, Tim!"

"I . . . ahh . . ." Tim wasn't sure what to say. "California Adventure opens an hour later today, at ten. I don't think our ID cards will get us in any earlier than that."

"I may know a way," Emily said, "but I'll need to get back into my suit." She eyed Tim, teasing him for his comments the night before. "And I'll need more battery life."

"I can help with that," Tim said.

"It's about time! I've only been asking you for forever."

"Sue me."

"With more battery power, I should be able to create a diversion for you at the Disneyland Hotel entrance to California Adventure."

Emily and Tim took off to work on her suit. Amanda looked over at Jess. "Now explain this," she said, touching the sketchbook.

"I think it's from back then. Charlene's there," Jess said pointing to her drawing. "And that's Maybeck, all dressed up."

"You must have been dreaming if you have Maybeck in a suit."

"Mandy, it was a bad dream. Something goes wrong. That's what they're all looking at. It's a . . . a witch or something. I was scared. It wasn't like the other Overtakers in my dreams. It had this . . . presence. I'm not sure what happens after this. You know the really strong dreams I've had? The super-dark ones? It was one of those."

"Great," Amanda groaned, defeated. "And there's nothing we can do about it?"

"I don't know." Jess paused for a moment, her fingernail tracing her drawing. "Maybe Nick will be able to help with this, too. He seems to know the history of the Legacy of Secrets."

"How do we know this has anything to do with that?" Amanda said irritably.

"If this," Jess said, pointing to the drawing, "is on or around Opening Day—and there's no reason to think it isn't—then it's back when there were no Overtakers.

If there were, they weren't well organized. Who was the bad guy then? I'm not sure, but we need to know everything there is about Hollingsworth. That's Nick. And we're going to have to tell Tim. He's Inspector Gadget. He's got to figure out how the Keepers crossed over into the past."

"You're allowed to say 'time travel.'"

"Not without feeling stupid, I can't. If Tim can figure it out, maybe we can get a message to Finn, to the others. If nothing else, tell them about Hollingsworth."

"And if we can't warn them?" Amanda sputtered.

"I didn't see the end of the dream," Jess said softly. "I don't have an answer for that."

21

CAT AND MOUSE

AT 8:30 a.m., an invisible Emily dragged a garbage can away from the Disneyland Hotel's private entrance to California Adventure. She moved it a few inches at a time. One turnstile was open at the early hour, manned by a single Cast Member. She didn't hear it at first. Or if she did, she convinced herself otherwise.

But eventually, she gave in and looked over. Emily let the garbage can stand. The moment the Cast Member looked back, Emily moved it again. Cat and mouse. The third time, the Cast Member snapped her head quickly and Emily spun the can in a full circle. The Cast Member froze, hand clapped to her mouth. Her state of rigidity allowed a brave Tim to duck and slip through the turnstile. In a flash, he was inside.

The next opportunity came when the Cast Member started talking to the trash can. "Okay! Ha, ha! I get it! So where are you?" She looked around for another Cast Member who might be controlling the trash can robotically—an attraction used in front of Disney World's Animal Kingdom. "I get it! I get it!"

What she didn't get was that Jess and Amanda had

slipped into the park behind her. By the time the Cast Member got brave enough to inspect a trash can that had moved nearly a yard on its own, Emily, like her friends, was long gone.

The door to the second cone to the left was cracked open a quarter of an inch. Tim had missed it the first time. He entered and kept an eye out for the girls. As far as he could tell, he'd beaten Nick to the rendezvous—though how the kid had arranged to have one of the food-stand doors unlocked was beyond him.

A wide cooler took up most of the small area. The curved back wall meant nothing fit. A broom and bucket, some shelves of supplies. A stainless steel sink.

"Nicholas?" Tim hissed. Jess and Amanda slipped inside; Jess released a chirp of surprise as the small boy wiggled out from behind a low cabinet.

"Can't be too careful," Nick said, brushing himself off. He wore blue chino shorts, a white polo, and running shoes without socks. He looked like he belonged on a yacht. Younger than the others—he might have been thirteen or fourteen, Amanda thought—he had a few freckles around his nose, widely set, expressive eyes, thin lips, and a round jaw that came to a somewhat pointed chin. His shoulders were so square you could have balanced a book on each; his legs were red and hairless.

"Apparently not," said Emily, who'd pulled on a skirt Jess had brought along for her. She had silver legs and a skintight silver top, but people in Disneyland dressed a lot crazier than that on a daily basis.

"What you all don't seem to appreciate," Nick said, "is what these people will do to protect the Legacy of Secrets. They don't care what happens to us. Not if we're in their way. They can be cruel, mean-spirited, and horrible to—"

"People?" Amanda said, drawing curious expressions from all but Jess.

"You expected . . . ?" Nick asked.

"Go on," Amanda said. "I shouldn't have interrupted." But she glanced over at Jess, and they shared a moment. *Mean to people?* she mouthed.

"They have an agenda. The mother of all agendas, if you're a die-hard fan of Disney, which I happen to be."

"What is it?" Tim asked.

"I have no proof," Nick said. He toyed with the cooler, but the sliding doors on top were padlocked.

"We deal a lot in theory," Jess said, "believe me."

"I don't know how much I can trust you," Nick said. He studied the three unsympathetic faces facing him. "Obviously, if you're asking me for help, then you have no idea either. Okay. Flashback fifty-five years: a megalomaniac kills himself after years of trying to take down his former employer. He leaves behind three sons, Amery Jr., Rexx, and Ebsy. Junior incorrectly blames his father's problems on Walt Disney. This son picks up where his father left off, doing anything and everything to bring down what is now an entertainment giant. His plans grow—they mushroom. Not only does he want to pit the Disney villains against the company, he wants spies and infiltrators as well. All of it is to be kept secret. Those who violate the secrecy will be banished from the group or killed."

"The Legacy of Secrets," Amanda said breathlessly.

Nick paused, meeting each of their eyes in turn. "That's my name for it. Again," he said softly. "Only theory, nothing proven."

"Hollingsworth's name is written on these clippings," Amanda said, passing them to the boy.

The only light inside the cone was a murky orange glow. It was difficult to read.

"Where'd you get these?" Nick asked, slowly skimming the articles. "They're yellowed. They must be fifty years old, practically ancient."

"We'll keep that source to ourselves for now," Tim said, cutting off Amanda's attempt to answer. "Since we don't know how much we can trust you."

Nick nodded, his thin lips grinning. "Very good."

"Thank you," Tim said.

If Nick had stood on his own shoulders he might have looked Tim in the eyes. As it was, it looked as if he was searching for a plane in a cloudless sky.

"Points of interest," Nick said. "The handwriting. I'd like to know who thinks these incidents might connect to Hollingsworth, wouldn't you? There must be ways to get handwriting samples from the Imagineers. Their autographs might be on the Internet. The stories," he said, flipping through the headlines, "all deal with—"

"Problems," Jess said. "But not all Disney problems. Only two. So, I mean, why bother?" She'd been quiet and withdrawn since arriving, arms crossed, face impassive. Somehow, her speaking up meant more to all of them. "Each article is about something going wrong. A library fire. A blackout. A trucker strike. A corrupt water union officer. In every case, it's a problem. But, I mean, it's a newspaper, and we all know newspapers deal only in problems."

"Someone must have suspected Hollingsworth was involved in these particular problems," Tim said, "or else why write his name at the top and file it away?"

"The lion spotted during the test run," Nick said, simultaneously reading one of the articles. "That's been in the rumor mill forever. He pooped by the edge of the water, and one of the boat operators smelled it. By the time she saw the thing, her boat had gone past, so they sent a Cast Member onto the island on foot. That's when it got interesting. That Cast Member was treed for over an hour. Guys from the zoo showed up and trapped the lion in a net. I guess they didn't have dart guns back then or something. It isn't in the article that way, but that's how I heard it went down."

"Hollingsworth?"

"A zookeeper admitted he'd taken a bunch of money to transport the lion at night and report it missing the next morning. They never caught the guy who bribed him, but years later, Amery Hollingsworth Jr. took credit. He was full of himself, so who knows? Still, your source kept the article, and it's in his pile, so maybe the Imagineers knew something the rest of you did not."

"Interesting."

"There was the Disney Railroad mishap," Nick said. "This is like the first week of Disneyland. Coming into Main Street Station, the train suddenly tilted and nearly dumped all the guests. Luckily, a bunch of Cast Members caught it in time and got it back on the tracks. No one knew what caused it. I'm betting Hollingsworth."

Amanda looked at Jess. Both knew what the other was thinking: Somehow, we've got to get messages to the DHIs.

"Whoever wrote his name on these articles," Nick said in a suggestive tone, "either knew of or was trying to find a connection between each of these events and Disneyland, the company, or Hollingsworth. I'll bet they tried to find a link to the Campaign of Darkness, what I call the Legacy of Secrets." He sounded somewhat in awe of the idea. "And if that's the case, then the Legacy is as big as or bigger than I thought. Their reach is longer, their numbers greater." He paused. "But can that possibly be true?"

"Lost me," Tim said.

"Please tell at least something about where you found these!" Nick said, clearly frustrated.

"They were filled with thousands of other documents and DSI research papers," Emily said. "Students. Former Cast Members. Except for the student papers, a lot of the files down there seem to deal with old employee records."

"Or maybe former Cast Members who posed problems for the company, like Hollingsworth." Nick faced Tim in direct challenge. "I'll bet you didn't find anything more on him, did you?" Without waiting for an answer, he continued. "That's because the real serious stuff on Hollingsworth and the Legacy is way too potent to be stashed away with a bunch of dusty old employment records. If anyone has access, it would be

Joe Garlington or the boss man, Bruce Vaughn. Maybe Craig Russell. They'd have it locked down tight, or they might have destroyed it. And I don't care how good friends you are with those guys, they'll never tell you the dirt on Hollingsworth. Forget it."

"No," Amanda said. "I can confirm that. I've spoken to Joe, and he's twitchy. He's afraid of us poking around. I mentioned Hollingsworth and—"

"You what!?" Nick shouted angrily. "You can't tell an Imagineer you know about Hollingsworth! Are you out of your mind? That's like telling Luke that Darth Vader's his dad—to his face!"

"You said Joe or Mr. Vaughn or Mr. Russell might know some of these secrets—if there are any."

"Oh, there are, Amanda," Nick said. "Plenty, I would imagine. What of it?"

"I was thinking how it would have helped Luke if he'd been inside Darth Vader's mind," she said.

"It would have freaked him out," Tim said. "Are you kidding?"

Jess caught Amanda's eye. Sisters being sisters, Jess knew instantly what Amanda was thinking. "Mattie?"

"It would save us so much time," Amanda said, "to go right to the source."

"Am I supposed to know what you're talking about? Who's Mattie?" Nick said.

"Shh! Someone's out there," whispered Emily, who'd been standing guard by the door. "I think I heard—"

Male voices carried through the sloping walls. At first, it sounded like a couple of boys trying to call a lost dog or cat. Then their words sharpened, cutting like little knives. "Come out, come out, wherever you are! We know you're in there." Oddly enough, they didn't sound close. It was more like they were moving cone to cone, saying the same thing and hoping. "Naughty, naughty. Someone's in trouble!"

Amanda and Jess gasped at the same instant. Amanda spoke urgently. "These guys are trouble. We need to get out of here!"

Nick pointed up. "This location wasn't chosen at random. I picked the only one with a false ceiling in place."

Amanda hadn't noticed the four ladder rungs running up the tapered wall, because they had blue-and-white pennants hanging from them. She nodded.

"Water filtration system for the shaved ice," Nick said. "Up you go!"

The girls went first, climbing the rungs and pushing open a square hatch well hidden by a cross-lattice of faux beams mounted onto the ceiling. Nick went next, then Tim, who lowered the hatch. Nick signaled

Tim to hang from a piece of steel mounted near the top of the nose cone. The girls kept their feet on the steel crossties that supported the filtration machinery. Nick clung to the ladder, bent awkwardly in order to keep one eye on the crack left by the hatch.

A moment later, the door below opened. The intruders had keys! Tim swore under his breath. Nick held up three fingers; a fourth.

"I swear I heard a guy's voice. Angrylike. Gave me the creeps," a boy said.

"I'll give your grill a remodel," said a gruff kid. "That'll take care of your creeps. Don't waste my time."

"It's my time, too," said the first kid.

"Shut up! You're hurtin' my head here."

Tim felt something tickle his hand. The air in the small space was gray, a dim fog that made it difficult to see clearly. He brought his hand closer to his eyes. "Cripes!" he shouted. A spider, its hairy body the size of a penny. He shook his hand, lost his grip and slipped, banging into the nearly upside down Nick, who fell off the ladder in a crouched ball and crashed through the hatch. The flying spider landed on Amanda's chest. Swatting, she lost her balance. Her right leg slipped off the steel beam and punched through the hung ceiling.

Tim followed Nick in a free fall through the hatch; he pushed off the wall to avoid hitting the smaller kid and propelled himself practically into the arms of one of the intruders. The Cast Member cursed and swung at Tim. Tim took a punch on the side of his neck and elbowed the boy, knocking the wind out of him. That didn't sit well with his cohorts, who piled on instantly.

Nick joined in the brawl, throwing and taking punishing punches. Amanda yanked her leg out of the ceiling, fell off the beam, and rolled to the hatch. She went out headfirst, caught a grip, and inverted, landing on her feet.

Shock and adrenaline—raw anger—had given Amanda her first glimpse into her particular strength. As a kid, she'd slammed the door to her room without touching it. With time and careful practice, she'd gained the ability to control her newfound "power"— but instinct still ruled. Unchecked, her emotions could become a formidable weapon—as they did now.

She shoved her left palm at the boy about to pound Nick. The boy lifted off his feet and slammed into a stainless steel cabinet. Her right hand thrust out at Tim and another of the intruders, who were tangled up like wrestlers. The two boys went over like bowling pins. Amanda lifted a third boy into the air and out the door, where the fourth among them was already running away. Tim sank his knee into the gut of the big guy. He had buzz-cut blond hair and red freckles on his arms. The guy expelled a gush of breath and bent over sharply. Tim pushed him out the door.

That left only the boy Amanda had slammed into the wall. Seeing he was outnumbered, he started to run. But he tripped, falling hard. He rolled, raised up to his elbows—and was smacked down hard again.

It took Amanda a moment to realize Emily and her invisibility suit were responsible. She'd terrified the boy.

"You want to see magic?" Amanda said in a cold, cautionary voice. "Watch those cups."

Invisible Emily caught on immediately. The stack of plastic cups separated, moved to the side, and re-stacked.

His voice dry and frightened, the boy pleaded. "I was only doing what I was told to do." He was wiry, maybe nineteen, with a home kitchen haircut and spaghetti arms.

"By who?" Nick said. He grabbed the guy's mobile phone and tossed it to Tim. "Who asked you?"

Three of the cups came off the stack and began moving in a circle—turned out Emily could juggle.

"Texts! I swear, it's all done by texts. We're paid by credit to Web site stores. I have no idea who it actually is."

"Password?" Tim said, showing the guy his phone.

Their hostage didn't hesitate. He spit out his password.

"You said, 'We're paid.' Who is 'we'?"

"I don't know the other guys. For real, I don't. A time and a place. That's what we get texted. This time, they told us to find you guys and tune you up a little. Hurt you. Make you think about quitting. That's all I got. I can agree or refuse. You refuse, sometimes you don't get asked again. It's mostly guys, but some chicks, too. Once or twice. Not that often."

"You've never seen the others before?" Tim asked. "Not buying it."

"Sure, I've done stuff before with one of those guys. They don't overlap us very often, though. I think that's part of it."

"They?" Nick said. "Or he?"

Amanda had run out of patience. She addressed the guy with her outstretched, open palm, shoving him against the equipment and holding him there from five feet away. "Answer!" She pushed hard—so hard that it was clear to the others that the guy was having trouble breathing.

"Mandy!" Jess said in a cautionary tone. "Ease up a little."

"I'm sick of this," Amanda said, her arm trembling, her face losing color. "Pushing," as she called it, exhausted her. "We don't have time for idiots."

"The things I've done . . ." the guy gushed, "were like, you know, sabotage. Vandalism, I guess you could call it. Always in the parks or the parking lots. Nothing to hurt the guests! Look, I'm a fan, a complete fan of everything Disney, right?"

"Ex-fan. Ex–Cast Member," Amanda said, still pinning the guy. "You quit and you turn in the names of anyone you've worked with, or we're coming after you."

"Okay!" He must have said the word twenty times. At last, Amanda relaxed her hold. His face studiously calm though he was clearly impressed, Nick asked the boy to describe the sabotage and vandalism.

"Small stuff. Fry power outlets. Flatten tires. Mess with an attraction just enough to get it shut down for a day or two."

"You came after us," Nick said.

"Yeah. But that's . . . I mean, that's not normal. We were supposed to scare you off. Find out who you were and what you want."

"Have you scared other kids off?" Jess again.

"Not exactly. There was a girl . . . this was a while ago. She was sneaking around the two parks. Lived inside Little Mermaid for a while. I was part of the team trying to keep track of her. But it wasn't for long. We lost her."

"Storey," Amanda said. Her whole body hurt. She

sagged back and propped herself up against the gear in the shop.

"Anything else outside the parks?" Tim said.

"No. I mean, not that we did."

"What's that supposed to mean?" Tim asked.

The guy didn't like the question. Nick repeated it. Amanda gathered her strength and pushed hard, just long enough to remind him. When she let go, he caught his breath and answered.

"It wasn't an assignment. It was . . . there was one time, just the once, when the text I got wasn't from a blocked number. Whoever sent it must have slipped up. I looked up the area code. It was four-one-oh. That's Maryland. A part that includes—"

"Baltimore," Jess said in a dry whisper. "Four-one-zero is Baltimore. Oh dear." She looked a little gray.

"When you were outside I heard you say, 'Naughty, naughty. Someone's in trouble.'" Amanda sagged a little at the knees. She choked on the words. "Where did you learn that?"

The guy shook his head, horribly frightened.

Tim was busy with the mobile phone. "The owner of the phone is Jason Ewart." The guy said nothing. "How did you become a Cast Member, Jason Ewart?"

"Whaddaya mean?"

An invisible Emily kicked him from behind.

Unnerved, Jason Ewart started shaking all over.

"Never answer a question with a question," Tim said. "Or bad things will happen to you. Do I need to ask again?"

"I know I look like a Cast Member," Jason Ewart said. "Dressed like this and all."

"And you've got the pin," Nick said.

"That, too. Yeah. All this stuff came with the job. An ID card, too, that gets me through the employee gates."

"From some guy you never met," Tim said, clearly unconvinced.

"Or a woman. Yeah. I was just . . . I'm a fan, okay? Was a fan. I applied like four times to be a Cast Member. Always got turned down. Then I get this text asking me if I'd like to feel like a Cast Member, look like a Cast Member, have all the access of a Cast Member, but make better money."

"The jobs you did," Nick said. "You felt like one?"

Amanda and Jess turned to one another. Both girls were frighteningly pale. Jess's hands were trembling. Amanda shook her head slightly. Both girls knew the boy was lying.

Jason Ewart shrugged. "It all went down like I was told. Day or night. Look, I get to hang out in the parks all the time. I'm asked to do something like once a week.

Maybe twice. It's nothing! And I'm paid almost like a full-time Cast Member. Did I know it was wrong? Yeah, sure. Did I know it wasn't Disney? Of course. But I'm a fan. I love it here. How was I supposed to say no?"

"You loved it enough to commit sabotage." Tim sounded disgusted.

"It was kinda give and take, admittedly. But on the whole I never did anything that bad."

"So you can't quit," Amanda said. "You told us you'd quit, but you can't because you aren't a real Cast Member, are you, Jason Ewart?" She raised her palm. Jason Ewart cowered. "Tell them the truth!" she said. "Tell them about the Major."

"No . . . No way." The boy's face went ashen white. "You can't possibly . . ."

"Can't we?" Amanda hissed. "Tell them about the Quiet Room or the Mirror Chamber or the Pipe."

"Who are you? I can quit! I promise! Here! Shred my ID! I swear." Still trembling, he produced his Disney ID card. Emily snatched it from his hand, held it so that it floated in the air in front of him. Seeing that, Jason Ewart's knees buckled and he collapsed, his eyes closed.

Emily reappeared, her hand on the battery pack on her leg. "Sorry about that," she said. "Overdid it, I guess."

"I'm out of here," Nick said, moving toward the

door. "We've been compromised. But at some point, Amanda, you're going to explain how what you said turned him to Jell-O."

Tim called out earnestly. "We still need your help with . . ." He glanced down at Jason Ewart, worried he might be faking. "That person we were talking about."

Nick turned. "If I help you? That's up to me."

22

SILVER LINES AND WHITE LIES

FINN DIDN'T CARE FOR THE PAST. He didn't care for two-dimensional projections and feeling at sea in Disneyland, of all places. He didn't like failure of any kind; he'd hoped to find Walt's pen right away and then focus on how the Keepers might return to the present. He was sick of looking stupid in clothes his grandparents would have worn. He didn't like what had happened at the Golden Horseshoe, nor did he appreciate that this guy, Hollingsworth, might be the father of the Overtakers. A man so awful Walt Disney had fired him, a man so reckless and mean-spirited that he'd use a celebration to threaten people.

But most of all, more than anything, he missed Amanda. He felt like his lungs weren't working, like he was sucking for air. His head hurt; his eyes stung, his throat went dry, and his heart sped up whenever he thought of her.

He had to do something about it—or go crazy. Cinderella hour, as Charlene now called it, approached—the hour or so after the park closed when power to Wayne's maintenance shop was cut. The projections ceased; the Keepers became real again, living, breathing teens. Although it might become more important later, it wasn't Finn's job to overthink the phenomenon. It was his job to take advantage of it.

The DHIs returned to the Opera House where they'd eventually settle down for the night. It was a strange reversal of how their projections typically worked. Once again, Finn wondered: How odd did the past have to be?

Maybeck told the two girls to go sit behind a pile of lumber.

"What for?" Willa complained.

"Hey. Don't treat us like that," Charlene said, the ice in her tone bringing Maybeck down a peg. She and Maybeck had been something of an item for a while now, and while no one had control of Terry Maybeck, Charlene definitely carried influence.

"I'm getting out of these stupid clothes," Maybeck said. "I didn't know you cared!"

The girls hightailed it out of sight.

Laughing, Maybeck explained himself to a puzzled Finn. "Look. My projection's my projection. That was set when we crossed over. But at least for the moment, I happen to be me, and those over there"—he pointed— "happen to be lockers. Workers' lockers. I found myself some blue jeans and a shirt. If I stay in this penguin suit for one more minute . . ." He stripped down to his boxer shorts. The jeans and shirt were a little big, but Maybeck was cursed, Finn thought, by looking good in anything. You could dress him in an apron and rubber boots and someone would put him on the cover of a magazine.

"I hate you," Finn said. "And I'm not kidding."

"Thanks, man. I do look good, don't I?"

"I have words for you that should not be spoken, so I'm going to keep it that way."

"The Phil-pill and me are meeting up with Wayne's World and heading to his place for a little late-night soldering. Philby's going to build a laser Wayne can use to make us 3-D."

"He can't do that. We don't have the parts."

"Actually," Professor Philby said, overhearing them. He dug into his pockets and opened his hand, revealing what looked like penlights. "Laser pointers," he said, and added proudly, "with laser lenses. I took them and some other stuff before we crossed. Stuffed my pockets. Last night, when you woke me, I didn't even notice. But coming back from the studio, I put my hands on my legs and felt them in my pockets. They became real when I did. Now, I have no idea what will happen when we project again tomorrow morning. But for tonight, I've got pretty much all I need to get cooking, provided Mr.

Artist here can keep a steady enough hand when soldering under a magnifying glass."

"Hey, I'm the Picasso of soldering," Maybeck said.

"Let's hope not," Philby said, laughing. "I can't recognize a thing in his paintings."

With Maybeck and Philby gone, Finn's mission would be easier to pull off. He nodded and smiled at them, hiding any trace of tension from his face.

"All-y, all-y, in come free," shouted Maybeck to the girls. "Coast is clear. Mr. Abs is clothed."

"Give me a break," Willa said, reappearing along with Charlene.

"What are you two up to tonight?" Finn asked. He tried to sound nonchalant, but it wasn't a question he ever asked.

"We thought we'd knit and sit by the fire while you men do the real work," Willa said. "Translated: we're going to look for some rags in the costume shop so that we can get out of these frills. You?"

"Maybe explore outside of the park some."

"But not too far," said Willa in a moment of motherly concern.

"Not too far."

If he'd been in middle school, Finn would have crossed his fingers behind his back.

23

Going In

Outside the gates of Disneyland, past the empty oceans of parking lot asphalt and onto the street, Finn left the quarter-mile of roadway familiar to him from his ride with Wayne. The air smelled bizarre, a combination of oranges and car exhaust. Neon signs took the place of streetlamps. Finn didn't recognize a single store or restaurant name. Not one chain. No McDonalds, no Starbucks, no Target, no GameStop here. Just donuts, "service stations," and mom-and-pop restaurants and stores with strange names.

There were too many phone poles holding too many wires, too many lights and too many cars going way too slowly—big, unruly cars, more like tanks, driven by teenagers smoking cigarettes and shouting car to car. Harbor Boulevard was the scene, as far as Finn could tell, and he'd walked right into it.

Surprisingly, it wasn't much of a town, just a few city blocks growing out of a central intersection of two major roads. Finn didn't recognize it as in any way related to the Anaheim of sixty years later. He moved through it, feeling like a ghost. No one seemed to take any notice of him; it was the first time he realized he'd come to feel like something of a celebrity in present time, and he didn't like the thought of that. He didn't want to become full of himself, to be so self-important that he started looking for other people to react to him. That seemed like more of a Maybeck or Charlene thing, not his.

When he spotted what he'd come looking for, he stopped. He was standing in front of a barbershop with a red-and-white spinning pole out front. The barber's pole dated back to medieval times, Finn knew, and the practice of bloodletting, tooth extraction, and surgery. The two colors were said to represent clean bandages and blood. Finn found it odd that, of all places, this was where he would first spot the thirteen-story hotel.

An odd and ungainly shape, it stood unevenly, like a set of poorly stacked wooden blocks. The upper floors were burned and damaged; they'd been struck by lightning twenty years earlier. Unoccupied and said to be haunted, the hotel remained in place, partly because Anaheim lacked the funds needed to tear it down, partly because the remains of at least one family had never been found after that fateful night. The surviving family members had repeatedly sued to leave the structure in place until the bodies were discovered, and proper graves dug. The lawsuits alone had, at one point, nearly bankrupted the small town. And still the hotel stood, just off the main intersection to the north, looking like a tower of terror.

Standing so close to a pole representing bandages and blood, Finn felt himself shiver. The shop was shuttered for the night, but inside he could see a series of three oversize leather thrones, which faced a wall of mirrors and a shelf of straight razors, combs, and colognes.

Finn shook himself. He was just standing here, staring. As much as he didn't want to be where he was, he'd made no effort to move on. This unsettled him. How much of him had actually crossed over to the past? How equipped was he to make good decisions? Was he mentally as two-dimensional as his projection by day? Was he wrong to have wandered outside the boundaries of his Keeper existence and into a time and place where a person like him did not belong?

These seemed like valid, important questions, ones that needed answering prior to his taking action. And yet, his feet moved almost independently, pushing him forward in a somewhat trancelike, near-catatonic state. He was going into that hotel.

The question weighing on his brain was: Would he come back out?

24

NOT ALONE

FINN FOUND ONE DOOR that wasn't boarded up, though it was marked DO NOT ENTER. It was around the side of the golden-brick hotel, with its flaked paint trim and windows scarred silver with grime. Only part of the warning board remained. It leaned against the wall, its stenciled letters a grayish white, a *T* handwritten into the empty space between words: NOT*T*E. Finn happened to know what it meant, thanks to an Italian babysitter in elementary school: *notte* was Italian for "night," as in *buonanotte*, or "good night." That struck him as far creepier than DO NOT ENTER.

To make matters worse, the doorknob moved easily and the door did not squeak on its hinges. Finn was no fan of the horror movie cliché, but since when did a door to a building closed down twenty or thirty years earlier not make at least a little noise when opened?

The answer was plain to his eyes: oil streaks ran like tears from the rusted hinges. Finn reached out and touched the streaks; not tacky or dry, but wet and smooth. Somewhat fresh oil, recently applied—and by someone who didn't want to be heard. A homeless guy, probably. Maybe a few of them. Finn wondered how a group of homeless dudes would take to an eighteen-year-old visitor violating their space in search of a particular room.

He took his time. He was in no hurry to get mugged. The hallway, off which was a disaster area that had once been the kitchen, was covered in litter, cigarette butts, and yellowed newsprint. He used one of Philby's laser pointers as a flashlight, which was a little like trying to fill a bathtub with a squirt gun. At a distance of twenty feet, the beam spread out enough to see an area about the size of a basketball. Up close it was nearly worthless, the beam of light about the thickness of a pencil.

The smells were horrid, a bouquet of cats and highway rest stop wrapped in an aura of stinking cigarette residue. Long, deep scratches marred the plaster walls, like the clawing of a giant beast. The laser caught a pair of three-inch banana slugs in a race from another dimension—not unlike me, Finn thought.

He had made two visits to Jess and Amanda's room in the months he and the Keepers stayed in Burbank, courtesy of the Imagineers. He remembered the fourth-floor commissary—a cafeteria offering all sorts of good food—and the game room down the hall. Finn thought that if he used this as his starting point, he just might be able to figure out which dorm room the girls would occupy sixty years hence. The old hotel felt like two buildings joined as one. He recalled confusing intersections of hallways; at one point the girls had led him into an area of narrower halls where, even in the present, the building's destruction by fire remained on display. Finn pushed all that aside for the moment, intent on finding the fourth floor.

The first time he felt a cold wind rush past, felt his hair lift and gooseflesh ripple down his arms, he thought of Maleficent. The dark fairy had made the destruction of the Kingdom Keepers a primary goal. She was gone now—Finn had seen to that himself—but remembering her fate was an effort. Finn also had to make a conscious decision not to believe the stories about the haunting of the Tower of Terror. It was said that five people had been riding the elevator when the lightning struck: a bellhop, a movie star and her husband, and a child actress with her nanny. The lightning strike had set the hotel on fire and caused the occupied elevator to free-fall thirteen floors. No bodies were ever recovered.

It was that last bit that had prompted the lore of the hotel, which was supposedly haunted by the ghosts of the five. In fact, if one believed all the stories, there were many more than five, but who was counting?

The second time Finn felt the cold, he was on the stairs. He spun around. Where is she? He couldn't stop his legs from carrying him up at a run. He reached the landing and grabbed the banister to swing himself to the next flight of stairs. His hand stuck to wood iced with frost.

This time the cold hit him like a pail of ice water tossed in his face. Something had moved through him. Experiencing panic as a DHI was one thing; Finn had learned the train-in-a-tunnel method to settle himself. As his real self, though, he'd rarely tried such techniques, especially while sprinting up a set of stairs. Plenty of times he'd made himself all clear; but that wasn't an option with Wayne's transmitter shut down for the night.

The splash of cold hit him again. This time he heard a voice.

"Danger . . ." A girl's voice. The child actress?

"Where?" Finn asked aloud. He arrived out of breath at the third-floor landing, shaking with fear, but convinced it was better to try kindness over terror, he stood his ground. He couldn't be sure it had been a voice, but it had certainly sounded something like one. How many people spoke back? he wondered. Wouldn't the "natural reaction" be to scream and flee?

But he wasn't natural, nor were so many of his experiences. He lived as a projection of light, which wasn't so far off from a ghost, all things considered.

Another blast of ice water. "Ahead."

The thing couldn't speak; he wasn't hearing it, not exactly. As it swiped through him, some kind of exchange took place. But it must hear his spoken words, Finn thought, because it had answered him.

"What danger?" he asked again, attempting to keep his voice from quavering.

"Ahead," he heard with the next chilly blast. And then it was gone; he knew without speaking another word.

Human or ghost? he wondered, thinking about the danger that lay ahead.

* * *

Slowly now, Finn climbed the stairs toward the hotel's fourth floor. His stomach was lodged somewhere near his Adam's apple; his heartbeat felt like a drum solo. He tried to swallow, only to discover his tongue was felt.

Ghosts. A burned-out, abandoned hotel with street people living it. Danger everywhere you looked.

He pushed on the door to the fourth-floor hallway. It didn't squeak, just like the door downstairs. Not good, Finn thought, his senses on high alert.

Stepping carefully around the trash and litter, so as to make no noise, he moved in the direction of the modern-day cafeteria. It shouldn't have surprised him to find an empty lounge half its present size, but it did.

The space had been remodeled in the future. When, if ever, was he going to get used to this time shift? It was one thing to look at pictures or video of the past; it was another entirely to live among its limitations, its fashion, even its language.

Finn thought he knew the way from this point and moved in that direction: down the bland hallway, left, right; look for the burned-out section and a stairway.

He turned a corner and froze, looking into a room where an Army-green canvas duffel bag sat on the floor. Fresh clothes were piled in heaps. Finn practically slammed his back to the wall; all that did was turn him around so that he saw into the room across the hall. More clothes there. They weren't the clothes of street people. His feet moved on their own, his eyes darting. At least two more of the rooms appeared to be occupied. He struggled to process the discovery. Who? Why?

He found the hallway to the right and took it; was about to take the left when he heard voices of kids his age—definitely not adults. He tiptoed. Three boys. No girls. They were sitting on inverted metal wire milk crates playing cards; they wore blue jeans rolled up over their ankles and white T-shirts. Each dressed exactly the same. Their hair was short and slicked back with oil or wax, Finn couldn't be sure which. To get where he was going, he had to cross the doorway. One of the boys could easily see him.

Danger, he thought. Now he knew. Where were the ghosts when you needed them?

At that very instant, he felt deadened with cold. The same windy voice of a young girl swirled through him: "Right here."

Not possible! Rather than excited by the communication, Finn felt paralyzed.

"We . . ." It sounded like a man's voice; ". . . can . . ." a girl's? ". . . help." Definitely a woman. Finn tensed like someone was choking him. But he'd learned so much as a DHI, as a Kingdom Keeper, that something allowed him to understand several things at once: these were the voices of the other people killed in the lightning strike, maybe even those in the elevator car; they were offering to help him, they weren't trying to kill him; he could communicate if he simply shared his thoughts.

Please, he thought, having no idea how any of this worked, or even if it would work. *Distraction. Diversion.*

Two drops of water splashed onto the wooden flooring. Sweat, running from his chin. He was talking to ghosts.

Within a second or two, the boys cried out from within the room. Playing cards flew into the air like windblown autumn leaves. The boys danced like witches around a fire, arms in the air. Finn zipped past the doorway, no one the wiser.

Instant cold. The girl's voice again. "Now we need your help," she said in the same chilly blast.

He hadn't realized that was part of the bargain.

* * *

Still reeling over the idea of speaking with ghosts and owing them a favor, Finn stepped into the fifth floor's long, dark corridor. He knew the room wasn't among the first few; knew it was on the right-hand side. Halfway down the corridor, he slowed, infused with a feeling of nearness: he was getting closer. He tried a door—it squeaked loudly on its hinges. Too loudly.

Would a group of boys recently scared out of their wits pursue a noise like squeaking hinges? He doubted it. Finn stepped inside.

The room looked like Amanda and Jess's. The same size rectangular box. A single window. Enough room for one resident, crowded for two. He didn't recall so much wall space to the left of the window. Amanda had decorated her half of the room with a string of Christmas cards strung near the ceiling, and an entire wall of book cover art. Jess's side was more stark and purposeful. A secondhand bookshelf, with maps of both Disneyland and California Adventure pinned to the wall. Finn attempted to mentally re-create the decorations in this space and couldn't make them fit; it was that darn wall space by the window.

He tried the next room. This looked better—much better! Once inside, he realized that even the door behind him was better placed according to his memory. The window was just right. Everything fit.

What he was about to do was probably stupid. Finn knew nothing of the space-time continuum, little about Einstein's relativity, was a newbie to time travel. Still, he had to try.

Finn stepped forward—and heard low voices from somewhere through the walls. Only then did he realize it wasn't the squeaking hinges that had kept the boys a floor lower. It was that someone—something—lived up here.

25

A FAMILY RECIPE

In the dank, underground cave below the foundation of what had once been Disneyland's Skyway Station, a small but dying fire burned.

The Creole woman, who had a dozen tattoos of strange symbols and shapes, nine earrings in her left ear, and thirteen in her right, cast a yellow powder onto the pyre. It flashed bright orange and red before settling into a copper patina green. She nudged two small bones together. No amount of flame seemed enough to warm them.

But the flashing catalyst had the desired effect. One of the bones stretched like a stick of licorice, bending and moving, snakelike, until it came into contact with the other bone. The movement stopped, but the first seemed to consume the second. The bones knitted into one.

The woman cackled, the sound more wild animal than human. Another pinch of power. Another flash. In the fire, the two bones found a third.

26

CARVING TIME

AMANDA AWOKE WITH A START, to the sound of squeaking and scratching. Rats! She'd heard the stories; she and Tim had even seen several when they ventured into the dorm basement. She adored *Ratatouille*, but it turned out not all rats were Remy. Most were ugly black sausages with tails, their darting black eyes beady under a coat of matted, sticky-looking hair. Ick!

From the sound of it, one of them was currently chewing on a desk or chair leg. The cracking of splintering wood overcame the fear-driven pounding in Amanda's ears. But she wasn't about to put her feet onto the floor and offer the animal a midnight snack.

It felt silly to wake Jess. What could she do that Amanda could not? But that sound! It was as irritating as Styrofoam rubbing on Styrofoam. Amanda's shoulders pressed into her ears; with chills sparking all over her body, she felt ready to scream. She reached out, fumbling for her mobile phone, unlocked the screen, and turned on the flashlight app, aiming the blinding blue light directly at the desks.

"What? What?" Jess came awake anyway.

"Rats!" Amanda said, though the thing had apparently moved so fast she hadn't seen it.

"In here?" Jess pulled the covers up to her neck. "Ewwww!"

The scratching started up again. Both girls craned their heads searchingly into the light from the phone.

"Over there!" Jess pointed toward the window.

"Down there!"

"No! It's over there!"

Amanda wrenched the phone's light in that direction. "See? There's not even wood on the floor."

"It's . . . not . . . on . . . the . . . floor!" Jess's voice sputtered in terror. "Up! Higher!"

Amanda directed the light up the wall. Her voice cracked as she managed to cough out, "What is that?"

Within seconds, both girls were up on their bare feet, Jess hurrying to the door to switch on the light. Amanda, meanwhile, walked unsteadily toward the window. "Is this really happening?"

"If it wasn't here . . . this place, you know, I would say we're both sharing the same dream." Jess's voice shook. "But I'm seeing it, too."

The window was framed by white wooden three-inch molding that stretched around the frame. With the light on, something abnormally strange was happening in the left molding. Before their eyes, clear as day, a groove was being cut by an invisible tool. Splinters of wood separated from the molding, floating to the floor like leaves falling from trees.

"Ghosts!" Amanda gasped. "I've heard the stories . . . I never believed them."

"I know! Or maybe it's like when the Keepers are in DHI shadow?"

Amanda stepped warily toward the unexplained carving. She swept an arm into the area where a person would need to be standing in order to carve the molding. Nothing.

The splinters of wood and paint continued to separate from the window trim, forming a straight line, perhaps an *I* or a 1. Then, at the top of the *I*, a horizontal line began to form. The carving was going more quickly now; whoever was responsible was getting the hang of it. That top line continued and stopped, much shorter than the long vertical line it was now connected to.

"Okay, so this can't possibly be happening, right?" Jess allowed fear to color her voice.

"I know, but it is. What's going on with that first line? Do you see the way it's changing? It's almost like it's been burned or something."

"Mandy, I—I think it's . . . aging."

The girls stood transfixed. For a moment, neither could speak nor move. Captivated, hypnotized, they watched in awe. It might have been a minute or two. It might have been a half hour. The cuts and grooves grew from a collection of meaningless lines to the letter *F*.

"No, no, no!" Amanda fell to her knees. "I am not seeing this. If this happened a long time ago, why hasn't it been here all along?"

"Because it's only happening now back then, I think. Not that I understand it at all."

When the next line began to form to the right of that first letter and on a sloping angle away from it, she knew what was coming. She looked over at Jess, tears in her eyes.

"It's him," Jess whimpered.

More minutes slipped past as a capital *W* took its place alongside the *F*. Quite quickly, two periods were drilled in to punctuate each letter. Below the initials for Finn Whitman, the carving began anew. The strokes were decisive now, strong, short, and deliberate. It took only a matter of minutes—or so it seemed—for the number 5 to appear, followed rapidly by another number 5.

It was Jess's turn to sink to the floor. The two girls sat side by side, chins resting on their knees, arms wrapped tightly around their bodies.

"It really is him. He's alive!" Amanda shook, and now the tears fell. Embarrassed, she slobbered through a few attempts at an apology for her foolishness until Jess threw an arm around her shoulder and pulled her in close.

"It's all right," she whispered. "It's okay. There's no reason to apologize. You were worried for him. So was I! And here he is, or at least his initials, his message."

Before their eyes, the carved initials and numbers continued to age dramatically, the pale fresh wood turning a dark brown, almost black, the paint chipping along the edges. It was like watching a time-lapse video.

F.W.

+

A.L.

55

"He's definitely trying to communicate," Jess said in an astonished voice.

"With me," Amanda said breathlessly. She couldn't explain to other people—even Jess—what her connection with Finn meant to her. It was a sense of family, of trust. Of safety. His reaching out like this turned her to mush.

"He had to find the place," Jess said. "He had to find this room. He had to know it was ours. Do you realize what kind of effort that must have taken? He's as desperate to hear from us as you were to hear from him. We've got to answer."

"How?"

"We carve him a message back." Jess rifled through her desk, came up with a pair of scissors, and handed them to Amanda. "Quick, while he's still there!"

Amanda placed the sharp end of the scissors on the wood, but hesitated.

"What? Come on! Hurry!"

"Think about it, Jess! He's carving something from the past, okay? It travels all these years forward in time and we see it. That makes sense. But it can't work the other way round. If I carve this wood for the first time now—time goes forward, not backward. He won't see it. He can't. It hasn't happened yet. It won't happen for sixty years."

Jess looked even more disappointed than Amanda felt. "We have to let him know. He's trying to connect with us."

"I don't think we can," Amanda said, discouraged.

"I don't accept that!" Jess grabbed the scissors. "We have to try. Wayne, Finn, everyone would want us to try."

She stabbed into the window trim and began drawing a heart around the lettering. But halfway through, she paused; the blond wood that formed the heart wasn't aging like the initials had.

"Come on," Jess said, pushing the scissor blade deeper into the wood.

Amanda stopped her. "It's all right. He's alive. We'll think of something. We know it's never easy—that it's always harder than we think."

Jess dropped the scissors onto the floor. "I hate this."

"No you don't. We are way better off than we've ever been, Jess. How can you possibly hate anything about this?"

"How can you say that? How can you possibly say that? That's your boyfriend!"

"And he's alive. We know where he is. Sort of. Now all we have to do is figure out how to let him know we heard him."

"You mean get a message to someone sixty years ago."

"Exactly," Amanda said, smiling at the improbability of it all.

27

To Grandmother's Shop We Go

Disneyland could barely contain its euphoric guests. Main Street USA swelled with bodies. Feverish excitement filled the air, its energy heard in the anxious cries of eager children, the joyous laughter, all mixing into the music trumpeted from a brass street band.

Sneaking out of the Opera House, the five Keepers kept their two-dimensional images pressed against walls and moving through shade. They did everything they could to be as inconspicuous as possible. They crossed Town Square and slipped past the fire station and held to the walls all the way down to the restrooms, then timed it just right to walk briskly past Town Hall.

It was all so different from present-day Disneyland that the Keepers found it difficult to orient themselves. Once through the gateway tunnels beneath the Disney Railroad tracks, they faced two ticket booths.

"This is going to be tricky," Finn said. They were basically Flat Stanleys that could walk and talk; it would be difficult to stand in line without their lack of three dimensions being noticeable.

Charlene came up with a solution. "We're going to have to wait for the line to be empty. That's the only way we stand half a chance."

"Well," said Maybeck, "Willa and I should be able to help make that happen."

A minute later, Maybeck and Willa, dressed in their nearly formal attire, had started directing guests to the second ticket booth. The line in front of the booth nearest Finn, Philby, and Charlene dispersed.

"I don't mean this the way it's going to sound," said Finn, "but a girl is going to have a much better shot at this than either of us."

"You mean I'm taking full advantage of my charm and beauty," Charlene said half-teasingly.

"Something like that." Finn smiled.

"I hereby volunteer." Charlene could add a few years just by the way she walked and carried herself. Sauntering up to the booth's open window, she began speaking before she arrived. Doing so put the young Cast Member inside on guard and established it was she, Charlene, who was in charge.

"So," she said brashly, "I have this problem. A friend of mine gave me this coin that she said was worth a whole bunch in the park, and I don't know where I'm supposed to spend it."

"Can I see it?"

In her attempt to project confidence, Charlene had neglected to have the coin at the ready. She figured her projection was probably blushing around now. Luckily, when she blushed, she looked like a ripe strawberry. "Oh, yeah! That would help!" She handed over the unusual coin they had found in Lillian Disney's purse.

The cast member flipped it over repeatedly, studying both sides.

"Nope." He passed it back to her. "I've never seen one of these before. I have no idea what it is."

"Never?"

"First time."

"So . . . what do I do with it?"

"Make a necklace with it, for all I care. It won't buy you any of my tickets."

"You have no idea? Seriously? You can't think of any place I can spend this inside the park?" Charlene asked.

"It doesn't work that way. Look, miss, you know how it is. You buy tickets to the various rides from me. I don't know, maybe Grandma's Baby Shop or the Emporium will let you use it, but I've never seen such a thing. Now, could you maybe ask your friends over there to stop doing that?" He pointed to Willa and Maybeck, who were still moving guests to the other booth. "They really have no right. It's not only impolite, it could get you all in trouble."

If she hadn't been strawberry already, Charlene would have turned purple. "Ah . . . yeah . . . sorry about that. I'll get right on it."

Now came the tricky part: if she turned sideways, she was going to disappear. Talk about getting into trouble, she thought. She fixed on a solution that might get her away from the booth without being spotted for the odd projection she was: she bowed, placed her hands prayerfully, and nodded as she continued to back away. Seeing this, Finn called off Maybeck and Willa.

The five Keepers met in the shade of a bushy orange tree, and Charlene explained her failed attempt.

"So," Philby said, "we'll try Grandma's Baby Shop first, and then the Emporium."

Discouragement had a way of spreading through the Keepers like the cold after sunset. You had to throw a blanket over it quickly and warm up before frowns and bad moods could prevail.

"We need to look at this as a victory," Willa said. "We've eliminated the ticket booth. That leaves two more possibilities—which is way better than facing a dead end, right? Come on! The more we eliminate, the better. We're narrowing this down."

"Since when are you Miss Sunshine?" Philby asked. The minute the words were out, he regretted them. Over the years, he and Willa had gone in and out of crushing on one another. For him to get on her case now was not impressing Willa one bit. "I mean . . . look . . . You're always sweet and—"

"Forget it!" Willa snapped. "You're only making things worse."

Philby looked like she'd slapped him. He opened his mouth to speak, but decided not to risk it. Girls are tricky, he thought.

The visit to Grandma's Baby Shop changed everything—and Willa's determined optimism paid off. The store was tiny. Baby clothes hung on the wall, were laid out on tables and in stacks on shelves. They might have been cute and adorable for 1955, but to Finn, they looked more like ugly doll clothes.

He and Willa approached the gray-haired woman behind the counter and showed her the coin. As with the boy in the ticket booth, she told them the coin could not be used to purchase anything. When an unhappy Finn took the coin back, the woman stopped him and asked to see it again. She measured its size and held it in her hand, trying to determine its weight.

"Golly," she said, "you know what you youngsters have there? I could most certainly be wrong about this, so don't you hold me to it, but one of my favorite pastimes when I get me a break is to stroll on down to Esmeralda and take a little chance on my fortune-telling."

"Esmeralda's still there," Willa blurted out to Finn.

"Still there?" the woman said. "We've only been open two days! Of course she's there!"

Finn shot Willa a disapproving look; they couldn't afford such time traveling mistakes. A few more slipups like that, and they'd have half the Cast Members in Disneyland out looking for them.

"Well," Finn said, lying, "that's a little disappointing."

"We hoped it was more valuable than that!" Willa said.

"I hope I've helped you all," the woman said, clucking her tongue.

"More than you know," Finn said. Taking care to make it look accidental, Willa pushed a baby onesie off the counter in the direction of the Cast Member. In the next instant, she profusely apologized.

The woman bent to pick it up. "Never you mind. Don't trouble yourself."

Finn and Willa spun around, so she wouldn't see them from the side.

The woman heard the door open. She lifted her head above the counter, but the two youngsters were gone.

"You're welcome," she said to herself. She had no idea she'd just changed the history of Disneyland forever.

28

An Unwanted Fortune

THE ESMERALDA WINDOW BOX stood in the front of the bustling Penny Arcade. It looked like a wooden phone booth with a set of metal legs. The top half was glass, with the fortune-teller's name painted in lettering across the top. Inside the window, Esmeralda could be seen from the waist up. She looked like something out of Pirates of the Caribbean: a puffy green satin blouse beneath a gold brocade black vest. The gypsy headscarf topped her shiny ceramic or wooden head, which had incredibly realistic facial features and makeup.

"If you squint," Maybeck said, "she could be real, she's so lifelike."

"We can't stay here," Finn warned. "Too many people."

It was true: they were being stared at. Some kids circled them, obviously intrigued by their disappearing act.

"I can help," Maybeck said. He faced the kids. "Pretty neat, huh? You ever seen something so cool-o before?" The kids shook their heads. "They're going to use us in a new attraction. Would you like that?" The kids' heads bobbed enthusiastically. "But right now, you gotta zip the lips, okay? We're kinda top secret—a secret only you know!"

As Maybeck kept the kids occupied, Finn tested the slot in the machine to see if their coin would fit. It did.

"So?" he asked the others. "If I do this, there's probably no getting it back."

Philby reached to stop him. "Why give one to Roy and one to Lillian? Are they supposed to know what to do with it? And Roy's is in glass."

"Glass can be broken," Willa said.

"If we have to," Charlene said, "we could go back to Roy's office and get his coin. I mean, if we lose this one. Right? So, as much of a hassle as it would be, we don't really lose anything by trying."

Philby kept his projected hand over the coin slot. "I don't know."

"Special coin," Finn said. "Special message. It feels like something Walt would do, you know? Esmeralda's always going to be here. For the next sixty years, she's in the park. Maybe he left specific orders to never remove her! Someone gets one of these coins, and whatever message Walt hid in here comes out. Doesn't matter how long it's been."

"A little help here," Maybeck said. He was running out of ways to keep the kids busy.

Finn and Philby shared a moment. They weren't

going to fight about it; it was going to be a team decision. At last, Philby pulled his projected hand away. Finn pushed the coin into the slot, and the five Keepers heard it roll down into the guts of the machine.

Esmeralda's head moved from side to side.

"Creeeeeepy," whispered Willa. "I've had her tell my fortune twenty times, I'll bet. It never feels anything but weird."

The gypsy's right arm lifted and fell. Her head lifted slightly, and her torso bowed toward the window.

Willa jumped back. "She has never done that! Never ever. Ever!"

Other curious guests collected around the machine, putting the Keepers at high risk. Esmeralda already had fans that knew her movements. The bowing forward and raising her arms was new to everyone watching. A great chatter arose, sounding like crickets and tree frogs on a summer's night.

A card slipped out onto the metal tray below the coin slot. Willa reached for it, but her fingers couldn't grab it. Finn tried and took hold. "One, two, three!" All the Keepers spun around in unison; it happened too quickly for anyone to believe the five might have briefly disappeared. Then they took off running.

Willa snatched the card from Finn, her hands functioning again. "This isn't right!" she panted. "Esmeralda prints out a whole paragraph on the card. This is just two sentences!"

"Proving," Philby said, "that it's special."

"What does it say?" Charlene asked. She'd had to slow down to allow the rest of the Keepers to catch up.

Finn stole the card back. Philby took it and skidded to a stop. The Keepers backtracked. "What?" "Tell us!" "Read it!"

Philby's voice faltered as he read, "'I named it after you. I hope it moves you as much as it does me.'"

29

A Friend Indeed

Being summoned to the lobby at the crack of dawn had an immediate effect on Amanda and Jess. First, they were tired from having been up in the middle of the night; second, they'd had no time to put themselves together, so they were deeply concerned about their appearances; third, this was not a request, but an order from the highest level.

It was impossible not to think they were in trouble—though they were always getting in trouble. Was this for carving the window trim? Amanda wondered.

For allowing files to be taken from the basement? Jess wondered.

In the lobby two men in uniforms met them. They had badges and arm patches. Definitely not a good sign. The two girls were led outside to a black SUV with dark tinted windows, put into the backseats and told to buckle up. The driver did not break the speed limit, but he was clearly in a hurry. The forty-five-minute drive took forty-five minutes, a first.

As they approached Burbank, the man in the passenger seat called someone on his cell phone. He spoke softly, too softly to be understood. Amanda nudged Jess, but Jess was off somewhere, staring out the darkened window, a frown on her face.

Upon arrival at the studio, the SUV maneuvered around a long line of waiting cars and irritated drivers. It was waved past the security booth, which stunned both girls. Every Cast Member and visitor had to stop and show an ID. What suddenly made Amanda and Jess so special?

Amanda figured it out first: the line of waiting cars had something to do with them. No one was being allowed into the studio until she and Jess arrived.

"What the heck is going on?" Amanda called into the front seat.

"I'm sorry, miss, but we aren't at liberty to say. Mr. Garlington will explain everything, I'm sure."

The SUV's tires yipped to a stop.

"Joe?" Jess said.

"Joe," Amanda echoed, seeing him standing all alone on the stone terrace in front of the Frank G. Wells building. He wore shorts, sandals, and a Disney company gray fleece, the morning air being chilled by a fresh breeze. As they drew closer, the girls were both offered similar jackets.

Joe had a team with him, all of whom looked grim. The girls slipped on the fleeces; Jess zipped hers all the way to her neck.

"Are we allowed to ask what's going on, Mr. Garlington?" Amanda asked. Her last meeting with him flashed through her mind; she hoped this wasn't payback.

"You are, and you are entitled to an answer, since apparently he'll only speak to one or both of you."

Joe motioned, turning the girls almost fully around. There, on a thick, gray concrete bench set on the terrace amid other such benches, sat a young boy. A dead boy.

"Dillard!" Amanda cried.

30

SPEAKING OF FRIENDS

AMANDA AND JESS APPROACHED slowly, unable to believe their eyes. Dillard Cole, Finn's neighborhood buddy and best friend growing up, had lost his life to the Overtakers, a tragedy that lingered for all the Keepers—and for the Fairlies, too. Just seeing the boy—a DHI beyond any doubt—forced a lump into Amanda's throat.

Following his untimely passing, Dillard's DHI had appeared before, once or twice. It was a rare occurrence, and both Jess and Amanda understood the significance of the boy asking to speak to them.

"Dillard?" Amanda asked, a few feet from the hologram. The boy sitting there wasn't a movie version of a hologram; he appeared absolutely real, his skin, hair and clothing opaque. His freckles, his green eyes, the smug expression were all Dillard. Two things gave away his projected state: his hair wasn't moving, despite the wind, and the girls could see an extremely thin blue line along his perimeter. It was only visible because they were looking for it.

"I will speak only to any of the five Kingdom Keepers,

including Amanda Lockhart and/or Jess Lockhart. State your name, please."

Amanda glanced over her shoulder at Joe. Now she understood the summons, and why other Cast Members were not being admitted onto the studio property. Joe regarded this appearance as a company secret.

Before she spoke to Dillard's DHI, Amanda returned to Joe. "What's going on?" she asked.

"You can see the situation we're in," Joe said.

"You did this?"

"No. He appeared sometime overnight. A guard spotted him this morning, just before sunrise."

"And you have no idea what's going on?"

"All I can do is speculate," Joe said. "Prior to his death, Wayne created a project he code-named 'Luke.'"

"Like the Bible?"

"More like Skywalker. Luke Skywalker saved the New Republic from the Galactic Empire. In the process, he discovered his true origins, learned the history of the Republic, and founded the New Jedi Order."

"I don't understand," Amanda said honestly.

"Wayne prepared a message in case anything happened to him. Those of us who knew him well believed it was probably something like the Stonecutter's Quill. Something some could decode, but not everyone. Remember when the Keepers—?"

"Yes! But I still don't understand."

"There may be more messages of his than this. Wayne was tricky that way. 'Luke' was to be triggered by an anomaly in the space-time continuum. In other words, someone, something time-traveling. Wayne claimed to have found a gateway to the past Disneyland. Some laughed, others, not so much. When this morning . . . Dillard shows up, I knew it had to be part of project Luke. He asked for the Keepers and you two by name. He'd obviously substituted DHIs at some point: the DHI of Dillard for himself. He must have felt having Dillard to speak to you or the Keepers would make more of an emotional impression."

"He was right about that."

"What exactly is the message?" Joe asked.

"I don't know yet," Amanda said. "I didn't answer him. I wanted to know what we were getting ourselves into."

"You won't know that until you answer."

"He's asking for the Keepers or us."

"Yes, I know. I've already tried talking to him. Believe me." Joe sounded exasperated. "I don't mean to be rude, but we're not opening up until we know if there's a threat or a problem, and that's up to you to find out."

Amanda nodded solemnly. "It's Dillard. It's not easy."

Joe placed his hand gently onto her shoulder.

"We've had our disagreements, Amanda. And listen, I know this is hard. But if you can do it for me, for the company, I'd be very grateful. Wayne means so much to all of us. Any message from him . . . well . . . it won't go ignored."

Amanda nodded and rejoined Jess, who looked at her expectantly. Her eyes were moist. Amanda squeezed her hand and said, "He basically told me Wayne came up with this. I didn't tell him about the carving, but I think that's what made this happen. Wayne had a plan in case the Keepers ever reached out from . . . back then."

"It's strange, seeing him . . . sitting there."

"I can hear you, you know," Dillard said.

The image's lifelike reaction nearly made both girls turn and run. Taking a deep breath, Amanda stepped forward and spoke her name, followed by Jess.

The projected eyes of Dillard's DHI shifted back and forth eerily. Computing, they seemed to say as they locked first on Amanda, then Jess. "Excellent! Good to see you both again."

"Same," Jess said.

* * *

"You understand we can't talk for long." Dillard's DHI voice sounded like he had a bad cold. "These people get nervous."

"The Imagineers?" Amanda said.

"They don't like being excluded. If anyone gets within hearing range, I will shut down until they leave. Just so you know."

"Got it," Jess said.

"Who sent you?" Amanda asked.

"You know."

"I guess so, yes."

"I'm sorry it's such a short visit. It has to be this way."

"Don't go!" both girls shouted, nearly in unison. In the background, Jess saw Joe take a concerned step forward.

All at once, Amanda understood the strange voice: some of the DHI's words were recordings of Dillard; some belonged to Wayne. She found the jumble off-putting.

"You can understand that this is important," Dillard said. "I had to count on you two. I am counting on you. If you are here, and you are, then our friends have succeeded in ways I wasn't sure were possible. One or more of them has broken through. It's a significant accomplishment. I don't have any way of knowing if the breakthrough involved you or not, so you will have to take me at my word."

"It did! Finn contacted me," Amanda said.

The DHI took time to process this information.

"If I am understanding correctly, you were witness to, or participated in, the breakthrough."

"Yes," Amanda said. Dillard was beginning to sound like an automated telephone operator: *Push one for customer service, push two for . . .*

"This was accomplished how? Please answer one of the following: visual, audio, other."

"Visual."

Dillard sat motionless. "You saw an image of: a person, an item, other."

"Other."

"Please describe in one hundred characters or less."

"A carving. On the window trim."

"Interesting. Let me think about that, please." A pause as the hologram's eyes darted. "Personalized or generalized?"

"Personalized."

"To you or someone else?"

"To me."

"Pay strict attention, please. Amanda?"

"Yes."

"Jessica?"

"Yes."

"Good. In case this is or has been intercepted, I have taken my usual precautions. Do you understand?"

This wasn't Dillard speaking. It was his voice, his

image, but it was Wayne's words. He meant he was speaking code.

"Yes." Both girls answered.

"For them, the street is only one way. Do you understand?"

"Yes." Jess and Amanda had talked about the Keepers being stuck in the past, that the technology in the past might not allow them to return.

"To reach them, you must follow them. Do you understand?"

"Yes. But how?" Jess said.

"Music was a favorite of Mr. Disney's."

"Okay . . ."

"It is imperative you and your friends know the truth now. Do you understand?"

"No," Amanda said. "What truth?"

"I am gone. Wayne is gone. Acknowledge only if both are true."

"Yes."

"It is imperative you and your friends know the truth now. Do you understand?"

The girls looked at each other, not having a clue what Dillard/Wayne was trying to say. Jess shrugged. Amanda answered for fear of losing Dillard. "Yes."

"The truth is not always easy to hear. Do you understand?"

"Yes."

"The truth must be disseminated. Do you understand?"

"We need to tell the others," Jess said. "Yes, we understand."

"Only those who can handle it. Only those who absolutely must know. Do you understand?"

"Yes."

"The truth can be dangerous for all involved. Do you understand?"

"Yes." Jess crossed her arms. The breeze had stopped and the morning air was a perfect 73 degrees. Still, she felt chills sweeping through her.

"What's he saying?" shouted Joe.

Jess spun around and signaled for the Imagineer to give them a moment.

"The truth must not be shared until it is known," Dillard said. His comment seemed to be in direct response to Joe's shouting.

"We can't share it with the Imagineers?" Amanda asked, her voice rising in astonishment.

Dillard took a moment to process her inquiry. "Please restate without any interrogatives."

Jess had to think about that request. "We should only inform those who need to know."

"Correct. Inform only those who must know the truth. Do you understand?"

"Only those directly involved," Jess said.

"Correct. Are you ready?" Dillard said.

The girls nodded at each other.

"Yes," Amanda answered.

"Memorize this, please. *Et quasi cursores vitai lampada tradunt.*"

"It's Latin," Jess said. "Repeat, please."

"*Et quasi cursores vitai lampada tradunt.*"

Jess told Amanda to memorize the first three words; she would memorize the last three. "Repeat, please."

Dillard repeated the expression twice more. "Say it back to me, please."

"*Et quasi cursores . . .*" said Amanda.

"*Vitai lampada tradunt,*" said Jess.

"Excellent. You will see me again if the next step is accomplished. With responsibility comes trial. Good luck."

Dillard's projection turned granular, and then vanished, leaving the bench empty and cold.

Joe came rushing forward. "What did he say? What was all that about?"

The two girls froze, neither certain of how to answer. Eventually, Jess took the lead. "It was Wayne."

"Of course it was Wayne! What did he say?"

"He has an assignment for us," she said truthfully. "But it's only for us. If we're successful, we can share his message."

"That's not how it works, Jessica," Joe said. "You of all people should know that."

Amanda looked over at Jess. "What's he talking about?"

"No idea," Jess said. Stepping forward, she challenged Joe, hoping he'd realize the mistake he'd made in referring to her Tink Tank participation in front of Amanda. "What's so special about me?"

Joe blinked furiously; he'd blown it, and he knew it. "Your . . . dreams. You know things none of us know."

Jess addressed him politely but firmly. "I have no dreams to share. This is up to Mandy and me. And I'm afraid that's how it's going to be."

31

WORDS DROWNING

THE FIVE KEEPERS FILLED the two front rows of a boat on Canal Boats of the World. They had the small dory to themselves. The boatman, a teenage kid with acne, ran a putt-putt outboard motor at the back, which exuded a gray stink and made enough noise to cover the sounds of their conversation.

"Lillian's coin takes us to Esmeralda. Esmeralda's fortune reads, 'I named it after you. I hope it moves you as much as it does me.'" Willa looked between the blank faces arrayed before her. "What's that supposed to mean?"

"He named Disneyland after her—and him," Charlene said. "He could have meant the park. He hopes it thrills her as much as it does him? Maybe he's trying to apologize for all the time the park must have taken him away from her."

"Always romance with you," Maybeck said affectionately. The others blinked at him in surprise; he wasn't usually so demonstrative. But then, Charlene had a powerful effect on him.

"What we know," Professor Philby said, "is what

it's not. It's not: Autopia, Snow White's Adventures, Peter Pan's Flight, this ride, Mr. Toad's, Mad Tea . . . What's left?"

"King Arthur, Casey Jr., Golden Horseshoe . . ." Finn contributed.

"Mark Twain, Jungle Cruise," added Willa.

"It doesn't make sense," Maybeck complained.

"Unless it's the park itself," Charlene said, repeating herself. "And remember, we don't know if this has to do with the pen or not."

"But it's something important," Philby said, "or why give one coin to Roy and one to his wife? Why have them lead to Esmeralda? No, the coin is highly significant. We're just not decoding the message correctly."

"Okay, okay, let's back up," Finn said. The boat was meandering through a canal; the view on both sides was mostly dirt. A few flowers and shrubs, very little else. No wonder they had the boat to themselves, he thought. And how much it would change in the years to come! He shook his head and refocused on the puzzle. "'Moves you as much as it does me.' Rides that move?"

"That's basically all of them," Willa said. "Only Golden Horseshoe doesn't move you around somehow."

"Maybe that means something," Maybeck said. "Maybe it's what doesn't move you that Roy or Lillian was supposed to figure out."

212

"You think his pen is inside the Golden Horseshoe? Really?" Charlene's tone was surprisingly sarcastic.

"No, it definitely sounds stupid," Maybeck admitted. "Look, I'm spitballing here."

"That's good," Finn said. "We need every idea there . . ."

His last few words were drowned out by a blast of the steam engine's horn on the Disney Railroad.

"Oh my word!" Willa said. "How incredibly stupid!"

"Me?" Finn said. "I only meant—"

"No, silly, not you! I know the solution to the clue!"

32

THE SMELL OF DEAD SKUNKS

SOMETIME AFTER MIDNIGHT, long after the last of
the fireworks had fallen from the sky like dying shooting stars, the Creole woman began her work afresh. The
castle was dark, the streets of Disneyland quiet. Having
tempered a young fire into a furnace of blazing coals,
she returned to the tangled assortment of bones from
her previous efforts. Sparks flew. Bone popped like fresh
kindling.

She stirred the gooey contents of the terra-cotta
bowl with the wing bone of an owl, adding last-minute
contents to the recipe. It had come to her in a nightmare. All the ingredients were various shades of green:
slime from inside a lobster, mucus from the nose of a
bull, the discharge from an infected wound—the most
difficult of all to collect. Though she could handle disgusting things without reaction, the last bit had made
her retch. She'd taken it off a dead skunk at the edge of
a roadway the night before. The animal had begun to
putrefy, making her task all the more foul. But there it
was, stirred into the pot with the rest.

The Creole woman poured the liquid carefully

along each of the burning bones. Watched as it congealed, turning nearly fleshy in texture but remaining green in color. It smelled of skunk and death and decay.

Delightful, she thought. Just right.

The more she poured, the more flesh disguised the bone. Soon the flesh sprouted small hairs, which showed no reaction at all to the heat.

"Attagirl," Tia Dalma spoke to the fire. "Come to mama."

33

No Explanation

THE DAY WAS AS BRIGHT and perfect as any Los Angeles day could be. No air pollution. No marine layer. Just pure sunshine, palm trees, and cars. Lots of cars. Too many. Los Angeles was a place to own a gas station or a tire shop. Car salesmen were everybody's friends.

"We're being followed."

Inwardly, Amanda sighed. Jess had had a rough time of it. She'd suffered first at Barracks 14, where she and Amanda had met. Then she'd been taken captive by Maleficent and held prisoner. Add to that the time when the Overtakers had, against her will, hidden her away in Animal Kingdom, and you got a young woman in her late teens who couldn't help but constantly feel people behind her, after her, chasing her, observing her.

"Yeah, well . . ." Amanda trailed off, unsure what to say. She was pretty much used to it, and she loved Jess like a sister. Who could blame her for being paranoid?

"Our seven o'clock, a girl in leggings and hoop earrings with a camo backpack. My three o'clock, guy on an electric bike." Jess had adopted military speak sometime back, which made it all the weirder when she went into

216

what Amanda thought of as "turtle mode"—trying to tuck her head inside her shell and never come out.

Still, the mention of an electric bike made Amanda look twice. For whatever reason, in a city that was mostly flat, no one rode bikes or motor scooters. Amanda hazarded a glance and saw the electric bike Jess had mentioned. She also saw the cute boy riding it. He looked like something off the tennis court or baseball diamond.

"Don't stare!"

"He's adorable."

"Stop!"

"I'm just saying."

"He's the enemy."

"Jess . . ."

"Every time our bus stopped, he stopped."

"He followed us all the way? On that thing?"

"From the bus station. Yes. And she showed up about three blocks ago. I don't know where she came from."

"You're serious about this?"

"The trouble with being in Imagineering School is that we seem to have forgotten we're escapees from a place that basically had us locked up. A place that would like to have us back."

"You think these two are from Barracks 14? That's clear across the country! It's in Baltimore, Jess!"

"I think," Jess said calmly, "that the kid yesterday, in Cars Land . . . what was his name?"

"Jason Ewart."

"All I remember about him is: 'Naughty, naughty. Someone's in trouble.'"

"Yeah. Why haven't we talked about that more?"

"Because we're scared," Jess said. "But you know the truth, too, Amanda. He's a Fairlie. He was at Barracks 14."

"No! We don't know that!"

"There's no other explanation. That was an expression the Major used. No one else. When have you ever heard that before? Jason Ewart is a Fairlie." She paused. "Thankfully, Tim and Emily don't know. This is all ours."

"You're freaking me out."

"Good," Jess said. "Maybe you'll take our secret admirers more seriously. Maybe they have to do with Jason Ewart, maybe our showing up this morning at dawn at the studios. Does it matter?"

"Do we try to lose them?"

"I don't think so. I think we want them to see what we're doing. They want to scare us? We'll scare them back."

"Listen to you!"

"I won't go back there."

"Of course not!"

"Ever." Jess had never sounded so angry.

"Me neither."

"If they are who we think they are, we can't allow them to bully us. If they get closer, we get farther away. If they get in our faces, we . . . I don't know."

"We say something random and walk away. Shouting is good." Jess looked at her curiously. Amanda smiled. "I actually paid attention in elementary school. We spent two weeks talking about how to beat bullies." She quoted: "'Show no reaction; feel your inner strength; walk your way around them; make jokes, but not at your own expense; reflect insults back at the bully; outsmart with laughter,' which is my personal favorite."

"And yet you ended up in Barracks 14."

"True," Amanda said, "but I won't take full blame for that."

The girls laughed.

"Better now?" Amanda asked.

"A lot. Thank you."

"No problem. You take Mr. Bike. I've got Little Miss Skinny Legs."

They'd reached the Flower Street entrance to the Los Angeles Public Library. Together, the girls headed up the concrete stairs leading up to the reflecting pond.

"This is such a long shot."

"It is not. It makes total sense." Jess was proud of her Internet search, which had turned up an exact match for the Latin phrase Dillard/Wayne had told them. It came from Lucretius's *De rerum natura*, and translated roughly as, "Like runners they bear the lamp of life." The same search returned several links to the Los Angeles Public Library. The expression, it seemed, was carved into the library's tower. "Look up."

Amanda shielded her eyes from the sun and caught sight of the rectangular tower, rising up above the rest of the library's facade. "Seriously, you can see that?"

"You need glasses."

"No doubt. So, let's say Dillard was trying to lead us here."

"Dillard was trying to lead us here."

"Ha-ha. Now what?" Amanda inquired.

"First, we lose these two behind us. We'll go inside through different doors. We get lost in there and meet in the children's library in ten minutes."

"There's a children's library?"

"There's always a children's library."

"Show-off."

The girls separated. They did so at the exact same moment without any signal. Such understanding had developed and grown between them, their souls braided.

For Amanda, Dillard's quest meant everything. It arose out of Finn's carving their initials into the window jamb, a message intended for her.

"To reach them you must follow them," Dillard had said. She assumed he was speaking metaphorically—to reach, as in "reach for," not "to touch or grasp." She would have liked to touch Finn's hand or kiss him. Just thinking about it made her blush.

Of course, she was nearly certain Wayne had no such intentions in mind. He wanted her to be able to communicate with Finn in the past: he wanted to warn the Keepers about something Amanda had no knowledge of. Not yet, anyway.

The cute girl in leggings followed Amanda at a comfortable distance. She was good at it; tailing someone was clearly not new to her. Amanda made no eye contact; in fact, she barely looked in her direction. Knowing she was being followed was enough. Losing her would require a combination of confusion, disguise, and misdirection, tools Amanda had been using since her escape from Barracks 14.

Disguise was the most difficult part. It required her to comb the reading areas for abandoned items; people often left a scarf or hoodie over a chair to save it while they searched the stacks. Amanda borrowed a Dodgers baseball cap and an atrocious tie-dyed shawl on the fly. She did so before her tail entered, and kept the items bundled at her waist to avoid them being seen. Then it was only a matter of racing up a flight of stairs—catching her tail by surprise, no doubt—and hurrying through an exhibition on polar bears and out the other side before descending a different set of stairs. She moved down a long hall fluidly, like a dancer, and ducked into a closing elevator, stepping into the back to avoid being too obvious. The doors slid shut. Amanda put on the hat and slung the shawl around her shoulders.

When they met up, Jess had on a headscarf wrapped like a hijab. She looked gorgeous, Amanda thought; no big surprise. Jess had a way of transforming her look with the slightest alteration. A change in lipstick could make her nearly unidentifiable, a rare and lucky quality.

"I was just asking Ms. . . ."

"Fabicon. Joanna Fabicon." The children's librarian was a round-faced woman in her early twenties with perfect, full eyebrows and a huge smile. Jess immediately felt comfortable with her. Her thin dark hair was long, brushing against her necklace of gold leaves.

". . . if they have a book on Lucretius."

"And I was telling your friend: not per se. But the general collection includes many reference works that would include bibliographical data on the author."

"It's the quote on the tower, in particular," Amanda said.

"Yes. Professor Alexander's theme of light and knowledge was beautifully chosen." Joanna would have made a good teacher, Jess thought. She had no airs about her. "The quote from Lucretius is such a great starting point for the theme."

"Starting point?" Jess asked.

"Well, yes! Have you seen the Hope Street quotation?"

"I don't think so," Amanda said.

"'A lamp to my feet . . . a light to my paths.' At various points on the building, Professor Alexander placed symbols that emphasize the themes of light and knowledge."

"The truth," Jess whispered.

"Interesting way to put it, but yes, I suppose." The librarian's oversize smile took over her face.

"Professor Alexander?" Amanda said.

"One of the designers of the original building. Included on the tower are representations of eight forward thinkers and writers of the time, each of whom contributed to the theme of light and learning. Professor Alexander called them his Seers of Light. We have a tour, if you'd like?"

As the words sunk in, Amanda knew what it had felt like to be Finn, facing the Stonecutter's Quill. This woman's explanation felt so much like something Walt or Wayne would invent; a puzzle too difficult and challenging for the boneheaded Overtakers to piece together, but just solvable enough for the Keepers.

"Is there anything written by him, the professor?" Jess asked.

"Let me think . . ." Joanna turned in her seat to face her computer. "There's the original guidebook from 1927. It's in our rare books collection on the third floor. Professor Alexander wrote an essay for it. Does that interest you?"

"That's perfect!" Amanda said. "Do we need an appointment or anything?"

"You do, as a matter of fact. But you've come to the right place. I'm connected." Joanna winked and placed a phone call. "You're in. Ask for Mallory."

The girls thanked her.

"We should split up again," Amanda proposed.

"Good idea."

"Five minutes?"

"See you there."

34

WHITE GLOVES

LITTLE MISS SKINNY LEGS was getting annoying. She hadn't identified Amanda's disguise yet, but she kept showing up anyway, like a mosquito around the campfire. Amanda could not risk leading her to the rare books room.

So she did what she had to do: she tailed her. It was like following a dog who could smell barbecue in the neighborhood, but was either too dumb or too easily distracted to hone in on it.

Amanda moved fast, not wanting to keep Jess waiting. Without looking at the title, she snatched a book from a shelf. Pulling her hat down tightly, she moved with agility and speed toward the girl. Amanda smacked into her hard and sent her tumbling. In the ensuing effort to help her back to her feet, Amanda slipped the book into her backpack. She apologized, gave the girl her hand, and, with the brim of the hat still lowered, pulled her up.

"Sorry 'bout that," she muttered, and moved on, already having singled out a man in a security uniform up ahead.

"You didn't hear it from me," Amanda said as she passed, "but I just saw that girl in the leggings put a book in her backpack."

She hurried ahead, reached the elevators and tapped the UP button. As the doors slid open, she heard a girl's protesting voice: "That's not mine! I swear! I swear!"

Amanda smiled.

The rare books room had the clubby appeal of a study in an old English manor house. The walls were rich with storytelling and meaning, iconography and symbolism. A few dark wood tables sat beneath green-domed law lamps. A hushed reverence muffled every turn of a page. From the moment Amanda and Jess applied their signatures to a journal scrawled with a hundred pages of names, most of which ended with initials like PhD, there was little question they'd entered a sacred space. This was where the ancients lived, the palace of the elderly.

Two librarians oversaw the activities, including a man named Ricky Hart, who hunted down volumes in a professionally accommodating way for the new arrivals.

Amanda, Jess, and the only known copy of Professor Alexander's original guidebook in the library were left to themselves at a large table. Wearing white cotton gloves, Jess turned the pages of the small book while

Amanda looked on. The professor's essay was so densely written it was nearly indecipherable.

"I don't know," Amanda whispered. "I don't think we're getting anywhere."

"Agreed. So what now?"

"You think there's a code in here? You think we messed something up?"

"If there is a code," Jess said, "then it has to have something to do with the original clue, right? 'Like runners they bear the lamp of life.' So . . . lamp . . . life . . . What are we missing?"

"His essay. It's got to be in his essay."

"Okay!" Jess turned once again to the yellowed pages.

Amanda saw it first. "Look at this!" Her chipped fingernail traced a line without touching the fragile paper. "'Light and learning are associated together by an impulse so natural that it pervades the great literature of the world. Knowledge is imagined as a lamp, wisdom as a guiding star, and the conscious tradition of mankind as a torch passed from generation to generation.'"

The girls stared at the page, rereading the quote. Finally, Jess whispered so softly that she might have been talking to herself, "I realize we have no way of knowing, but that's got to be it. That's got to mean something."

"'Generation to generation,'" Amanda said. "Wayne and Dillard passed the torch to us, because the Keepers aren't here. That much I get. But the generation stuff doesn't make sense, does it?"

"Maybe it's the message we're supposed to deliver. Something about . . ." Jess had continued turning pages past the book's brief index. An old yellowed pocket was glued to the inside of the back cover. It had probably once held a library card. Something had been sketched in pencil onto the paper pocket.

"What is that, a hand?"

"Looks like a Q-tip," Jess said.

"It's a torch!" Amanda said too loudly, earning the attention of the librarian. "It's not a good-looking torch, but it's a torch."

Jess rubbed her gloved thumb over the drawing ever so lightly. It smudged. She gasped and jerked her hand back. The smudged pencil left a small horizontal line in the middle of the torch.

"Wait a second," Amanda said. "There's something in there." She reached for the page.

"Shh!" Jess slapped her hand back, reprimanding her. "You don't have to tell the whole place, you know?" She delicately lifted the fragile paper pocket. She couldn't get her finger inside without risking tearing it.

"This is so Wayne," Amanda wheezed.

"We need a tool, something flat like a letter opener," Jess said. "Tweezers." She closed the book.

228

"What are you doing?"

"I'm going to ask for help."

"What? You can't do that! Whatever's in there . . . that's for us! If you ask, that guy's going to keep it."

"It's a rare book, Mandy. I'm not going to damage it."

"This is Finn we're talking about!"

"And I'm the one wearing the gloves!"

"Turn it upside down. Please, try gravity first!"

Jess, embarrassed not to have thought of it, flipped over the book. Something slipped out of the pocket. Amanda grinned.

It was a lined card inscribed with handwritten names and numbers.

"It's been cut with a pair of scissors or a razor blade," Amanda said, lowering her eyes to examine it. "The cut edge isn't yellowed like the rest of it."

"Why?" Jess said, picking it up gingerly with her gloved fingers. The back of the card was blank.

"There has to be a reason. Wayne doesn't do stuff for kicks."

"The name!" Jess said. "By cutting the card, he's telling us to read the last name."

"Which is unreadable," Amanda sighed. "If that's someone's signature, you'd never know it."

"The number!" Jess said, standing, the book in hand. Together, the girls marched to the reference desk where Ricky the librarian sat, his head down.

"Excuse me," Jess said. She showed him the card, explaining that they'd found it in the back of the book.

"Interesting. This is from so long ago! We haven't used this system in twenty years or more. You say it was in the back, in the pocket?"

"Yes," Jess said, and nodded eagerly.

"Even more remarkable given that this card is not for this book. Some kind of mistake, I assume."

"What do you mean?" Amanda asked.

"The title has been cut off the top. Names, cut off the bottom. But it's a yellow card. In the old days the rare books collection used blue cards. Yellow was reference."

"Like dictionaries and things," Amanda said.

"All sorts of reference materials. Maps. Encyclopedias. Almanacs. Scientific journals. On and on."

"Yellow," Jess said. "Should be blue if it's in here."

"Right. But really, the cards were pulled from all the rare books a long time ago. There shouldn't be any card in here at all."

"You can't make out that signature, can you?" Jess asked.

The librarian looked first with his naked eye, then with a magnifying glass. "No, I'm afraid not. It's a bunch of scratches."

"The number?" Amanda inquired.

"Good one!" Ricky Hart said. "Should have thought of that myself. Look at that number, would you?"

"I beg your pardon?" Jess said.

"How low it is! It's three digits. Three!" The man could barely contain his glee.

"Is that good?" Amanda asked.

"Are you kidding? That early a number? The person is practically a founding member!"

"Can you look up the name for us?" Jess asked.

"I wish! Sadly, anyone with a membership number that low has surely passed away by now."

"Are there any records anywhere?" Jess asked.

"Well . . . yes. Of course. I could look it up manually, I suppose."

"Could you, please?" said Amanda, flirting a little. It worked.

"Well . . . why not?" Ricky asked the other librarian to cover for him and went through a door. He called back, "This could take a while."

35

NAMES, DRAWERS, AND A WIFE

WHILE RICKY WAS THUMBING through a dusty card file in a basement archive, Amanda and Jess were left in the rare books library. As Jess copied down the exact quote from Professor Alexander's essay, Amanda wandered the room, reading titles off book spines and sneaking glances over the shoulders of the other patrons working at the tables.

Whatever Wayne had left them qualified as difficult to solve. She assumed they were on the right track, but wouldn't know for certain until some obvious piece of evidence jumped out at them.

Generation to generation. She wanted so badly to believe that line meant something, but maybe not. The torch the runners passed . . . She'd seen a torch on the library roof; another on display in the library lobby.

Still sorting through possibilities, Amanda ducked back and away from the room's main door as the boy who'd had the electric bicycle walked past. She was sure it was him; he was too cute to mistake for anyone else.

Heart in her throat, she waved, trying to win Jess's

attention. But Jess was bent over the reception desk, writing and reading from the guidebook. A shadow fell into the room from the hallway—a shadow in the shape of a man. The bicyclist had stepped back to get a look inside.

"Hey," Amanda heard. "I've just spotted a friend of mine. Could I . . . you know? Just for a minute."

"I'm afraid not."

"I'm not going to steal anything."

"Good! Then I won't have to arrest you. . . . Just kidding! Do I look like a cop?"

"Oh, phew!"

"You turned so pale!"

"Ha-ha," the boy said, snidely sarcastic.

"I'm sorry, though, answer's still the same. You'll have to wait out here until she's through."

"She'll be through soon enough," the boy said. The guard missed the menacing tone, but it sent chills through Amanda.

It took Amanda three more tries, but eventually Jess looked her way. After a frantic effort, Amanda was able to move her forward, out of sight of the doorway.

"You're not going to believe who it is!" Jess said excitedly.

"The guy on the bike is waiting at the door for us. He's our new best friend, according to him."

"Wait? What?"

"Your guy," Amanda said truculently. "He told the guard you and he are good buds."

Jess's excitement was such that she couldn't focus. "The member's name on the library card? Her number identified her as Marie Bounds."

"Is that supposed to mean something?"

"That was my reaction, too. I asked what the last book she checked out was. No record of that. But while he was checking, Ricky-the-librarian turned out to be smarter than he looks. He's Willa smart; Philby smart. We could have spent the rest of the day in here trying to figure out what Dillard was trying to tell us, but we've got Ricky Hart on our side, and Ricky Hart is a Disney freak. Spends his weekends in the parks, goes to D23 and movie premieres and anything Disney he can do in his spare time."

"Speaking of time, we're a little short. Maybe we can talk about Ricky's love of Disney later?"

"Later? No! We're not done here."

"I was afraid you were going to say that."

"Marie Bounds, as in Lillian Marie Bounds, her maiden name before she married Walter Elias Disney. This is from Ricky. Here's the thing, though: He first recognized the name as being one of the library's early big-time donors. Then this light went on in his head and he made the connection; he's muttering stuff about how they probably used her middle name and maiden name to keep a low profile on the contributions. The Disneys were big supporters all along, he said—huge—and still are, but Lillian had this thing about reading. Maybe they gave the money early on under her maiden name for some reason that made sense to them."

"Why would Dillard/Wayne want to lead us back to Walt's wife? That seems so odd, to make us work so hard."

"We're not done," Jess said.

"Meaning?"

"There's a wall of card file drawers downstairs—"

"Let me guess. Ricky?"

Jess nodded. "Each drawer represents a big library donor. Ricky is positive there's one for Marie Bounds. The drawers are fake, but who cares? Maybe there's another clue. Alexander's book gave us light, truth, and Marie Bounds. We're not done."

"We are if the guy in the hall doesn't move. We can't lead him to our next clue. And what if he calls in reinforcements?" Amanda looked frantically around the room. "This is the only door."

Jess pointed toward an exit sign over the door behind the reception desk.

Amanda nodded. "Yeah, and right alongside it says,

'Emergency Only.'" She got into a staring contest with Jess, who was clearly waiting for her to make the connection Jess already had. Jess's eyes said, *Come on!*

"Ricky . . ." Amanda said.

36

SLIDING BOOKS

CONVINCING THE LIBRARIAN to allow Jess and Amanda to use the rare book room's emergency exit wasn't easy. Ricky proved to be a stickler for rules as well as a Disney fan. "There's a public entranceway," he told them, "so use it. The exit through the back stacks and offices is in case of a real emergency, not to ditch some boy waiting for you in the hall."

"Have you heard of the Kingdom Keepers?" Jess asked in a hushed voice.

Ricky looked around cautiously. "Of course. And you aren't them."

"We work with them," Jess said.

"Uh-huh. Sure you do."

"We're doing this for them," Amanda said. "Whether you believe it or not, that's the truth. The Imagineers sent us. Joe Garlington."

"You know Joe Garlington? I'm supposed to believe this?"

"No one can make anyone believe something they don't want to," Jess said. She whispered to Amanda, who shook her head. "Please," Jess said more loudly.

"I don't do tricks. And I won't do that. It's too risky. I could hurt them."

The librarian looked worried. "If we're all done here, I have an actual job, you know?"

"Ricky," Jess said, "you're all-in when it comes to Disney."

"I said so, didn't I?"

"So some part of you believes in magic—no matter that your mind may tell you differently. Do you deny it?"

"Of course not. What about it?"

"My friend here can create an emergency, at which point it won't be just us going through that door behind you. If she does that, though, something bad could happen to the books, so she's refusing."

"Are you threatening me? I'll call security, you know. Don't think I won't."

"Magic," Jess said, giving Amanda the signal. Amanda resisted for a second, then slowly lifted her hand off the counter. Ricky could barely contain his anger.

"See those four books at the end there?" Jess asked.

Amanda closed her eyes and pushed as gently as she could. Six feet away, at the end of the counter, the four books slid off and hit the floor. Some heads lifted and swiveled, trying to find the source of the sound.

"Now," Jess whispered, "picture every book on every shelf."

"You had me at 'magic,'" Ricky said, moving to open a piece of the countertop and admit them through. "No need to be mean-spirited." He asked Amanda how she'd done it, adding, "It's a trick, right? But I don't get it."

Amanda said only that the boy in the hall was going to try to follow them. When he did, it would be good if security showed him to the front door and didn't let him back into the library.

"In other words," Jess said to the man, "it may come down to you to stop him from following us."

"I can do that! The Kingdom Keepers, seriously?"

"She's Finn's girlfriend," Jess said.

"No . . . way!"

"We've lost him," Amanda told Ricky honestly. "But now, thanks to you, maybe not."

37

AN OPEN DRAWER IS
AN OPEN BOOK

THE DONOR WALL, a repurposed card catalogue, was all golden oak drawer fronts with brass pulls—hundreds of regimented drawers with the names of various donors in small brass frames mounted to their fronts, where once there had been alphabetical listings like "FICTION Aa-Ak."

Jess tugged on a few. They were fixed shut.

"They're fake, you goofball," Amanda said. "I mean, they're real, but glued shut. It's art or something."

Jess found the drawer marked Marie Bounds and pulled. It opened. "Yeah, fake," she said.

There was but a single item in the long drawer. Jess reached in and pinched it between her fingers. Amanda leaned in alongside her. "It's names and a number!"

"No, it's a picture."

The photo, a black-and-white, showed a man proudly posed before a window in a hospital maternity ward. At his side was a young man, about ten years old. In his arms was a boy of four or five. Inside the room behind him was a cradle holding an infant in a dark gray knitted cap, a darker gray than that of two other babies nearby.

"That's a blue cap. A boy. The others are pink. They're lighter." Jess flipped the photo over. Written in flowing blue ink were the words:

March 13, 1965, Glen Cove Hospital, New York Amery (standing), Ebsy (holding), Rexx

343 He 38

"That's not a zip code," Amanda said. "Not a phone number, either."

"If it's an address, it's incomplete."

"Could be a license plate."

"Yes!" Jess said excitedly. "New York State. We have the date. We should be able to figure this out."

"It's a card catalog number," a male voice said from behind them.

The girls jumped and spun around quickly.

"Nick? What are you doing here?" Amanda asked accusingly.

"I told you: I make these people and their precious Legacy my job. There have been messages sent back and forth about two girls at the library."

"Texts? You can read other people's texts?" Jess blinked, shocked. "You've hacked people's phones?"

"What I'm capable of, what I can and can't do, is nobody's business but mine," Nick said. "You can thank me later. What you're holding is a card catalog number. Appropriate, given what's behind you. Trouble is, the library stopped using cards decades ago. So if we want to know what book that's referencing, you're going to have to ask a librarian."

"We, not you?" Amanda said.

"I'm glad you're paying attention, Amanda. I'm a regular here. I practically live at this library. I don't need to be asking questions like that. You two, on the other hand, are entirely forgettable."

Jess pursed her lips and nodded angrily. "Man, you're a real charmer, Nick."

"My point, in case you missed it," Nick said, "is that people I can associate with the Legacy are aware of you two. They know you're here. You got one of them thrown out for stealing—nice job, incidentally. Another got asked to leave the library for entering an unauthorized area. I don't know if that was you or not—*and I don't need to know!*" he added, shutting up Amanda. "But, again, my point: others will be coming, are probably already on their way."

"What do they want from us?" Jess pleaded.

"I doubt they have any idea. They want what you have, or are about to have. They want to protect themselves and the secrets of their Legacy. They probably perceive you as a threat. What *are* you after, anyway?"

"We don't know," Amanda said cautiously. "Not exactly."

"Not exactly?" Jess said. "More like, not at all. We got—"

"—a message!" Amanda said, interrupting. "From a . . . friend. Seriously, we have no clue if it means anything."

"Oh, it means something," Nick said. "The first name? The boy in the photo standing alongside his father? It's Amery. Someone wasn't paying attention in class," he chided. "Amery, as in Amery Hollingsworth."

38

THE TREE

IT TOOK THE LIBRARIAN at the second-floor information desk less than five minutes to translate the call number on the out-of-date index card.

"That's located in our Genealogy Room. Although we still maintain many of these books in our collection, you'll find the computers there of far greater use. A librarian there can show you more about our online system. I wouldn't imagine you'll have any trouble with it."

Jess looked back occasionally; Nick followed behind the two of them like some kind of spy. In the Genealogy Room, a combination reference room and computer lab, the three reunited. The librarian on duty was a ginger-haired guy in his late twenties who seemed to only see Jess and not Amanda. Amanda asked the questions; Jess got the answers. He worked the computer's keyboard like a pianist, showing off by looking up in the middle of his typing. He punched ENTER on the machine and a smile filled his face.

"There!" he said, without looking.

Nick groaned audibly. Jess blushed and thanked

him. Amanda cleared her throat to remind him she was still there; if he noticed, he didn't show it.

"The images are scanned?" Nick asked.

"Exactly! Seventy percent of our genealogy collection is digitized, with more coming online every few months."

"And we are looking at . . . ?" Nick asked.

"*The American Guidebook of Genealogy*, volume four of seven."

"It's like an encyclopedia," Nick said.

"Correcto-mondo!" the guy said, still working to impress Jess. "The call number is for this volume. It starts with 'Ho' and ends at 'Ku.'"

"H-o as in Hollingsworth," Nick whispered. The girls leaned in.

"Have at it," the guy said. "I'm right over there if you need anything." He meant this only for Jess, who blushed.

Nick worked the keyboard, arriving in short order at the listings for the family name of Hollingsworth. The image scans of the original pages could not be text searched, requiring the three to read carefully.

Amanda was thinking more than reading. All this effort on Wayne's part to lead her and Jess to the genealogy of the Hollingsworth family—why? Wayne had to have set this all up weeks, perhaps months, before the

Overtaker attack on Disneyland, something he couldn't have seen coming. He would have ranked this information as being of primary importance—Wayne didn't kid around with stuff like that. Without a doubt he was signaling, intentionally or not, that Nick's weird stories of the Legacy of Secrets were for real.

"Wayne had no way of knowing we would meet you," Amanda said aloud. "This . . . scavenger hunt is supposed to tell me and Jess about Hollingsworth. Who he was, and who he's related to."

"I think I'm just about there," Nick said, continuing to scroll through all the Hollingsworths.

Jess took her eyes off the screen. "I see what you mean," she said to Amanda. Their conversation continued with Nick caught between them. "No Nick, no Hollingsworth."

"So, is this all a waste of time?" Amanda wondered.

"Can't be. Everything meant something to Wayne, and it was always deeper than we thought. Much deeper."

"Got it!" Nick said.

Together, the three began to carefully read and study the document, a family tree that began in the 1700s at the top and carried down. Outside the scanned image, in the margin, a Web site address had been penned in blue ink.

Nick took charge—no surprise there, Amanda thought—placing his fingertip on the screen and working across the horizontal and vertical lines that connected one name to another. Below the bigger brackets were oversize equal signs representing marriage. To the right of the wives were listed any children born and, to the right of that, a more detailed explanation about the children and their baptisms and burials. Nick's finger stopped on Amery, one among three children in the bottom listing on the page.

"Oh . . . my . . . *gosh!*" Amanda gushed far too loudly. She stepped back from Nick and Jess, leaving them to think it was for dramatic effect. In fact, she was having trouble maintaining her balance. She searched for a chair, finding one among seven others neatly spaced around a long rectangular table. She plopped down into it with a thud.

Jess hurried over. "Mandy? Are you all right?" She reached to take her hand. "Your hands are freezing!"

"I think my heart stopped."

"Thankfully not."

"Did you read? *Baltimore!*" Amanda was shocked white. "It's in the notes! Read the notes!"

Jess hurried back to the screen. Nick was watching their interaction. "Is she all right?" he asked.

"I don't know." Jess ran her eyes over the lines of

typeface. She found Douglas Archibald Hollingsworth and an oversize equals sign connecting him to his wife, Bethany Blair Longfellow. The branch connected to three children, all boys: Amery Hatcher, Ebsy Balwin, Rexx Upton. The first two had been baptized in the Old Otterbein Methodist Church; the youngest, Rexx, in the Baltimore Basilica of the National Shrine of the Assumption of the Blessed Virgin Mary.

"Oh, dear," Jess moaned.

"Is one of you going to tell me what's going on?" Nick complained.

"It's . . . it's just so Wayne. I mean, this is how he operates. Everything is always right there in front of you, and yet so easily missed. It's as if all he could ever think in were puzzles. Even when you think you've got it, you don't. There's always another layer to peel back. He puts stuff out there. He puts it right out there where anyone with a decent mind can solve it, yet it seems to go beyond that, to this place where either you get it or you don't."

"Well, at the moment, I don't. A little help?" Nick continued to look across the room at Amanda. He was obviously worried about her, which touched Jess.

"We . . . Amanda and I . . . share a past. An awful past. Every so often we get reminders. We're currently being hunted like criminals. At least some of the time we are. The Imagineers have tried to help us, to make things better. I'm not so sure it's helped as much as it's hurt. We've never fully understood what we were part of, what our pasts had to do with anything. Wayne rescued us. Helped us to escape. At least we think he did. We don't really know."

"I'm so lost."

"You never knew him, did you? He was a great man. Really amazing. The kind of person that once you meet him, you want to hang around him. You don't want to let him get too far away. He was like a grandfather and mentor, a friend and teacher. He was that way to all of us. The word *love* is thrown around a lot, but I loved Wayne. I think Amanda and the Keepers did, too. And the thing is, he never stopped caring. He never stopped working to defeat the Overtakers. He didn't care how much people laughed at him, questioned him, disliked him. Nothing was going to stop him from trying to protect Walt's dream. One Man's Dream? You know, the museum in Disney Hollywood Studios. That sounds like a name Wayne would have thought up. That's what he lived for."

She paused, took a deep breath, and fixed Nick with a steady gaze.

"You're wondering about the Legacy, Nick. You're wondering if some guy named Hollingsworth could have gotten so hateful toward Walt and the company that he passed that hatred along to his children, to his family. I don't know how to explain this yet, but I can tell you that Amanda and I no longer think you're crazy."

"That's hardly reassuring."

"You're onto something. You are absolutely, one hundred percent onto something."

"And you know this because . . . ?" Nick asked.

"One word!" Amanda called from her chair. She'd been listening to the exchange. "A word that brings back a million horrible memories. A word that makes a link, a real link, between your world and ours, Nick. Something simple. Something massive. A conspiracy. I don't think there's any other way to describe it."

"You're killing me here! What word, Jess? What am I missing?"

"Baltimore," she said.

39

FAILURE

FINN'S RETURN TO the dilapidated Hollywood Hotel began in much the same way as it had the night before. He reached the back door, whose oiled hinges had given him so much concern. This time he had the luxury of knowing the fourth floor was being used as a dormitory, though by whom, he couldn't be certain. He climbed the stairs slowly and quietly, avoiding the area of concern and working his way through darkened hallways by the pinpoint red light from his laser pointer.

On the final turn, which steered him toward the future dorm room of Amanda and Jess, he heard a crunch behind him. There was no mistaking it for a rat or cat. It was a human crunch, a foot stepping on a piece of litter. Either that, or the rats were the size of bears.

If only the ghosts would help me again, Finn thought, recalling his last visit. He repeated the thought several times, believing he'd communicated in this way on his first visit. Nothing. No voice in his ears. No help.

Please! he thought. Still nothing.

He tried a door to his left. Locked. The next door opened, though no one had oiled its hinges in far too long. It sang like a choir. Finn stepped inside a dusty, cobwebbed room, swatting away sticky silk, which stuck to his face and clothes. He wanted to scream.

No one arrived. He'd been all set to spring out into the hall, scaring and tackling his pursuer. He felt tremendously let down. The adrenaline in his system had no release. It sickened him like a poison, making lead of his arms and legs and sending his brain into three-mocha overdrive. He eased out into the hall and continued toward the Jess-Amanda room.

"Boo."

Finn jumped a foot off the floor.

Charlene was pressed back into a doorway.

"What the—?"

"I followed you. Not last night. I had things to do. But tonight I was worried. Two nights in a row, leaving like that? Off on your own? You know the rule. You, of all people."

The rule was for them to always partner with another Keeper; too much trouble came when they did not. Charlene was right: Finn was typically the one reminding everyone else.

"You followed me inside?"

"Yeah. A little creepy for me. I almost turned back. But hey, I'm better now." She stepped quite close to him. Charlene was beyond cute; she dwelt more in the realm of adorable. More infectious than her cheerleader good looks was a kind of light that surrounded her. A presence. She touched Finn on the arm.

"It's nice not always being DHIs, isn't it?"

"What's going on, Charlie?"

"I can't be worried about you? I worry about you all the time, Finn. I'm *constantly* thinking of you. You know that."

"You're constantly thinking of Maybeck." Finn was feeling nervous and out of control of the situation. "I like Amanda. You know that."

"I like Terry. I do. Very much."

Finn wondered if it was the hotel, the place, that was getting to her. Ghosts. Strangers in rooms. Charlene acting weird.

"Well, I appreciate the company. I do. But there's two things you need to know: I'm pretty sure I spoke to ghosts last night, no kidding. And there are a bunch of guys—Cast Members, I think—living on the fourth floor."

"Living here?"

"I know, it's gross. But, yeah, they're down there. I thought you were one of them. My guess, and it's only a guess, is that they aren't real Cast Members. They're the imposters we've been chasing around the park."

"I've been worried about you, ever since Dillard,

Finn. You have been so . . . I don't know . . . driven. I felt so bad about that, Finn. We all did. But you've got to put it behind you."

Finn didn't appreciate thinking about his friend's death, a death he had caused. Even if the others didn't see it that way, he did.

Finn stopped in front of the door. "Behold," he said, his voice and manner intentionally dramatic. "The room where Amanda and Jess will live sixty years from now."

Charlene was awestruck. "Seriously?"

"This is it."

"This is why you're here?"

"I'm trying to help us return, Charlie."

"Are you going to tell me this has nothing to do with Amanda?"

He smiled. "Maybe just a little. And, listen, Amanda and Jess happen to be the only two people in the present we can work with."

"True."

"Why were you flirting with me just now?"

"Was I?"

"As if you don't know."

"No, I do know, and I'm sorry. It's embarrassing. Not that I don't like you, I do. But I want Terry to notice me more."

"Maybeck doesn't notice anyone other than himself."

She looked sad.

"I'm joking!"

"But you're right."

"Well, come on. Cheer up. This is a big moment." Finn led the way into the gloomy room. Charlene followed, mindful of the dust balls on the floor that looked an awful lot like mice. At the window, she examined the wood and scrunched up her nose.

"Aww, you carved both your initials. How sweet."

"I carved this to let them know we were here. I had seriously thought . . . I could have sworn . . . the reason I came back tonight is that I was sure one of them would have carved something back."

"But how could that possibly work?" Charlene said. "I understand if you change their room now, in 1955, that maybe there's some chance it'll show up sixty years from now. But if they do something, how is it supposed to go backward?"

"None of us knows how any of this time travel stuff works, I was hoping . . . that's all."

"So maybe she has seen it," she said. "And if she sees it, then what's she going to do?" Charlene asked rhetorically. "She's going to try to find a way to get a message back to you."

"Good luck with that."

"Think about it. What would you do?" Charlene

pressed, continuing to stand too close to Finn for his comfort. "You're always thinking up the best solutions."

He wanted to contradict her, felt the need to contradict her, but she was tired or something, not acting like herself. Her leg touched his. "Joe, I suppose. Maybe the Crypts. I'd try to figure out where the five of us were last seen together. How we crossed over."

"Exactly. I totally agree! Meaning, we should be checking the same place every night."

"Jingles."

"Jingles," she said, nodding.

Disappointed, feeling stupid, Finn headed out of the room, Charlene close on his heels.

"Finn," she whispered.

He turned around.

She pecked him on the cheek. The kiss puzzled him briefly. "That's for putting up with stupid me," she said. "I hope you know I respect you and Amanda. I still want to sting Terry, but this isn't the way." She hesitated, obviously thinking something. "Still, it might just work."

"We should get out of here," he said.

"Agreed. It's spooky and disgusting in here. But what about the Cast Members downstairs? Don't you want to know more about them?"

"I suppose, sure."

"So why don't we go have a look?"

"Because there are more of them than us?" he said. "Because they know this building much better than we do? We can't just walk up to them and ask them what they're doing here."

"I can," she said emphatically. "Of course I can. I'll tell them I'm looking for a hobo named Alfonzo. I heard he was sleeping here. I'm pretty, Finn. Not that you've noticed. Other boys notice that. While I have their attention, you'll get into one of the rooms and look for a name, a piece of mail, a wallet. Anything you can find."

"They could hurt you."

"So you do care!"

"Of course I care. It's something like one a.m. What if they don't like surprises late at night?"

"They'll like me," she said. "And I promise you, I can run faster than any of them. You know it's true."

"You're different, Charlie. What's going on, anyway?"

"No idea. You and Philby got us here, and now no one seems to have any clue how to get us back. Our projections are horrible and are going to get us in trouble. Our only ally is a guy who's going to be a Disney Legend someday, but isn't close to even being an Imagineer at this point. He's barely an intern. We can't find the pen we came to find. Without it being in One Man's Dream, we'll never find it. That's bad for everyone.

We have to find that pen. We don't seem any closer."

"That's why I tried to make contact with Jess and Amanda. We definitely need help."

"Jingles," she said.

"You distract them. I'll search the rooms," he said.

Charlene smiled wistfully. She gently touched his cheek using her whole hand. "Yeah, let's get on with this."

40

OF PAST AND PRESENT

FINN AND CHARLENE returned to Disneyland at 2:30 a.m., an iron-on laundry name tag in hand. Finn had pulled it from the collar of a dirty shirt he'd found in a heap of clothes on the floor of one of the dorm rooms.

The name on the tag, Declan Little, meant nothing to either of them, but they hoped that by sometime tomorrow that would change: the Keepers were good at research.

They entered the wood shop behind the Opera House quietly, expecting everyone to be asleep. Instead, four anxious faces greeted them, including Wayne's.

"Where have you two been?" asked Maybeck, his voice rising accusingly. "We've been trying to brainstorm on Esmeralda's fortune. We could have used some help!"

"I discovered a cell of—"

He caught himself; Wayne wouldn't understand what he was about to say. He explained the idea of Overtaker Kids, OTKs, to him—kids recruited as spies by the villains. The Keepers had previously confronted such kids—and not always come out on top. "There are guys living in the old hotel. They have Cast Member clothing. I think they're some of the guys who were at the studio."

Philby looked the most shocked. "How did you find them?"

"Chance," Charlene said. "He left a message for Amanda, carved his initials into the room they will occupy in sixty years."

"Interesting idea," Philby said.

"It was worth a shot," Finn said. "No evidence it actually worked."

"I was his backup," Charlene said.

"The hotel?" Philby said. "The Tower of Terror?"

"That doesn't sound promising," Wayne said.

"It's actually a cool ride," said Willa. "Very fun. But it won't be around for a long time."

Finn said, "I'm not giving up. And I did speak with a ghost. . . . Plus I got the name of one of the squatters."

"A ghost?" Willa said.

"I think she's one of the people who died in the Tower of Terror elevator crash."

"No . . . way!" said Willa.

"Yeah, she helped me. She spooked those guys and basically saved me."

"We have news, too." Wayne turned to Philby. "Are you going to tell everyone? I could use some shut-eye."

"Tell us what?" Finn said.

"We've been waiting to hear," Maybeck complained.

"Waiting for *you two*." He placed heavy emphasis on the last bit.

"Okay! First, using the names Finn and I dug up at the Golden Horseshoe—Hollingsworth's handlers, his posse—Wayne looked up three of them."

"They all work for him," Wayne said. "One used to be an animator at Warner Bros. The woman is a well-known psychic, the daughter of a man who correctly predicted the Lindbergh kidnapping."

"That doesn't sound great," Willa said. "Especially considering his speech about wrecking Disneyland."

"The other thing," Philby said, "is a lot better. Wayne and I—mostly Wayne—have generated our first three-dimensional projections." Philby was not known for his modesty, nor for sharing tribute, so the Keepers quickly paid attention. "We used the circuitry from my laser pointers, 'borrowed' some equipment, reengineered it, and set up a second transmission. We had to cannibalize Willa's phone—"

"I didn't mind!"

"—and one of the network television cameras here for opening day will need a repair, but the end result is pretty spectacular. As convincing a 3-D as we're going to get in 1955." Philby smiled widely. "I have a feeling holography is about to take a giant step forward. The first decent laser is still five years away from discovery, in 1960. But we're using laser technology in 1955. In about ten years or so, some major discoveries are going to be made. No one may ever know that Wayne Kresky, the Keepers, and Disney were behind them!"

"Nor will anyone care," Wayne said. "Enough of that beeswax! What's important is that, thanks to Philby's laser pointers, you'll all be able to move more freely about the park. No more of the bother. They're still going to shut off the radio towers after closing, but during park hours, you're going to be just dandy!"

"One thing about Finn's attempt," Charlene said. "He and I were thinking what would *we do* if we were in Amanda and Jess's position? What if Finn's initials suddenly appeared in the window like that?"

"They might try to retrace our steps. They'll talk to Joe or Brad. They'll look for us on park security footage. They'll see us enter Walt's apartment, see us running to King Arthur Carrousel. They'll see that we never get off."

"Jingles," Charlene said. "If they leave a message for us, it's going to arrive on Jingles. It's going to be sometime during the night. We have to post a watch. Take turns."

"There are a couple of boys on our night patrol I like

a lot," said Wayne. "Trustworthy. I could ask them to keep an eye out."

"Sure, as long as you've known them a long time," Finn said. "But we know now what we're looking for. As for the guys in the hotel, I think we should get to know them better, starting with this." He held up the laundry tag belonging to Declan Little.

41

SOLUTIONS ARE OFTEN
THE PROBLEM

THE KEEPERS MOVED THROUGH the Disneyland
crowd with confidence and ease, their 3-D projections
and period costumes blending in with the tens of thousands of park guests.

Willa had followed the hunch she'd had in Canal
Boats and solved Esmeralda's riddle: *I named it after you.
I hope it moves you as much as it does me.*

"Walt named it for Lillian," Willa had told them
triumphantly. "The operative word is the verb."

"*Moves,*" Maybeck said. "We've been over this
already!"

"We left out the railroad," Willa said.

"Santa Fe?" said Charlene.

"Disneyland *Railroad,*" Maybeck said. "That doesn't
help."

"Lilly Belle," Charlene said. "*I named it after* you. I
always thought how romantic that was." She squeezed
Finn's arm. He couldn't take it anymore and broke away
from her, making a bit of a scene.

Maybeck looked ready to split open Finn's face.

Wayne, oblivious to the Charlene antics, brought the conversation back to where it needed to be. "*Lilly Belle*, the parlor car he built for her! Wonderful, Willa! So much like Mr. Disney!"

The Keepers split up. Finn told Charlene and Maybeck to board the Santa Fe railroad's freight train while he, Philby, and Willa rode the passenger train that left from above the park entrance. Charlene didn't appreciate the snub and took it badly; her behavior made Maybeck feel about two inches high. Finn could see behind Maybeck's cockiness to know how it stung.

Glad to be rid of her for a while, Finn walked briskly. They waited ten minutes on the platform, the last few impatiently. Finally, the train approached.

"So many people," Finn said. He, Willa, and Philby stood away from the others; they couldn't risk someone bumping into their projections only to discover there was nothing to bump into. The trouble was, by standing clear, they were last in line. As holograms, there was no way for them to push onto the crowded parlor car. Willa found an open space to the left inside the door; Philby followed Finn in to the right.

"Jammed," Finn said, his voice clearer and more normal sounding than when he'd been 2-D.

"We need to spread out," Philby said.

"Good luck with that."

"Yeah." Philby rose to his toes as the train doors shut and the car jerked, beginning to move.

The parlor car was decorated to resemble a Victorian sitting room. Down the left side was a row of plush red-velvet seats with dark wood arms. The wood-paneled ceiling had floral inlays, brass fixtures, and a glistening polish. The windows were double hung, flanked by red-velvet window curtains edged with golden tassels. At the far end, a gleaming oak door with a glass window looked out on the receding landscape. Another ornate chair, a marble-top card table, an imitation gas lamp with a smoked glass flute, and a long wood shelf made up the car's right side.

Finn pushed deeper into the car, the shelf cutting into his projection. Presumably because of his angle, no one could see the wood knifing several inches into his back.

He reached the marble-top card table, hoping he might find something to do with Walt's pen. A set of leaded glass decanters were glued to the marble. Nothing else.

Finn spotted a brass drawer handle near the wall. He reached over to it, his full concentration on making his right hand material, not a projection. He failed.

He and the other Keepers were guinea pigs for Philby and Wayne's new, untested device, cobbled together from stolen parts of equipment engineered for technologies in the Stone Age of the information revolution. Without thinking, he'd expected his hologram to perform similarly to his three-dimensional projection in the present. It was not cooperating.

He eye-signaled Willa, who joined him a moment later. "I can't open that drawer," he told her. She tried. She couldn't, either.

"This isn't good. We can't play the fear game all the time."

"No. That wears me out."

"Cover for me," she said. Dropping to her knees and fluffing her skirt to the side, Willa tucked herself under the small table. Finn stepped over to screen her from view. A moment later, her hand appeared by his pants leg, and he moved to let her up.

"Drawer is empty," she said. "It was dark in there, but not pitch-black. No photographs. No documents. How can finding a man's pen be so hard?"

"There must be a clue in here. Or the pen itself."

"Agreed."

"If it's here," Finn said, "he could have hidden it out in the open. We could be looking right at it. It might be in pieces." Finn checked the lamp. Nothing. He searched the visible areas of the car for anything that looked like a disguised part of a black fountain pen. "The barrel would be easy to hide. Maybe the cap. But the actual guts of the thing . . . I don't see how you hide that."

The train's track was laid in a circle around the property's perimeter. It moved slowly, guests pressing their faces to the park-side windows, oohing and aahing at what they saw: the Riverboat lagoon, the Stage Line, the Casey Jr. roller coaster. As they circled around the speedboat rides and Autopia, they faced the Rocket Ride to the Moon, an attraction that drew the most number of lookie loos. That freed up space, allowing the three Keepers to meet at the marble-top.

"Nothing," Philby said.

"Same," Finn said. "And we have technical problems." He swiped his fingertips through the tabletop.

Philby imitated him, to the same result. "Oh my . . ."

"Yeah," Willa said. "We're going to need Wayne or someone with us. This is not going to work."

"Worse," Finn said, "Maybeck and Charlie may not know their limitations. We're kind of lucky we figured this out now."

"We need to get word to them," Philby said, sounding panicked. "You know Maybeck, always biting off more than he can chew."

Willa said, "I'm more worried about Charlene. Did anybody else notice how strange she's been acting?"

Finn hung his head, feeling his cheeks warm.

"Not me," said Philby.

"You never notice anything about people's feelings!" Willa complained.

"Ouch," Philby said.

"Finn?" Willa asked.

"Hmm?" He looked up. "I . . . ah . . . I think we need to warn them for sure."

Willa leveled a gaze that cut right through him. "Finn?"

"It's complicated," Finn said.

42

FAKES

MAYBECK SPOTTED THEM FIRST: two boys dressed as Cast Members, doing a poor job disguising their interest in him and his adorably dressed escort.

The costumes had worked well for Opening Day. But though all women visiting the park wore dresses and formal shoes like Charlene, and most of the men donned coat and tie and pressed slacks like Maybeck, *none* of those guests had black skin. Zero. Maybeck was not only young and good-looking, he was a "colored boy" dressed in rich clothing, sitting alongside a gorgeous, equally young white girl. It turned out at least two young Americans in 1955 found this combination off-putting, even unacceptable.

"They're fakes," Charlene said. "Their shirts and pants are wrinkled. I haven't seen a single other Cast Member with their clothes in that shape."

"No."

"They're looking at us."

"Yeah, I caught that. I think I kinda stand out."

"You think they know who we are?"

"I sure hope not." Maybeck looked around for

escape options. The train turned the corner toward Main Street station, where the Disney Railroad train carrying the three Keepers was currently sidetracked.

"Our stop's coming up," he said.

"I don't mean to freak you out or anything," Charlene said. "But last night when Finn and I were at the hotel, I kind of . . . ran interference for Finn."

"Meaning?"

"I may have acted lost in order to buy Finn time to search a couple rooms. What I'm trying to say is: I recognize the guy on the left, and maybe, just maybe, he remembers me."

"I've got news for you, Charlene. There's no 'maybe' about it. Guys don't forget you."

"I can't tell if you're trying to give me a compliment or if you're mad at me."

"Maybe a little bit of both. For one thing, I didn't actually love seeing you hang all over Finn."

"Do you think we could talk about this another time?"

"Not really."

"I was afraid of that."

"Besides," Maybeck said. "I know a way to beat these clowns. If they make a move for us, you stay with me."

"No problem."

"Did you happen to notice when we sat down—"

"Yes," Charlene said, interrupting him. "I didn't feel the bench under me."

"Exactly. We're sitting, but not actually. We just look like we are to everyone else. And that means—"

"We can run away, but we can't stay and fight."

"Yeah. That."

"If we try to take them on," Charlene said, eyes darting nervously, "it'll reveal our DHIs."

"They'll think we're ghosts. But that won't help us," Maybeck said.

"Hadn't thought of that. So it's hide-and-seek."

"More like tag. They're 'it,' and we can't let them touch us."

"Well, all I can say," Charlene said, "is I hope they're looking at us because of me and not because of you."

"And here I am hoping we'll never find out."

Charlene turned and scanned the car again, looking for a possible way out Maybeck might not have considered. She saw framed photographs on either side of the doors at both ends of the car. They looked like pictures of trains, but she was too far off to see clearly.

"I'm sorry if I upset you, Terry."

"I don't think you are," he said. "I think you did it on purpose, and I don't exactly get what I did wrong."

"It's weird having this conversation while looking straight ahead. I want to see you."

"That's just an excuse."

"I suppose," she said.

"Okay," Maybeck said, "they're moving. You'll be happy to hear that we'll have to talk this out later."

"That's not fair."

"You ready?" he asked.

"Terry." She tried to touch him tenderly on the arm, but her hand passed through his hologram. "Oh, come on!" she said, annoyed.

"Here we go," Maybeck said, standing. The two boys—hardly boys given that they looked to be in their early twenties—moved down the center aisle. Maybeck turned toward the back of the car, Charlene right behind him.

"He definitely recognizes me," she said over Maybeck's shoulder.

"Told you so," he said. "This is what we're going to do. . . ." He stepped aside to allow her to share the narrow aisle with him. "What we're counting on here, is that everyone is looking in the direction we're moving."

It was true, Charlene realized. Passengers were either looking forward or out the windows.

"Terry?" she said, sensing his intentions as they drew within three strides of the car's back door. "Look!" She pointed to one of the photographs.

"I don't have time for the art gallery!"

"It's Lilly Belle! And it's not the parlor car." Her brow wrinkled as she read the caption aloud.

Walt Disney's Carolwood Pacific Railroad #173
Lilly Belle *miniature live steam locomotive replica. Disney's railroad hobby was the inspiration for the Disneyland Railroad.*

"We've got to get going!" Maybeck said emphatically.

"It's the same name: Lilly Belle! 'Named it after you. Moves you . . .' It's a locomotive!"

"It's a model!"

"Walt Disney's Carolwood Pacific Railroad. That's not Disneyland. What is that?"

Maybeck took a fraction of a second to absorb the photo and what she was trying to tell him. "No way."

"'. . . as much as it does me.'"

Maybeck said, "If we don't get out of here right now, they're going to catch us—or try to—and that's going to win us a lot of attention we don't want or need."

Charlene nodded. "Yeah. Okay."

Together, they faced the train car's wooden door. Their projections stepped through it and outside. With the passengers' attention elsewhere, Maybeck assumed only the two guys had seen them vanish. He wondered what they were thinking.

Next, his and Charlene's DHIs passed through both the iron banister on the car where they stood, and the banister on the trailing car. Their projections moved through yet another door and into the crowded train car, with its rows of benches on both sides.

Maybeck and the Keepers had come to learn that the human brain does not want to process the impossible. It will look for any reasonable explanation to an event, even going as far as to invent it.

If two teens walk through a closed door to a moving train car, then you blink and look again. Seeing the two teens, you laugh or look away . . . because *there's no way that could have happened.*

Problems arise with agreement. If *two or more* people agree they witnessed the same phenomena, then the incident is given weight. The good thing about train cars is that most of the passengers are strangers, which greatly reduces the chance for discussion and agreement. Few people want to nudge the person next to them and say, *Did you see those two kids just vaporize through the door!?*

Maybeck and Charlene saw a few pair of wide eyes, saw two passengers point at them, but those same people looked away quickly, embarrassed by what they thought they'd seen; the pointing fingers dropped, and heads turned. The train car was slowing for the station. It was time to get off.

Behind Charlene and Maybeck, it was the same but different story. Their pursuers had struggled; opening the train car door, climbing over two railings and opening a second door had slowed them down. By the time that door came open, a mob of passengers filled the center aisle. The colored guy and the blonde had disappeared.

Fighting through the crowd proved a hopeless effort; there were too many people in too small a space. Turning and joining the throng, they moved out onto the platform, eyes alert. Nowhere. The two were gone.

"Did they actually . . . ?" one of them said to the other.

"The door?"

"It looked like . . . nah . . . Did you see—?"

"No! No, I didn't see nothing. They got through that door quickly though, I'll give you that, bud."

"Super-duper fast. It was almost like . . . nah."

"Nah."

"But that was the same girl at the hotel, right?"

"Looked like her to me."

"Do we tell . . . *him*?"

"What? Are you cuckoo crazy? How we gonna

explain we lost them? He'll tell us to hit the road. He'll can us."

"So we keep this private," the other said.

"Far as I'm concerned, this never happened. And if you've got any brains—which is questionable—you think so, too."

"How am I supposed to think something never happened when it did?"

"There you go again. What did I tell you? Dumb as a doorknob. As smart as a rock."

"Shut up!"

"You shut up!"

One boy punched the other in the shoulder. The two of them laughed. But they were forced laughs. As they started down the stairs from the platform, they both looked back over their shoulders at the train and shook their heads in disbelief.

43

The Right Touch

"You're our secret weapon, Mattie. Get it?" Amanda said.

Mattie nodded, her lips twisted wryly. "I didn't think you asked me up here to have a pedicure."

"You are so nice to do this!" Jess said.

"My internship currently involves carrying trays of hot cinnamon rolls from the kitchen to the counter. I get fat just looking at them! I'm glad for the break, believe me!"

The three girls walked beside one another across the Disney Studios lot in Burbank. Mattie was hardly fat. Short, yes, but with athletic legs and a swimmer's shoulders. She wore her dark hair unusually short, with no makeup, a look that was both feminine and strong.

Amanda had made the appointment with Joe Garlington, saying it was urgent. He'd squeezed her into his morning schedule, something that spoke to the influence of the Kingdom Keepers and the weight of recent events. Not everyone could get a last-minute appointment with an Imagineer.

"You understand what we're after?" Amanda said.

"This guy Hollingsworth."

"Exactly. Any images or thoughts Joe may have. No matter how small, we need them," Jess said. "And you'll have to ask quickly about the Keepers, because you may not get a second chance to touch him."

"I'll need help, if that happens," Mattie said. "They're hard to stage. One trick is to hand the person something."

Amanda slipped a zippered purse out of her back pocket and opened it. "I've got just the thing! And a story to go with it."

Jess saw what she was holding. "Yes! That's amazingly perfect!"

"What is it?" Mattie asked.

"Better if you seem surprised," Amanda said.

In the long second-floor hallway, Amanda and Mattie sat on a padded bench while Jess studied the original Disney artwork that decorated the walls.

"You're missing out!" she called.

"We're waiting patiently," Amanda said. Enduring twenty minutes with nothing to do but tap her foot had unnerved her.

"What do you think's going on?" Mattie said.

"He's busy, that's all." Amanda saw the stern look Mattie was giving her. "Look, I confronted him about Hollingsworth, okay? My guess is, he's in there studying up on everything they know about the Keepers, and Jess and me at DSI. He took the meeting, which means he's still worried about me. That's good for us."

"You are seriously twisted, girl." Mattie looked scared.

"He'll see you now," announced a male secretary. He wore a collared shirt with "Walt Disney Studios" in red stitching over the chest pocket, and looked about twenty-five. He stared long and hard at Amanda as the three girls entered Joe's office.

Now came the hard part. Amanda counted on Joe Garlington, a proper and polite gentleman, coming around his desk to shake hands with the three teens. The problem was that the handshake might be the only time Mattie had a firm hold on him. Her Fairlie strength, like all Fairlie abilities, was unexplainable. Mattie could read thoughts with just the faintest brushing of skin to skin, an ability that dated back centuries to fortune-tellers and seers, sorcerers and sorceresses capable of reading one's past. If one accurately heard one's past, he or she might be more accepting of predictions for one's future.

Sometimes the person Mattie touched felt something like a drain opening. Sometimes not. The trick was to put the correct thought into the subject just prior to contact—tricky when shaking hands for the first time. Today, the seeding was left to Amanda.

As Joe came toward them, he shook Jess's hand first. Amanda made sure he shook hers next—she literally bumped Mattie out of the way. Looking mildly confused, Joe suggested they sit on the small couch in a sitting area along the wall.

"You remember Mattie," Amanda said, as Joe reached for the girl's hand. "She's come to ask about Amery Hollingsworth." There! She'd planted the thought.

Joe hesitated a fraction of a second before he and Mattie shook hands. Mattie squinted, looking like she'd eaten something gassy. The handshake released. Joe offered no indication that he'd physically sensed her reading him, but he squinted in a way that expressed concern. The girls crammed in next to each other on the sofa.

"Of course! Mattie. How's the internship working out?"

"I think I've gained about five pounds, but otherwise I have a newfound respect for cinnamon buns."

Joe laughed along with Amanda and Jess.

"So, what's this about Amery Hollingsworth?" he asked Mattie, looking and sounding slightly angry, or at least confused. He directed his attention to Amanda. "It wouldn't have anything to do with your little visit from your friend Dillard Cole, would it?"

"Amery, Ebsy, and Rexx Hollingsworth," Amanda said.

Joe sat up straighter, taken aback. "O . . . kay. This is from Dillard, or this is your question?" he asked Mattie.

Mattie had memorized the information from Amanda. "Amery and Ebsy were baptized in a place called the Old Otterbein Church."

"I'm afraid I'm still not following," Joe said.

"I might have missed it," Mattie said, playing her role perfectly. If Joe had looked over at Amanda, he might have seen her lips moving in nearly perfect sync with Mattie's voice. "If it hadn't been for Rexx, I wouldn't have . . ." She stumbled here, but regained her memory and composure. ". . . bothered to look up the address of the church."

"What church?" a nervous Joe asked.

"It was Rexx who changed all that," Mattie said. That had been Jess's line, a stinger. Joe knew he'd been read.

"I thought we were all on the same side," he said to the girls. "What's the meaning of this?"

"Rexx was baptized in the Baltimore Basilica of the National Shrine . . . of the Assumption . . . of the Blessed Virgin Mary." Mattie exhaled audibly.

"Well, that's a mouthful," Joe said, trying to make light of it.

"Emphasis on *Baltimore*," Amanda said.

"And you know this because?"

"Dillard. Wayne's fortune cookie."

Joe sat back, nodding. He looked like a man trying to figure out what to say. "Baltimore. I admit, I didn't see that coming. You know this how?"

"He had foresight," Amanda said. "We are concerned about sharing this, about who we can trust—"

"'Whom,'" Jess said, annoying Amanda.

"I'm honored," Joe said.

"We need you to promise that, for now, you won't share this." Amanda stared at him intently.

"That's a difficult promise to make without knowing the nature of what you're about to say."

"But that's the deal," Amanda said.

Joe considered each of the girls carefully. "Deals typically involve two sides. What do I get?"

"Information. Knowledge of what was so important to Wayne that he left a clue even as he was dying. He directed us to documents. We have proof."

"Baltimore," Jess said.

Joe pursed his lips. This was not a conversation he wanted to have, but it was information he craved. "I promise I'll keep this to myself. But there's a caveat: if it threatens the company or any individuals, I will make a judgment call, and it may not be to your liking."

"Barracks 14," Amanda said, silently accepting his

conditions, "is clearly Hollingsworth's baby. We know he's connected to Disney. We know for a fact that at least one Fairlie—a boy—is currently posing as a Cast Member in Disneyland. We know the Keepers have time traveled. We can prove that as well."

"Finn has contacted us," Jess said. "We have to let him know we got his message."

Mattie took a chance. She reached out and took hold of Joe's hand. "You're the only one we can think of who can help us."

It took Joe a long moment to look down at his hand in hers and realize what was going on. He jerked it away. "You're reading me! You tricked me!"

"We needed a backup plan in case you wouldn't cooperate," Amanda said.

Mattie silently looked over at Jess and nodded. "Walt's apartment," she said.

Amanda remained focused on Joe. "Will you help us?"

His face flushed with anger, his voice tight, his head spinning, Joe addressed the three girls. "I never break a promise if I can help it."

44

AN UNEXPECTED VISITOR

WILLA AND PHILBY hid among the Mad Tea Party's cups and saucers. The spot afforded them a perfect view of King Arthur Carrousel. It was going on 2 a.m., and their knees were starting to cramp. They'd become their "real selves" at the stroke of midnight—they were just now getting used to it. Every thirty minutes, right on schedule, a security guard strolled past, forcing the two teens to lay low and not utter a sound.

At the end of one such pass, as the guard turned toward the castle, the carousel began moving, the music blaring out into the silent night. The guard turned, dumbfounded and perhaps a bit afraid. Philby saw it, having poked his head just high enough to make out what was going on when the music started.

Willa tugged on his shirt. Philby slapped her hand away, which made her tug all the harder.

"What?" he whispered, his voice covered by the loud music.

"Jingles! Look for Jingles."

"Duh!" he said nastily, then, "Ouch!" She'd punched him.

The guard appeared to have little idea how to

handle this unexpected occurrence. He took a step toward the suddenly moving ride, followed by a step back. He stood still. Finally, after prolonged consideration, he called out. "Hello? Who's there?"

No answer. Slowly, the guard found his courage and approached the ride. He hopped on as it was moving and walked toward the carousel's stationary central hub. "HELLOOOOO?" he shouted. He found the hub's well-disguised door, opened it, and stepped inside, calling out again.

"Philby! Jingles!" Willa hissed excitedly.

A piece of paper, taped to the neck of the carousel horse with a distinctive golden mane, flapped in the wind generated by the spinning platform. It made a fluttering sound that could be heard despite the music.

"I see it!"

"I hear it!" Willa said.

The guard emerged from the ride's hub, his head angling in curiosity. He stood less than five horses from Jingles and the piece of paper. "And so does he."

"I swear it wasn't there a minute ago," Philby said.

"Of course it wasn't. We know where it came from."

Philby snapped his head in Willa's direction. "Yeah, I guess we do."

"We can't let him get it."

"No."

"I'm faster than you," Willa said, "by a long shot."

"Maybe, maybe not. But it doesn't matter. I can't let you do it."

"Baloney! You mean you can't stop me." Willa rose up on her haunches. "Cover me."

Philby reached out for her, but too late. Willa was off and running.

Several things happened at once. Willa had cleverly waited for the guard's movement on the carousel to turn his back to them. She sprinted and jumped onto the revolving platform, arriving 180 degrees from where she needed to be.

The carousel came around, the guard now two horses from the mysterious flapping sound. Philby stood and moved off the Mad Tea Party, allowing the guard to see him. Carefully, he offered only his profile, not his full face—he didn't want to be easily remembered. Around came the carousel, Willa moving in a crouch toward the guard and Jingles.

Philby had blown it—having spotted him, the guard was now moving counterclockwise to the carousel's movement—directly toward Willa.

The carousel spun. The guard kept pace with the speed of the platform's revolution, effectively standing in place, now two horses from Willa. She stood. The guard stopped and turned. The two disappeared on the far side.

Philby advanced toward the ride.

Willa, crouching alongside an outer horse, saw the guard's leather boots heading toward her. Jingles was four horses ahead. At this rate, unless she moved, he'd catch her before she reached Jingles. . . .

NOW!

She stood and hurried ahead. The layout of the carousel put a half-dozen fixed horses between her and the guard. It was a game of tag with an unexpected twist: her world was moving around in circles.

The guard lunged over a moving horse and grabbed her sleeve. Willa screamed. The music surged; the horse lifted and broke his grip. She jumped ahead, snagged the flapping piece of paper. It tore.

Suddenly, there was Philby, waving his arms. The carousel had completed another rotation. "HEY!"

He bought her just enough time. Willa's brain could function at the speed of light. In that nanosecond standing alongside Jingles, note in hand, she ran through the consequences of leaving a torn piece of the note taped to the wooden horse: any evidence would support the guard's claims about what had happened; if Walt's team became curious, they might study that evidence; they might discover that the tape used to stick the note to

Jingles's neck was not like any tape available in 1955; and most importantly, the note had been handwritten and was missing at least two words—what if those words were important?

Willa took only a second to reach out and peel off the length of tape and the torn piece of paper stuck to it.

A massive hand clamped down around her wrist. She let out a squeal.

"Who . . . what . . ." said a man's deep voice, "is going on?"

"Hey!" Philby shouted, now inches from the guard.

The man's shift of attention ever so slightly loosened his grip on Willa. She broke free and jumped off the moving carousel. Lost her balance and went down hard. Her shirt was grabbed from behind. She spun to slap the guy. Philby ducked at the last second.

"It's me!" He yanked her to her feet. The guard had to work his way around the horses. In the few seconds it took him, the carousel had rotated half a revolution.

Philby led the way through the castle at a run. Willa was soon in the lead.

"Left!" he instructed. She slipped to the left once out of the castle, stopping short on a drawbridge beneath a wrought iron torchlight. Water churned beneath her feet. The sound of the guard running echoed in the castle tunnel.

"Down!" Philby hooked her by the arm and dragged her over the edge of the drawbridge. She and Philby hung from the side, their feet dangling above the water.

"If I fall, genius, the note is ruined," Willa whispered.

The guard sprinted out of the castle and across the drawbridge, sliding to a stop on the stone bridge that connected the drawbridge to the park.

Seeing no one, the guard began a slow-motion turn back toward the castle. When his head came fully around, he looked to either side of the drawbridge and saw no indication of the two kids. They'd vanished.

Dangling from a heavy black chain underneath the drawbridge, Willa and Philby were face-to-face, their knees touching. Philby, one-handed, had transferred his hold from the edge of the drawbridge to the chain below.

"Thank you," she whispered into his ear. "I'll never doubt you again."

45

PRISONERS

THE IDEA WAS TO TURN Amanda's note to Finn into a hologram and stick it to Jingles's neck. Whether it could possibly result in sending the note into the past was entirely theory. It was believed worth a try. The job was left to Brad and Joe's creative team. At the urging of the Cryptos—an elite group of highly technical Imagineers who worked out of a basement bunker at the studio—the Fairlies weren't included in any of it. They were told to return to the dorm and go about business as usual. Joe would keep them informed.

Tim, Jess, and Amanda had other ideas, but it soon became clear that they were temporary prisoners in the dorm. Under constant watch by dorm proctors, saddled with evening assignments, there was no way for them to escape.

Emily was a different story. Tim's battery upgrade to her invisibility suit doubled the time she could move around unseen. She used three minutes of battery life to leave the hotel, rode a city bus fully visible (though somewhat embarrassed by her body-conscious outfit), and met Nick Perkins alongside a fence to the south of the park.

"I'll stay with you until it's too risky for both of us," he said. "At that point, you'll go invisible. Put your phone on vibrate. I can send you a text if things get hairy, and you'll feel it."

"Done. We're good."

They climbed over the fence, and Nick put them in position to watch the stairs to Walt's apartment. It was among the last places Finn or the Keepers had been seen.

"By my recollection," Nick said, "this is the first time two people who've never met the Keepers are doing work for them. A new era. Historic, you might say."

"Let's worry about the history books later, kiddo," Emily said. "Lay it out for me."

"We're assuming Joe or one of the Imagineers, maybe more, will climb the stairs to Walt's apartment. When they do, you need to be right behind them. You have to get into the apartment when the door's open. Once inside, watch everything they do. Everything. You need to memorize it all, and you need to get out when they leave."

"Oh, is that all?" Emily said sarcastically.

"I know it's not easy," Nick said. "Once outside, you can conserve your batteries as soon as you feel it's safe. I won't move from where you leave me. We'll join back up and follow them. You may need to go invisible again. Who knows?"

"I was hoping you did," she said.

"Piece of cake," he said, trying to sound encouraging.

"Uh-huh. Sure it is."

They waited nearly forty minutes. At last, two men in khaki pants and white shirts—Cast Members? Emily wondered—entered a gate by the firehouse and walked backstage. Nick and Emily were hunkered down behind a pair of smelly trash bins with a good view of the stairs leading up to Walt's apartment, as well as the apartment's outdoor patio alongside City Hall.

Nick tapped Emily on the shoulder. She disappeared. He tried to picture her catching up and staying right behind the two men.

When one of them turned suddenly, Nick held his breath. The man had to be inches from Emily. He'd heard her or sensed her. Nick waited. The man reached out, by which point Emily had either stepped down the stairs or ducked. His hand swiped only air.

The other guy called out, "Paranoid!" and continued climbing. Five minutes later, the men left the apartment in a hurry; they raced down the outside stairs and took off at a jog into the park. Nick kept his eye on them as they rounded the corner.

Immediately, Emily appeared, her back against the building's brick wall. She waved Nick out from his hiding place.

"I saw everything," she said, breathless. "They're wearing Imagineering shirts, not Cast Members'. It's Walt's music box. They got it going, and one of them said they had to hurry. I think I should stay with them."

"It's too far to the carousel. Your battery will run out. We can stay backstage, cut behind the Plaza Pavilion. It'll be a sprint through the Plaza, and you'll have to go it alone, but at least we buy you a couple minutes of battery."

"Okay. Let's go!"

They followed Nick's plan, and it nearly worked. But the men stopped at the Plaza. Emily went invisible in order to get closer, leaving Nick unable to join her.

The Plaza was dark and empty. The two Imagineers just stood there. Emily felt her battery draining. What were they waiting for?

And then one of them pointed. The hologram of the note had crossed over into the Plaza; it lay alongside the street's curving curb. One of them rushed over, but discovered he couldn't touch it. His hand waved through the projection. He called on a walkie-talkie. The hologram disappeared.

The men hurried through the castle, Emily following close behind. She skidded to a stop when she saw the King Arthur Carrousel moving. It was the *only* ride moving. The *only* attraction lit up.

The two Imagineers stopped as well. They had a conversation she was unable to overhear, followed by more discussion over the walkie-talkie. The hologram of the note appeared about five yards away from them. She could feel their tension as the men continued the radio conversation.

"Twelve feet to the left . . ." The note vanished and reappeared as directed. One of the men consulted his phone. "Five feet, two hundred degrees." The note moved again. And again, this time hovering along the outside of the spinning horses. "Apply the algorithm."

An instant later, the note began revolving with the platform at the exact speed of the ride. More directions. The note was now inches from a horse and perfectly timed with the carousel's rotation. "Looking good. Slow now, and be ready. . . ."

The note slowed. Jingles approached. Each time the carousel lapped and passed the Imagineers, small adjustments were made through the radio. At last, the hologram gave the appearance of being attached to the neck of the horse with the golden mane.

Emily's phone buzzed at her hip. She looked down: her suit was sparking. Nick was trying to warn her that she was no longer invisible.

46

THE KINGDOM ON HIGH

WAYNE'S PICKUP rolled to a stop in a quiet neighborhood overlooking a valley of lights. "There are laws, kiddos. Trespassing is one of them. You be careful."

"It's for a good cause," said Maybeck through the truck cab's sliding window. He, Finn, and Philby had ridden outside in the truck bed, as before.

"We can dazzle Walt with astounding facts," Willa said from the far side of the bench seat. "For instance, It's a Small World hasn't been built yet, but you can bet he's already thought of it. Stuff like that."

"It won't be Mr. Disney you're talking to," Wayne said. "It'll be the police."

"It's almost one in the morning," Charlene said. She was squeezed between Willa and Wayne, with Maybeck's chin nearly resting on her head. "It'll be quiet."

"I wouldn't count on that," Wayne said. "The Disneys like to socialize. I heard they were having that radio guy, Ronald Reagan, over to dinner tonight. I guess what I'm saying is, be careful. Stay alert. Jeepers, you sure as heck don't want to be caught. Anything happens, you run down the hill. The minute I see you, I'll get the truck up and running, and we'll be out of here lickety-split."

The Keepers climbed the hill before them, arriving at a row of bushes and flowers. Beyond was an enormous sweeping lawn. To their right, a sprawling one-story ranch home.

"That's the house," Finn said.

"So much property!" Willa said. "It's way bigger than I thought."

"Big enough for the Carolwood Pacific Railroad," said Philby.

Wayne had confirmed that Walt Disney owned his own backyard railroad, but he'd been unaware that Walt had named a locomotive after his wife. Charlene's discovery had surprised everyone.

Nearing the top of the hill, they lay flat on their stomachs and crawled. The grass was damp with dew, but smelled fresh-cut and sweet. The five scrambled up the hill and took their positions, moving like the well-oiled team they were. Charlene and Philby advanced across the lawn while Maybeck swept left through a curving flowerbed that ringed the backyard. Willa moved opposite of Maybeck, finding a lookout spot that allowed her a view of Wayne's truck as well as the Disneys' driveway. Finn held back, pretty much where he was, with a view of the terrace and the sliding glass doors leading out to it.

Philby and Charlene stayed on their stomachs, moving as fast as frightened lizards. From their perspective in the grass, the miniature train, rising up in the distance, looked eerily to scale—a gleaming red-and-black locomotive trailed by a coal car and then two long boxcars, the first of which was open and able to carry two or three people straddling it. The locomotive had a single seat; Philby could almost picture Walt Disney sitting in it, wearing a blue-and-white-striped engineer's cap.

Once they were alongside the train, Charlene spoke in a whisper. "What exactly are we looking for?"

"A Walt-type clue, or the pen itself, I suppose." The train was spectacularly real looking. The locomotive was six feet long, the trailing cars slightly longer. Every detail was perfect, right down to the rivets holding the locomotive together. "Amazing. It's a working steam engine," Philby whispered.

"I don't think I care. I don't love the idea of being arrested for trespassing in Walt Disney's backyard. Maybe we can just get on with it?"

"I'll start in the front and work back. You take the caboose and work forward."

Philby took his time studying the locomotive, admiring the attention to detail involved. He should have moved faster, but every brass band, fixture, and wheel was functional and gorgeously rendered. Charlene made some noise pulling on one of the seats, seeing if it would move.

A dog barked from within the house.

Finn saw the curtain covering the sliding glass door move, as did Maybeck, who signaled Philby. A dog's wet nose smeared the glass.

Charlene froze the moment the dog barked. She didn't appear to hear Maybeck's whispered warning: "Take cover!"

"Psst!" Philby struggled to remain calm while trying to win her attention. "Charlie! We've got to move!"

Finally, Charlene heard him. "What?"

Finn saw a light turn on behind the curtain and whistled softly. A yellow haze spread across the back-yard. Charlene turned toward the house as a man's hand appeared, gripping the curtain. Finn heard Maybeck whistle twice, sharply. Floodlights came on from either corner of the roof.

Philby rose up and dove over the locomotive. Something clattered loudly—what was it? Charlene practically flew above the boxcar on her way to the other side.

Finn ducked. He peered through a bed of yellow flowers. A man walked out onto the deck wearing a satin bathrobe and bedroom slippers. He was backlit;

Finn couldn't see a face, but who else could it be? Transfixed by the thought that he was once again looking at Walt Disney—*the* Walt Disney—Finn paid no attention to the other Keepers. He watched the great man come outside, a tall poodle with him.

"Hello?"

There was no mistaking that crackling voice. Finn had heard it so many times. It was Walt Disney himself. Finn could barely move.

"Anyone there? I don't appreciate people nosing around my property, so skedaddle, would you please? I'd hate to have to call the police. Now, begone and good night!"

Finn realized they probably weren't the first Walt Disney fans to pay the legend an uninvited visit. The man and his dog went back into the house. The sliding glass door closed and clicked. The floodlights remained on.

Philby, lying flat on his stomach, heard the condemnation and found it hard to breathe. Walt Disney himself, about to call the cops. The low point of his life.

When Maybeck whistled once, softly—*coast is clear*—Philby started crawling toward Charlene, who was on her back, breathing hard, terrified of being caught.

Something slipped off Philby's leg. He looked back.

It was a *piece of the train*! He'd broken Walt Disney's beloved locomotive!

He pivoted, trying to grab hold of the object. What—no! Of all things, it had to be the sign: LILLY BELLE. His pants had caught on it. Just great! Philby thought, in total misery now. He kneeled, keeping his head low, wondering if there might be some way to reattach it. Running his hand along the back, he felt cold metal on either end. Magnets!

Charlene reached him. "I think I'm dying," she said.

"You and me both. I broke his train!"

"We're doomed. This is the worst night ever."

"Wait a second!" Philby lifted the nameplate higher into the light. Charlene swatted it out of his hands.

"Are you crazy?" she asked hoarsely. "We need to get out of here."

"We need Maybeck to memorize this," he said. "Go get him."

"It's probably a serial number or something. We are *not* sticking around for that."

"Tell Maybeck I need him, Charlie. Then you, Finn, and Willa get back to Wayne's truck. We'll meet you."

"That's not going to happen, and you know it." Charlene scurried off on hands and knees toward Maybeck's hiding spot.

Philby angled the nameplate to catch the light, allowing him to more clearly see the words inscribed on the back.

It was not a serial number.

47

REIMAGINING

INSIDE WAYNE'S WORKSHOP, under the dim illumination of three flashlights, Wayne and Philby worked late into the night. On the table before them was a flickering image, mostly blue and white and black, courtesy of a small, battery-powered transistor radio Wayne had rewired to transmit. The device was just strong enough to project the sparkling hologram of what looked like a piece of paper. The same piece of paper that had been discovered attached to the neck of Jingles.

"It's no surprise this arrived," Wayne said. "After all, you five made it through. The challenge will be to send something back."

"We have analog transmission," Philby said. Wayne looked at him, confused; he backtracked, trying to explain. "Basically, it's this: climbing onto Jingles ourselves would kill whoever tries it. We can maybe send a few small objects, but we have nowhere near the bandwidth we need to transmit a human."

"I don't get it," Maybeck said.

"I don't think anyone does," Wayne said. "It seems that by carving his initials, Finn created a change in the present that carried into the future. This note isn't like that. It came from the future, where the technology exists to allow its transmission. Gee whiz, we're barely able to *see* what they sent, much less duplicate the process in reverse. But we're working on it."

"We're thinking," Philby said, "that it's just unstable. Wayne thinks he can fix that. Let's give it a try."

Wayne pointed at the floating image. It looked like a magic trick, the way it hovered a quarter inch off the worktable. The piece of tape and the torn bit of note hovered at the top. Wayne continued to work, a tiny screwdriver in one hand, the oversize knob of some kind of power supply he called a rheostat in the other. The equipment hummed and buzzed loudly.

"I love that smell," Philby said, mostly to himself. "Like after a thunderstorm."

"Or a burning wire, but yes, it is rather pleasant." Wayne continued to tinker. Philby watched as the scratches on the hologram began to connect. Another few adjustments by Wayne and the lines became fuzzy and indistinct. Philby wanted to coach him—*A little more this way! Now that!*—but knew firsthand how annoying such advice could be.

A final adjustment . . . and it was like a PowerPoint projector's lens focusing. The note came suddenly into view.

Message received. Castle has sparkling spires.
Missing you and our four friends. Beware of A.H.
Mattie read Joe. A.H. has been Public Enemy #1 since
your time. Joe's thoughts about A.H. are woven in with
OTs. Be careful! How can we help you return?—A

Wayne couldn't hold it; the image vanished.

"That's okay! I've got it!" Philby said, lifting a pen from the back of a sheet of sandpaper. He'd written it all down.

"What does it mean—'Castle has sparkling spires'?" Wayne asked.

"She's telling us the date. For the sixtieth anniversary of Disneyland," Philby said, "they changed the castle. She's just telling us it's the sixtieth. If the note had been found by someone else, they wouldn't understand. Call it code."

"Amazing." Wayne stepped back and sat on a high stool. He stayed silent for a long time. "I keep waiting to wake up," he said eventually, his voice very soft.

"You and me both."

"I just read a message written in 2015? Am I supposed to believe this?"

"It's up to you, I suppose. The first time you brought Finn back here, it was in the 1960s. You brought him through a television set. He returned the same way."

"No idea how I did that."

"You'll figure it out."

"Not without a lot of help from Philby," Wayne said.

"It's weird to me, too," Philby said. "I'm not saying it makes sense in terms of physics."

"A.H.," Wayne said. "It's Mr. Hollingsworth, isn't it? Amery Hollingsworth."

"Must be?"

"'Beware of A.H.' We all know him. The same Mr. Hollingsworth who gave that speech in the Golden Horseshoe. The same man fired by Mr. Disney for stealing animation cells from the studios. He said he was innocent, of course, and he made up all sorts of lies about Mr. Disney stealing his ideas. Foolishness! There were other people in those meetings! Mr. Disney didn't steal anything. Some of his villains and stories go back to the European fairy tales, but golly, who cares about that? Mr. Hollingsworth's lies never made sense. There were lawsuits. Mr. Hollingsworth never won. But he doesn't stop trying. He's jealous, that's all. The people who work here, we all love Mr. Disney like a father. Other people don't get it. There will always be sore folks like Mr. Hollingsworth, I guess, but it's not fair to great men like Mr. Disney. Not one bit."

"I agree completely. But let me get something straight: Amery Hollingsworth is alive and kicking in 1955?"

"Very much so. Why? And who is O.T., anyway? I can't think of anyone with those initials."

"It's not a person. It's more like a group."

"And you know this group?" Wayne asked.

"I know this group," Philby whispered, wondering at the message Amanda had been trying to deliver.

48

EZEKIEL

THE THREE FAIRLIES SAT in Amanda and Jess's
dorm room with the door closed. Jess was on the bed,
Mattie and Amanda in desk chairs. A grim air filled the
room, the kind of silence that follows a team loss in a
championship match.

"When Finn described his first time travel experience, *after* he got his memory back about what had happened, he talked about being chased into the TV set by
a Dapper. What if it was the same guy? What if he was
trying to help Finn, not hurt him?"

Amanda spoke first. "We need to find the Dapper
Dan. This guy Ezekiel."

"Overtakers play all sorts of tricks," Jess said. "You
put any faith in that?"

"This is my fault," Mattie said. "It all happened so
quickly."

"Tell us again," Jess said.

"I've told you three times!"

"Once more. Please."

"I touched Joe right as Hollingsworth was mentioned. Things went crazy. His mind went all frantic,

which makes it so difficult to read. He was inside a vault, like a bank vault. He reached for a drawer—second row, third from the left. There was a brown folder inside with Hollingsworth's name. A black-and-white photograph of a man. There were Disney villains like Maleficent and the Evil Queen, too. Superclear and colorful. Animated, for sure, not the characters in the parks. There was a photo of a gravestone. And yeah, he was thinking about a Dapper Dan—a thought, not a photograph—Ezekiel? Ebsy? Some name like that. And a businessman of some sort, and this other guy I can't really describe except to say he was maybe the same age as the others. I don't know."

Mattie took a deep breath, eyes half-closed, hand slightly lifted as if she were physically reaching back into her memories.

"To reach the vault, there was a curtain," she said. "When you mentioned Finn crossing over, I saw steep stairs, a jukebox or an old record player, and the King Arthur Carrousel—especially this wild-eyed horse."

"That last part matches what our friend Emily saw when she was spying in Walt's apartment," Jess said. "The music box. King Arthur. That's how Finn crossed over into the past. We should be able to duplicate it."

"Don't change the subject, Jess," Amanda said. "Joe saw a Dapper Dan. Mattie got a look at his face." She aimed the words at her friend, eyebrows raised, expecting an answer.

"That's true," Mattie said.

"He doesn't know us," Amanda said. "The Keepers, maybe. Willa and Philby for sure. But not us. We find him, and maybe we find someone willing to help us like he offered to help them."

"And maybe we get caught and are never heard from again," Jess said. "Look, I know you want to get Finn back, but—"

"They . . . need . . . us!"

"But he could be Barracks 14, right?" Mattie said. "Maybe the thing to do is find him and let me read him. There's no way he knows me."

"It's a risk," Jess said.

"Worth taking," Amanda said, her face alight with hope for the first time.

"Easy for you to say," Jess said.

"I don't mind," Mattie said. "I want to help."

"We can play backup," Amanda proposed. "Something goes down, we're there to stop it."

"AMANDA LOCKHART, YOU HAVE A VISITOR IN THE LOBBY." The announcement rang out through the dorm's hallway.

"That's interesting," said Jess.

"That's Nick," said Amanda. "Who else?"

49

MR. MYSTERY MAKES
AN APPEARANCE

NICK PERKINS WAITED, legs crossed, arms out-stretched across the back of the red-velvet couch in the dorm's throwback lobby. He carried a thin briefcase, making him look official despite his youth. The three girls sat down, facing him.

"Mr. Mystery makes an appearance," Amanda said.

"Mr. Mystery figured it out," Nick said. "At least he thinks he did."

"We're listening," said Jess.

"There are two Amery Hollingsworths," Nick said. "Amery the first, and Amery Jr. A. the first was fired from Disney for stealing animation cells. You want to guess which ones?"

"Surprise us," Amanda said.

"Villains." The word exploded in their ears, hanging in the air, filling the room like a shock-and-awe grenade.

"He killed himself," Nick said. "Amery the first. That angered his sons, as you can imagine, especially firstborn Amery Jr., who never liked being called Junior.

He blamed it all on Disney. He moved to Baltimore."

Nick opened the briefcase and withdrew a number of sheets of paper, some stapled, some not. "I ran some background information. The usual stuff: Web searches, credit scores, public company financials, investments. You can't get everything, but no one can hide completely."

He held one of the stapled stacks of papers to his chest, taking a moment to look at each of the three Fairlies. "You may find this painful, but I think between the three—four!—of us, we should be able to figure stuff out that we couldn't decipher on our own."

"Nick," Amanda said, not bothering to hide her irritation, "just show us, would you?"

He passed her the information. "One of Junior's companies entered a government auction twelve years ago. They won the bidding. It was for a piece of property, a former—"

"Army barracks and training facility," Amanda said. She flipped pages, reading more quickly with each one. "Photos . . ." she muttered.

"Look! Look!" Jess said. "The number on that building!"

Mattie snatched the sheets of paper away. "Fourteen."

50

FLIPPING THE SIGN

PHILBY READ WHAT HE'D scribbled down from the encounter in Walt Disney's backyard, the words inscribed on the back of Lilly Belle's sign.

> *"Within the park*
> *a day's not done*
> *Until our guests*
> *"read for fun"*
>
> *Letters make up words of three*
> *dnaehtnepnactifoot*
> *easily*
> *into one of these so freely'"*

"What's that even supposed to mean?" Finn complained to Philby as they walked toward the Jungle Cruise, dodging crowds as best they could.

"Focus on the first half, remember? One step at a time."

"None of this makes sense."

"It must mean something. It wasn't hidden on the

back of the sign for nothing, you know. Esmeralda's fortune led us straight there! It's Walt's next clue."

The first half of the riddle had led them here, to the Jungle Cruise. "Read for fun," the Keepers had concluded, had to mean the things people read in the parks: signs, maps, souvenir books highlighting the attractions. To cover as much ground as possible, the five of them had split up. Finn and Philby went to check out Jungle Cruise and Snow White's Adventures, while the girls and Maybeck headed to Mad Tea Party and King Arthur Carrousel.

Finn and Philby boarded a boat at the last second, doing their best not to attract the attention of their fellow passengers, though two Cast Members their age gave them an extra-long look.

The boat set off, the Cast Member "skipper" at the helm yelling his spiel through a megaphone. He warned his passengers about the "dangerous voyage" they were about to embark upon. To Finn's surprise, no one laughed at his serious tone. It dawned on Finn then that it wasn't meant to be a joke, that the audience was really buying into the idea that the animals lining the banks were real and ready to attack the boat. Such a strange thing to witness on an attraction that would become known for its comedy!

"Look for clues," Finn whispered to Philby.

"Remember the Stonecutter's Quill; it'll be tough. Keep your eyes peeled. Anything that can be read."

The boat floated by Audio-Animatronics of tigers, a wrecked campsite. There were words on the side of some of the crates there, but none big enough to read. Throughout, to Finn and Philby's amazement, the guests acted as though they were actually on a treacherous journey through the jungle.

Before the boys knew it, the boat had passed a shrunken-head trader and returned to the dock. Neither boy was any closer to solving the riddle.

"Well, that was a bust." Philby sighed.

Together they set off toward Snow White's Adventures. They were halfway across the hub of the park when Philby nudged Finn.

"Behind us."

"Yeah?"

"Those Cast Members, they were on the Jungle Cruise with us."

"Are you sure?" Finn glanced backward, trying to catch a glimpse.

"Absolutely. Besides, what are Cast Members in Frontierland costumes doing on the bridge to Fantasyland? It doesn't make sense. So what do they want?"

"We're not going to stick around to find out."

"Who knows? They could be on our side."

"Philby, since when has any suspicious behavior *ever* been an indication that someone's on our side?"

Philby shrugged at that. They were almost through the castle by now, and the Cast Members had shown no signs of wavering from their tail.

"We're almost there," Finn said. "Stick close and don't get lost."

They cut immediately left, past the castle, and stepped their holograms through the wall into the Snow White attraction, sliding into the empty backseat of a car departing the station.

The ride flew by in a blur of colors and lights, but no words. Emerging back into the daylight, Finn and Philby still had no more clue as to the riddle's answer than when they'd begun.

What they did know was this: someone wanted them followed.

51

THE ABCS

SINCE THEY'D SOLVED the Stonecutter's Quill, the five Keepers had worked out the puzzles and mysteries that challenged them as a group. With this one still baffling them, they reconvened at an empty table, wedged in a corner outside the Red Wagon Inn. Their attempts at getting some food had failed miserably. They were starving.

"You know what's crazy?" Maybeck said. "Fifty years from now, we're going to be seven years younger, sitting in a restaurant right next door to this one in Florida, and we'll still be trying to solve crazy riddles that Wayne and Walt left us."

"Shush. You're making my head hurt," Charlene said, playfully tapping him on the arm.

"Yeah, well, no veggie burgers in 1955, but we have everything we really need. Pen, paper, and the five of us," Philby said.

"Let's focus," Finn said, grabbing their attention. "Charlene, Willa, Maybeck what did you find?"

"Nothing," Willa reported. "We kept our eyes peeled for every little detail, but nothing stood out. I wrote some stuff down. None of it matters. I'd have thought after all these years, we'd be a lot better at this, but here we are. The carousel and Mad Tea Party don't even have writing on them."

"There was some writing on the Jungle Cruise, and books in Snow White's Adventures," Philby offered. "But I agree with Willa—nothing that mattered."

He pulled out his ticket stubs and laid them on the table, fanning them back and forth as if they held the answers.

"So no one saw anything?" Finn asked.

"What if we're too focused on the attractions themselves?" Willa said, brow wrinkled. "These puzzles are always about the bigger picture. So what led us to the attractions?"

Charlene was playing with Philby's ticket booklet, spinning it on the table. Giving it an extra spin, she stopped—and gasped. "Wait a second! Check it out! The clue is 'Until our guests read for fun.'"

"Yeah? So?" said Maybeck.

"'Read for fun,'" she repeated, and tapped the table. "Get it?"

"Maybe not," said Maybeck in a snarky voice. "I wouldn't ask otherwise."

Charlene tapped again, her fingers flicking the pages of Philby's ticket book. A light went on in the professor's eyes.

"It's not about the attractions!" Philby cried. "It's about the ticket books. You read to have fun. On opening day you bought different tickets for different rides. A-tickets, B-tickets, C-tickets! That's brilliant, Charlie!"

Charlene smiled proudly. "But what exactly is the clue saying? I have no idea."

"Anagrams," said Willa. "It's always anagrams when it comes down to a few letters. Remember Stonecutter's?"

Philby said, "What I wouldn't give for an iPhone right about now. . . ."

Charlene, the Scrabble whiz, was already creating letter tiles out of a torn napkin.

"Acronyms aside, the only word in the English language formed only with ABC is 'cab,'" Professor Philby said.

"But it's never that simple," Finn said.

"Maybe it is?" Maybeck said, helping Charlene with the letters now.

"If Walt was trying to guide Lillian or Roy to the pen, then it's designed so they can solve it," Willa said. "It's not going to be impossible, just difficult. Tricky. Something the OTs or OTKs would have serious trouble with."

"Okay . . . so CAB. Cab. Taxicab? An attraction with a cab?" Willa said.

"The Haunted Mansion! The invisible horse," Maybeck said. "The hearse could be a cab."

"That might work," said Philby, "except it hasn't been built yet."

Maybeck looked crushed. "Oh, yeah, there is that."

"The horse-drawn carriage on Main Street!" Willa shouted out the words like a game show contestant. People at other tables turned and looked over. She lowered her voice and slouched down in her chair. "A horse-drawn carriage, like Terry said . . . the back part, the part you ride in, is a cab."

"What about the second half of the poem?" Charlene said. "We can't just ignore it!"

"We take it in order," Philby said. "It's a puzzle. You solve puzzles in order. We've done this before. Finn? We inspect the cab first."

"I'll distract the driver. Charlene will go under the cab to look around, while Willa and Maybeck get inside to check it out. It's an open-door carriage, so it won't present problems for our holograms. No handles to turn."

"We're getting better at that," Charlene said, demonstrating her superiority by spinning a pencil on the table.

"Some of us, not so much," Maybeck said, waving his hand through the pencil and the wood beneath it.

"The point is," Charlene said, "I can help out, if needed."

"You're thinking about the guys in the old hotel," Finn said.

"I am. I doubt we've seen the last of them."

52

UNDERCOVER, UNDER WHEELS, UNDONE

THINGS STARTED OFF WELL. As Maybeck and Willa climbed into the horse-drawn carriage at the Plaza, Finn approached and spoke to the driver.

"Excuse me, sir. Can you explain the story behind the carriage?"

"Why, yes, son! Happy to. Mr. Disney grew up in a wonderful small town in Missouri. He saw many Main Streets just like this one, Main Street USA. He loved the old carriages and horses, and the reminder of a simpler time in America. The idea is to give you, our guest, the chance to relive those days."

"Gee whiz," Finn said, trying to sound like Wayne, "that sounds just super!" He thanked the man as Charlene came out from beneath the carriage. She gave Finn a thumbs-up and headed for the sidewalk.

"So?" Finn said, joining her.

"I'm not sure what it means," Charlene said, "but I've got something."

"Like what?" he asked excitedly.

"Yeah, like what?" came a voice from behind them.

Turning, Finn saw the mistake they'd made. Among the park guests waiting in line for the carriage were four older boys in dress pants and button-down shirts. They were apparently in disguise, dressed as normal people, not Cast Members, in order to close in on the Keepers. They'd nearly gotten away with it.

"Heads up! Four OTKs working undercover, coming for us!"

Two of the boys went for Finn, two for Charlene. Grabbing for the holograms, the hotel boys encountered an agile Finn, who managed to shove both back. The two grabbing for Charlene came up empty, then looked at one another in astonishment.

"Fast," one of them said, believing she'd jumped out of the way in time to make him miss.

"Ghost!" called the other, reeling violently away from her, trying to process the fact that his hand had swiped through what should have been her body.

Charlene could have run away right then; she had the few milliseconds required to turn and flee. But she had a competitive streak, and it was especially strong when she was pitted girl against boy. She wasn't going to be the loser in any one-on-one situation. Finn had seen it enough times to know. So when the one boy called her a ghost, she shouted "Boo!" and jumped at him.

It might have worked, but the other boy stuck out his leg, and Charlene tripped and fell. Exactly how that was possible escaped Finn; if she'd been all clear—pure hologram—there was no way she could have tripped. It reminded him how unstable and unpredictable an existence they lived in 1955. It was an existence he had no desire to further test.

He sprang forward and helped her up, as first one, and then two of the boys attacked. Finn ducked, and the two OTKs embraced each other.

People in line laughed at the sight of two young men hugging. Kids had gathered around as the whispers of "Ghost!" continued to rustle along on the breeze. Throwing caution to the wind, Finn pulled Charlene through the kids, who screeched, shrieked, and giggled.

Something flashed in the corner of Finn's eye. A reflection off the glass, Finn thought. Or maybe it was more like he'd imagined it—like having been in the Golden Horseshoe Saloon, he'd mingled thought and reality, holograms, and his real self.

The reflection, or image, was of a man: Amery Hollingsworth, standing among the crowd, enjoying the "staged fight." Finn imagined, or perhaps it was real, that he and the man locked eyes, that in those dark sockets he saw hatred and cruelty the likes of which even Overtakers like Maleficent and Chernabog hadn't possessed.

Venom seeped across Main Street USA as if shot from a snake's upturned fangs. Witchcraft and sorcery. The kind of savage, primal loathing that had somehow festered into a yellow, stinging pus, oozing from a mental wound. In that gaze, Finn saw real, unmasked hatred.

Terrified, he grabbed for Charlene and led her down Main Street at a run. A dozen young kids broke away from their parents and followed, calling out, "Wait!" "Come back!" "Golly gee!"

"Don't look now, but we're a kite with a tail," Finn hissed to Charlene.

"I don't like running away!"

"They're following us, Charlie. They're back there. Think of something!" They passed the Intimate Apparel shop, Ruggles Glass and China Shop, and Grandma's Baby Shop.

"Not easy," Charlene said.

"No fooling."

"I've got it! How stable do you think our projections are?"

"Not great."

"Willing to take a risk?"

"Such as?"

"Little piece of Disney trivia you may not know . . ."

"You going to talk trivia while we're running? I can barely breathe."

"Then you shut up. I'll talk. In 1955, all the lakes and lagoons in Disneyland were connected."

"What!?"

"Yes. It's one big water system."

"Not possible! So you're saying . . . ?"

"We're going for a swim."

At the end of Main Street, they'd lost all but a handful of the kids. The four older boys dressed as guests were right on their tail, however. Body humming with tension, Charlene steered Finn toward Adventureland. Reaching a bridge, she dove. Finn did as well.

In the murky water, their DHI projections glowed like goldfish. The kids left the path and chased the shifting colors as they moved underwater. The four fake Cast Members pushed a few of the younger kids aside and moved closer to the water's edge.

"We've got 'em now," one of them said. "This pond is tiny. Surround it! All sides!"

The remaining three spread out.

What Willa had told them about being a projected image underwater proved true a second time. Still no pressure on Finn's chest; no sense of urgency to breathe. Charlene, twice the underwater swimmer he was—

surprise!—hesitated a moment, a great darkness ahead of her. She looked like a blond mermaid, except none of her clothes and none of her hair was waving in the water.

He rose and sipped some air, but there was no sense of suffocating. It was incredible to swim this way, Finn thought, and freeing. Charlene motioned Finn ahead. His vision adjusted; he saw what she intended for them. A conduit pipe three feet in diameter, dark as a well and scary as all get-out.

He shook his head vigorously, as if to say, *Not me!*

Charlene stuck her glowing tongue out at him and led the way into the pitch-black pipe.

Soon after, Finn surfaced again for some air. They were passing the bandstand. Charlene nudged him back down and through another pipe. Together, they entered the water in front of the castle. Finn could hear people shouting—he thought passersby had probably seen what appeared to be *giant fish* in the castle moat.

The next pipe went on forever. Reaching the end was the first time Finn felt certain they weren't being followed. He gulped more air and returned underwater. Charlene, recharged as well, stayed near the lake's sandy bottom and soon Finn understood why: motorboats from the Speedboat Rides zoomed by repeatedly over-head, though from what Finn could see, they weren't exactly speedy. She led Finn down an arm of the lake, which narrowed quickly. At last, the two crawled out onto dry land. Autopia cars zoomed around a sharp corner not twenty yards away.

"We can get out through Tomorrowland," she said, and reached out to take Finn's hand. But her hologram was incapable, and Finn was glad for that. No more hand holding. No more trouble. "Aren't you going to ask what I saw underneath the cab?"

"I'd almost forgotten," Finn said.

"A brand, you know, like hot metal burned into wood? Small, but easy to make out. A famous mouse, one hand on his hip, the other in the air."

"Mickey!" Finn said.

53

IN THE FLESH

TIA DALMA, THE BLACK MAMBA, fanned the flames, her chipped teeth parting in a craggy smile. At last, the conjuring formula was working. The bones had accepted the flesh. The flesh had re-formed into an ugly entity, like something she imagined pulling out of a cracked dinosaur egg. Like a young animal.

Her hands worked busily, putting the finishing touches on the straw-and-grass doll she'd been working on for nearly two weeks. Its feminine form was unmistakably adult, sleek, and refined, like that of a dancer. The chin was pointed, the neck long and thin. The Black Mamba had woven the grass to form beautifully braided skin, as green as a chameleon lizard in the garden. The eyes had been plucked from a living bat, and the fairy wings from a dead one.

Tia Dalma painstakingly wove the wings into the straw figure's upper back. The doll's hair was made from clippings of her own matted locks, ensuring that the two would share a physical trait forever.

Forever, she thought calmly, was such a nice long time.

54

GIBBERISH IN REVERSE

"WITHOUT WAYNE, we'd have never figured out any of this," Willa said. She'd noticed that the boys—especially the boys—tended to take credit where it wasn't always due.

"That's not entirely true," Philby said.

They'd timed their mission to their advantage. It was the first time they'd employed the strategy of entering a structure as holograms, so as to be there when they turned back into normal bodies. That way, no one could follow them inside without unlocking a door, making noise, or drawing attention to themselves.

Their destination was the park's wood shop. Wayne knew the Mickey brand that Charlene had seen on the bottom of the carriage. When the wood shop built an original piece, they liked to mark it with their own version of a hidden Mickey.

"All this time, we were sleeping about twenty yards from where we wanted to be," Finn said to the others.

"How bizarre is that?" Maybeck said.

"There's still the second half of the poem," Charlene

reminded everyone. "I still think we should have solved that riddle before we got here."

"It's the right place to solve it," Philby said. "You'll see."

"But Wayne isn't with us."

"The poem wasn't left for Wayne. It may have been left *by* Wayne—an older Wayne—maybe even the Wayne we knew. Or it could be from Walt himself. But right now we are the ones solving it, and solve it we will."

Their projections had passed effortlessly through the wood shop's locked door. The shop was an open warehouse space about the size of three garages. It housed all kinds of industrial saws and planers, drills and lathes and routers. Special vacuums and lights and power cords dangled from overhead. It took ten minutes for them to find the metal brand and the butane torches used to heat it.

The Keepers searched the area thoroughly, but found no pen, and no clue as to where they might find it. A baby stroller nearby, nearly completed, carried the burned Mickey brand. Two benches. A set of window shutters. None offered any further clues.

Discouraged, they took a moment together to regroup.

"It's got to be the second half of the poem," Willa said. "The answers are there."

"That second line is gibberish," Philby said, "in case you hadn't noticed."

He unfolded the clue and they studied it again.

Letters make up words of three
dnaehtnepnactifoot
easily
into one of these so freely

"Letters make up words of three. DNA. EHT. Nep. Nac. What's that supposed to mean?"

"Hold on a minute," Maybeck said. He grabbed the sheet of paper and took it to a nearby desk, digging around in the messy drawers until he turned up a broken shard of mirror. He held it over the paper. "Take this down, somebody!"

Willa grabbed a pencil and a scrap of paper.

"*T, o, o, f, i, t* . . ." Carefully, Maybeck spelled out the gibberish in reverse order.

Philby was ahead of everyone else. "Too fit can pen the and . . ."

"It's backwards!" Finn shouted. "And the pen can fit too—"

"And the pen can fit too easily into one of these so freely." Philby spoke barely above a whisper.

"One of what?" Maybeck asked.

"A cup with other pens?" Willa suggested.

"A drawer?" said Charlene.

"A hand!" Willa said. "A pen fits easily into a hand."

"Keep looking!" an excited Philby cried.

They separated and started a fresh search, their focus now much different than before.

"I think I've maybe got something!" Willa whispered. They joined her in the far corner, where a high drafting table and wooden stool faced backstage. A glimpse of the top of the castle was just visible in the distance.

"This is for drawing," Maybeck said. "Check out the initials." A wooden plaque read: WED. "Walter Elias Disney. This was—is!—his desk!"

Reverence filled the air. Finn's arms rippled with goose bumps; his neck tingled. "It doesn't get any cooler than this," he murmured.

The five stood there, unwilling to approach the desk.

"I'm not messing with Walt Disney's stuff," Maybeck said firmly. "I mean, we messed with Roy's and Lillian's. That was bad enough. But this . . . this is different. You know the expression 'This is where the magic happens'? Well, guess what . . . forget his office." He threw his arms out wide, taking in the space around them. "This is where he sketches the stuff that counts. This is Walt the designer, the artist, da man."

"Where the rubber hits the road," Philby said, voice quiet and impressed.

"That's what I'm talking about," said Maybeck.

"We've got to do something." Charlene, ever practical, was the first to issue a call to action. "But Maybeck's right: I'm not touching anything of Walt's."

"Even if it'll save the parks?" Finn said, stepping forward.

"They're his parks," Charlene said. "Who am I to decide what's right and what's wrong?"

"There are others deciding that," Philby said, stepping forward alongside Finn, "and we don't like their vision. If we did, we wouldn't be here."

"Guys?" Willa's voice carried certainty; a single word spoken crisply, with authority. It said, *You're going to listen to me.* It said, *Stop what you're doing*; it said, *I know something you don't and you want to hear it.*

The others turned to her, silent and mindful.

"We don't have to mess with anything," she said. She pointed to the window. A bare wood sculpture of what had to be Mickey Mouse stood there, but it wasn't the mouse they knew. He had the same skinny legs and arms, the oversize shoes and gloves, but his nose was longer and more rodentlike, and his eyes resembled round buttons. He stood in a welcoming pose—one hand at hip level, palm out, the other, his left, held up as if waving.

But he wasn't waving.

He was holding a fountain pen.

55

LIFE-OR-DEATH

AMANDA NUDGED MATTIE and head-gestured toward a quartet of Dapper Dans coming down Main Street USA in their colorful striped jackets, white pants, and straw hats. That made nine since the girls had started looking.

"Oh my goodness," Mattie said. "Second from the left. That's him. That's the man Joe was thinking of. The one with the two names."

"You're the expert."

"That's the face Joe saw when I read him. I'm sure of it." Mattie blinked, then nodded firmly. "He's a little older than the guy in Joe's mind, but it's him! He must be the brother."

"And if he is, then he knows stuff. You're sure you can you do this?" Amanda asked.

"Yes!" Mattie sounded confident.

"I'll be right here."

"All right, then." And with that, Mattie charged off to intercept the quartet. Amanda stood back, admiring her courage. Mattie had proven herself far more independent than Amanda or Jess. At Barracks 14, she'd been a loner, aloof, and often caustic when not with the two girls. She hadn't said much outside their circle, and when she had, it was typically cutting or cruel. Her eyes were always dancing, always looking for a way out. She'd proved herself the girls' ally when they needed her; and in the end, she'd escaped Barracks 14 to join them.

Now Amanda saw her walk up to the four men, singling out the second from the left. She spoke to him as she shook his hand. Invading another's thoughts was when things could get dangerous. Amanda hugged herself tightly, trying not to let her nerves get the better of her.

The Dapper Dan said something to his friends and nodded to Mattie. They walked over to Amanda.

"Hi," Amanda said.

"Hello there," he said, standoffish.

"I see you're wearing the name tag 'Ezekiel,'" Mattie said.

"That's my name, as I told you a moment ago when we met and shook hands."

"But when I asked you about it—when we shook hands, as you've just said—you thought of the name Ebsy," Mattie said.

The man appeared blindsided. "But how could you—?"

"It's such an unusual name," Amanda said, interrupting. "A friend and I happened upon the same name, the name of a man about your age: Ebsy Balwin Hollingsworth. Son of Amery senior, brother of Amery junior and Rexx."

The Dapper Dan blinked and doffed his hat. "I have nothing to do with my brother. I disapprove of everything he's doing. I don't know who you work for, young ladies, but you have this all wrong."

Amanda wondered why Disney would ever hire Amery Hollingsworth's son. "You're a spy for Joe Garlington," she said, theorizing. "You keep your eyes open for people who might be working with your brother."

The man blinked rapidly. "I know Mr. Garlington. That's a ridiculous accusation."

"One you didn't deny, I noticed," said Mattie.

"You can't hold a brother responsible for his brother," the man said.

"So you've helped Joe out with that."

"Maybe, a little."

"You know of the DHIs."

"Yes."

"Of their *work* in the Disney kingdoms."

"I am very much aware. I met two of them recently, I'm proud to say. I respect them all."

"They need your help. We need your help," Mattie said. She reached out and put her hand on his wrist.

"We need to know about *a vault that's here in the park.*" A moment later she removed her hand and gave a slight nod to Amanda.

"I think you overestimate me," he said.

"You won't help us unless Joe tells you to?" Amanda sounded angry.

"Let's say I was who you think. Then what do you suppose my answer to that is?"

"The Kingdom Keepers need you," Amanda said. "This is life-or-death."

Mattie spoke, giving no indication she'd just gained this information by reading the man. "The vault is in the Disney Gallery. It contains important information. There's a curtain," Mattie added.

Ebsy Hollingsworth appeared impressed. "Interesting."

He was far more cautious than Amanda had expected. "Both my friend and I spent several years in Barracks 14." She paused, staring into his eyes, waiting for him to nod. "It's outside Baltimore."

Ebsy looked deeply saddened. "I . . . I know my brother acquired a former military training base outside of Baltimore. He's trying to continue my father's legacy. I don't approve of what he's doing. You must know that."

"Which is?"

He glanced around nervously. "Complicated." He added, "If you were there, I'm assuming you're both . . . talented."

Amanda just stared. "What do you think?" She paused. "No, that was rude. I'm sorry. Yes. 'Talented,' that's us."

He nodded, considering. "May I ask what your talents are?"

"If you won't laugh," Mattie said.

"I can promise you that."

Amanda spoke first. "Telekinesis. I move things."

"I can read people," Mattie said. "I've read you. I saw the vault, but I don't understand exactly what I saw."

He addressed Mattie. "That's . . . somewhat incredible."

"Work with us here," Mattie said. "I only saw a few pictures of the vault. We need more."

"I feel partly responsible for all that's happened here in the Kingdom. And I want to help. I do know the vault you're asking about, and what it contains. It's said to be a record of disturbances within the park, but I can't verify that. It's not money, I know that much. So it must be information of some kind. There's a certain Cast Member who visits the site each and every day."

"In the Disney Gallery," Mattie said, repeating herself from earlier.

"It used to be the Bank of America. Now it's the gallery and the vault door is left open for visitors."

"How could they keep anything secret with the vault door open?" Amanda sounded suspicious.

"It's typical Disney. An illusion. Since it's not shut, one would never think to try and open it."

"What's that supposed to mean?" Amanda asked. Her mind was spinning, trying to make sense of all the hints and half-answers.

Something or someone caught the man's eye. He snapped his head to the left and spoke faster. "If the stories I've heard are true, the combination is put into the *open* vault door, just as if it were closed. That opens an interior wall. It's only rumor; I can't vouch for it." He glanced in the same direction, face flushing with excitement—or fear. "Now, pretend I'm giving you directions!"

He turned them both, pointing off toward the castle. The girls played along, nodding. They thanked him and shook his hand. Then Ebsy Hollingsworth rejoined the crowd in the street.

"What just happened?" Mattie asked.

"I think," Amanda said, "he just told us how to open a vault that's already open. You're going to have to read a Cast Member to get the combination. But then I think," she said, barely containing her excitement, "that we're in business!"

* * *

As the final sparkles fell from the sky, ending the evening's fireworks display, and guests flooded down Main Street toward the exit, an average-looking man with an average walk entered the Disney Gallery. He wore khakis and a white Disney Cast Member shirt, and carried an average-looking briefcase.

The Cast Member behind the register walked over to the door and locked it. She drew down window shades that were easy to miss—reflective film that eliminated any chance of the events inside being witnessed from the street. She nodded, which translated as, *Good to go.*

The man with the briefcase heaved against the old bank vault's open door. It moved one inch. He pushed again. It moved two feet. He stepped between it and the wall and began to spin the combination lock. The Cast Member, used to the routine, stood a distance away with her back turned.

He spun the dial to the left, right, left, right. Then he jumped violently as someone—or something—brushed against his back. "Whoa!"

"Excuse me?" the woman said.

"Never mind."

"What?"

"You know those Disney myths? Like Cast Members who heard a sneeze inside Snow White, right before they closed it down?"

"Or the ghost in Haunted Mansion."

"That's no myth," the man said. "And whatever just touched me on the shoulder isn't, either."

"Uh-huh."

"Funny thing is, I'm serious. Something touched me on the shoulder."

Mattie stepped back as they continued speaking, working to memorize the numbers 131, 3, 71, and 3 stolen from the man's thoughts—the combination to the vault.

Emily's invisibility suit barely fit her. It bulged where she didn't want it to bulge and stretched where she didn't want it to stretch. The girls had warned her that because of this, the suit wasn't perfectly invisible from the sides. The plan had been for her to leave the moment she had the combination, but now she couldn't resist the opportunity to discover more.

The man moved around the safe's two-foot-thick door and into the vault. Mattie followed. He drew a curtain aside on the left, exposing a section of wall, and a second thick door popped open a few inches. He pulled it open with some difficulty, revealing a large square room beyond, two of its walls lined with neatly ordered shelves, the third filled with smaller doors—file drawers, Mattie realized.

Aware of the battery's limited charge, she headed for the gallery's front door, only to remember the female Cast Member had locked it. This was nothing short of a disaster. She had three to five minutes remaining; then she'd be exposed—a girl in a silver glitter suit that fit her like a leotard. What now?

The Cast Member stood by the door, waiting idly for the man to finish. Did Mattie dare turn the dead bolt and knob with the woman just a foot or two away? Would it be taken as the act of a ghost, scaring the woman and sending her running, or would she think someone was opening the door from the outside and block the entry? The ghost option would work beautifully for Mattie. Blocking the door could backfire horribly.

Stuck with those choices, Mattie lost her nerve. Staying well away from the woman, she crossed the room and crouched behind a display stand just wide enough to hide her. She switched off her suit to save her battery. And she waited, counting down the seconds.

She looked like a silver Spider-Man. Face hood, gloves, booties.

She heard a clunk—the vault handle being turned.

"All set?" The woman's voice.

"Right as rain. Thanks, as always."

"One last loop and we're out," the woman said.

Loop? Mattie wondered, her finger returning to, but not pressing, the battery's button. Mattie looked toward the window and caught a distorted reflection off the Mylar window shade.

Something yellowish moved toward her end of the room: the woman Cast Member. How do I handle this? she wondered, unsure if she had more than a few seconds of invisibility remaining in the battery.

Heart in her throat, she peered around the display case. The man was reading his phone, head down. She decided to risk it. Watching the moving yellow orb on the window shade, Mattie waited until the woman was only a step away from seeing her. Then she turned on the battery, going instantly invisible, and moved around the display case, like hiding behind a tree in hide-and-seek. Her arms and legs flashed. If the man looked up, he'd see her.

The Cast Member walked past; Mattie slowly circled the display case until she was back where she'd started. The Cast Member was at the far wall now, passing the cash register, reaching the vault.

"All good!" she said. She switched off all but one row of ceiling lights, unlocked the door, and left with the man. Mattie heard the key turn in the lock, then silence.

Her suit's battery dead, she waited several minutes before trying the combination on the vault door. It took her two tries; the second time, the handle moved and the door inside popped open.

Thankfully she knew exactly what she was looking for—Joe had shown her.

* * *

They reviewed the documents in the dorm library—Tim, Nick, Amanda, Jess, and Emily. Mattie had an important internship project coming up. She was desperate to be included, but keeping the internship was critical to her.

Hollingsworth's history with the company read like a Shakespearian tragedy. He had started low, as a runner on the studio lot, and risen up through the ranks to become a member of WED Enterprises, the earliest version of Imagineering.

"It looks like once his plan for the park got turned down," Tim said, reading, "he turned sour. He started making false claims and bad-mouthing Walt Disney."

Hollingsworth had been accused of trying to recruit a fellow member of WED into the occult. He'd told this Cast Member that he'd learned to cast spells and was working on summoning the dead, that his power and abilities far outstripped those of a "cartoonist" like Walt Disney. His twisted ambition was to make the parks darker. He criticized Walt for sugarcoating the experience and underestimating the average park guest.

Among the secreted papers were testimonies from Cast Members who'd been intimidated into joining up with Hollingsworth. Photographs in the file appeared to be the work of private investigators, which suggested that the WED employees had begun to take the Hollingsworth threat seriously. They were right to worry: soon, animation cells went missing—always of villains.

Eventually, WED set up a film camera to shoot frames every fifteen minutes—very likely the first security camera ever built. It was on this film that a man named Adrian Chesborogh was caught stealing. Chesborogh had been arrested and questioned by the police; no connection to Hollingsworth was proved, but the man shook with fear at the mention of Hollingsworth's name. Without ever naming him specifically, Chesborogh went on to describe satanic worship, animal sacrifice, and worse. He escaped police custody his first night in jail—it was reported he'd "disappeared" from within a locked cell.

"Well? Thoughts?" Nick said, reading along with the others. "Cat got your tongue?"

"It says here that one of Hollingsworth's sons was

admitted to an asylum," Jess said softly. "They thought he was bewitched and tried to cure him with a priest."

Jess and Amanda exchanged a look of confusion and fear. They'd been treated much the same way as children.

Nick said, "What do you want to bet Hollingsworth was working on a few spells of his own, trying to bring the villains to life? I'm betting he tested one on his son. That his ultimate goal—the destruction of Disney—having failed in the courts, in the company, in everything he tried, came down to battling Disney from within?"

"The Overtakers." Jess had dreams to back up this theory, but didn't want to take the time to explain.

"We already knew that at some point the villains broke away from the Disney 'family,'" Tim said. "That was the start of the Overtakers."

"But we didn't know why," Jess said.

Emily cleared her throat and waited for everyone's attention. "Anyone remember eighth-grade language arts? How do you incite action? Through conflict. Hollingsworth cursed or created or reinvented certain villains to go inside Disney and recruit the same way he was. What if he wanted to create a divide between Disney villains? That divide would be like splitting the atom—excite it enough and you create a burst of energy capable of bringing down the house. In this case, the House of Mouse."

"That's what has to be stopped," Tim said. "The divide. The early conflict that results in empowering the villains—"

"Turning them into the Overtakers," Jess said.

"Yes! That's what we have to tell the Keepers," said Amanda. "They have to know it's not as simple as getting Walt's pen back."

"What pen?" asked Nick.

"Never mind." Amanda shook her head vigorously.

"They stop the divide," said Jess, "and maybe they prevent the Overtakers from ever existing."

"I hate to say it," Nick said, "but that makes sense."

"Trouble is," Amanda said, troubled, "how do we tell them?"

56

MISSING, MISTAKEN, DUMBSTRUCK

THE EXCITEMENT OF the moment led to a giddiness among the Keepers. The search for the pen had consumed them for days. Now the five teens and Wayne were about to test it out.

It was well past midnight; they were human, not hologram. Only Finn was not at his best. His connection with Amanda, across a million miles and sixty years, left him feeling melancholy and anxious. While the group celebrated their discovery, he was looking ahead to the reality of their situation: there was no way to return. The five of them were Dorothy without the ruby slippers. Stuck in 1955.

His feelings for Amanda, his yearning for his family, overcame him. Though he overheard the conversation, he was a reluctant observer, pushed into the corner of Wayne's small workshop.

"So, are we ready for this?" Maybeck asked. As resident artist, he got the honor of testing the pen.

"I am so ready," Charlene said, ruffling her skirt. "I've had enough of crinoline for about sixty years." Willa laughed. The boys didn't get it.

No one was talking about the fact that the last test of a pen, nearly identical to this one, had failed. The connection of the pen to Walt's drawing table gave them all added hope this time might be different. Wanting to test it on a blueprint, they used Wayne's diagram of a floating head in a haunted house, an attraction he hoped to pitch to WED Enterprises sometime soon.

"Aren't you coming over to watch?" Charlene called out to Finn. Finn got up and joined them—picking a spot at the table far away from Charlene.

Maybeck uncapped the pen. "There is a difference. This one has gold trim."

Finn sensed something wrong, someone nearby or present. "Have we checked the workshop?" he asked Wayne.

"For?"

"Unwanted guests."

"Finn, this place barely holds us," Willa said. "What are we waiting for? If this is the right pen, if we make sure it's on Walt's desk to stay, then it should be on his desk in One Man's Dream when we solve the Stonecutter's Quill in sixty years. This is epic!"

"Here we go." Maybeck lowered the pen's bulbous nib toward the diagram and used the lever to release a drop of ink. Everyone but Finn watched him closely. Finn's attention was elsewhere, on all the places a person could hide in the cluttered workshop.

"Try again."

"Maybe draw a line?"

"Try another blob!"

Finn looked at the unchanged diagram.

"Another piece of paper," said an anxious Philby.

Wayne dug one out of a drawer. Maybeck drew a mouse, then a rabbit. Nothing changed.

"Wayne, you try," Philby ordered. "The first time we saw this thing do anything, you were the one holding it."

Wayne gave it his best. The pen drew lovely lines, Finn thought, but nothing more.

"It . . . doesn't . . . work!" Maybeck declared, exasperated.

"All this for nothing?" Charlene moaned. "Again!"

"Try again," Philby said, taking the pen from Maybeck and scribbling madly. "It's got to work!"

"We're missing something," Finn said.

"Duh!" Charlene and Willa said in unison.

"We're not thinking it through," Finn continued, undaunted. He addressed Wayne. "What do you think?"

"Cause and effect," Wayne said. The Keepers settled a bit, leaning in to hear his words. "The story you tell about me using the pen. There was a need at the time. Yes?"

"I'd say so," Maybeck snapped.

"Maybe that need doesn't exist in the same way at present," Wayne said.

"There is a great need, an urgent need, that we make sure this pen is eventually in One Man's Dream," Finn explained calmly. "It's missing in the future. Something happened to bring it forward to the right place, and we think that something is us."

"Perhaps you're mistaken," Wayne said.

"Perhaps we're not," Philby said. "In which case, it's the pen that's not working."

"Not working *properly*," Wayne said, correcting him. His eyes widened. "How foolish of me!"

"What?" Willa asked.

"I wasn't thinking!" Wayne said. "How did Mr. Disney get hold of such an enchanted pen in the first place? Hmm?"

The Keepers were dumbstruck.

"He enchanted it himself," Maybeck said. "He's Walt Disney, for crying out loud!"

"Mr. Disney appreciates a good magic trick," Wayne said, "but he's no sorcerer. He's a person just like the rest of us. That's what makes him so special." He paused and scratched the side of his nose with his index finger. He would carry that same habit with him for the next sixty years, Finn realized. There was only one Wayne.

"There is a story, probably more myth than fact, that Mr. Disney encountered a gypsy when he was driving ambulances in the Great War. It's said that this woman sensed the greatness in him that was to come and enchanted him, blessed him with creative powers as her line had enchanted others before, like Leonardo da Vinci and Michelangelo."

"Enchanted his pen."

"What ambulance driver carries a fountain pen?" Wayne said. "And what gypsy has one lying around to offer as a present?"

"I'm totally lost," Maybeck said.

"The body is an instrument," Wayne said, "but it is nothing without spirit and—"

"Blood," said Philby.

"Someone's paying attention," Wayne said. "Go ahead, Philby, tell them."

"Ink," Philby said. "It wasn't the pen she enchanted, it was the ink!"

"Enchanted ink that Walt Disney would have kept handy, but would have used sparingly."

"It's in the wood shop!" Charlene said.

They all heard the sound of scuttling feet.

"Outside! Spies!" Finn shouted, connecting the sound with his earlier sense of an unwanted presence. The Keepers raced out of the workshop in time to see four older boys running away at full speed.

Heading in the direction of the wood shop.

57

ARMING THE ENEMY

"Do you have any idea what we've done?" Philby panted, racing toward the wood shop. A pink sky was forming in the east. The park's radio antennas would be turned back on at sunrise—any minute now.

"Maybe we could discuss this later?" Finn said, working hard to keep up.

"If those punks get hold of the ink, we've given them the very tools they need to create real villains from the Disney drawings. We've created the—"

"Overtakers." Finn went white.

"Wrap your mind around that one."

"If we don't stop them from getting that ink, we're the ones to blame."

"And if we do, then the Overtakers may never exist, which means Disney doesn't need us—Wayne doesn't need us—and—"

"We never meet. We never become friends."

Finn and Philby skidded to a stop, both in shock. The others saw them and slowed, then stopped themselves.

"What?" Charlene shouted, well ahead of the rest of the Keepers.

"There's good news and bad news," Philby said.

"Really? Now?" Willa said, impatiently. "Guys? They're getting away!"

The five took off again, but Finn and Philby exchanged a telling look of panic, fear, and remorse. Save Dillard, the Keepers and the Fairlies were the only friends Finn had known for the past several years. They had been his world. His universe. He'd walked the parks as a hologram. He'd done things, extraordinary things he couldn't imagine a life without. He'd made friends he couldn't live without.

How did the universe work? he wondered. If they recovered the ink, would the Overtakers find another way to exist, or would it mean the end of them? If the Overtakers failed to exist, would he and his friends find a different way to meet, or would they never know each other's names?

As torn as he'd ever been, he reached the door to the wood shop. In front of him, Philby, Maybeck, and Charlene were already fighting the hooligans.

Finn took a deep breath, and dove into battle.

58

PAIN AND CONSEQUENCE

THESE GUYS MEANT BUSINESS. Philby took a fist to the face and went down to his knees with a bloody nose. Charlene cut out the knees of the boy responsible, but all her blow did was cause him to stagger. The boy spun, fist raised, and . . . hesitated. His brain apparently couldn't process that a girl had hit him and now he had to hit her back. In that instant, Charlene performed a martial arts pivot on one foot and delivered her opposite heel into his abdomen. A whoosh of air went out of him, yet he still remained standing.

A leg tripped Charlene from behind, the work of yet another of the boys, on his way to club Maybeck with an elbow to the back. Willa was crouched into a ball, hands on her head, as a third boy brought both fists down, screaming at her, "Mind your own beeswax!"

The Keepers had lost the advantage in a matter of thirty seconds. Two of the hooligans fled through the door of the wood shop.

The ink! Finn thought. Resolve shot through him; he found a strength he hadn't experienced in a long, long time. He'd first felt it after an electrifying experience on the Disney Dream cruise ship. Now, it entered his veins like warmth; he recognized the familiar glow immediately: he was twice, maybe three times his normal strength. Blinded by the rising sun, he was reminded of what an endlessly long night this had been. Only then did he make the connection to the tingling he was feeling.

"All clear!" Finn shouted. "We're DHI!"

The Disneyland radio transmitters had been turned on.

The next blow to Willa's head went straight through her. She stood and kicked the boy in the shins, but her poorly projected leg passed through his. Off-balance, she stumbled and fell.

The teen who'd elbowed Maybeck should not have stuck around. Maybeck's hologram proved impossible to strike.

"Ghost!" the teen shouted, terrified.

Maybeck focused intently on his hands. He felt them tingle and struck the kid in the jaw, the belly, and on his back with an elbow, driving him down to the pavement.

"You . . . don't . . . play . . . fair!" Maybeck said, kicking the kid, though nowhere near as hard as he could have.

"You'll never beat Hollingsworth!" the boy spat up

at him. "Once he has that ink, his power will be greater than any of yours!"

"Yeah? Well, he doesn't have it yet." Maybeck headed for the wood shop at a sprint.

Finn had already reached the door. He hurried inside, only to see a 2 x 4 piece of lumber flying through the air, aimed at his head. It passed through him. But his fear of the thing gave him substance. He grabbed hold, yanked it from the kid on the other end, and swung for a homer. The boy went down with stars in his eyes. One to go!

Maybeck blasted through the door behind him. His hologram charged right through Finn's, both of them racing toward Walt's desk in the back. Solidifying, Maybeck knocked into a kid who had the rough wood statue of Mickey in hand. The statue flew up into the air. A narrow glass jar slipped out, spinning and flashing as it tumbled down. Maybeck caught it with one hand.

The ink.

Finn sped to a stop at his side. He bent and used twine to tie the hands of the kid Maybeck had leveled.

Trying to catch their collective breath, still shaking from adrenaline, the two boys looked at the dark ink inside the vial. It was thick as blood, dark as the Evil Queen's cape.

"Perhaps we can come to some agreement," a man's deep voice called out.

The boys looked toward the door. An older man with an upturned chin and fierce, narrow-set eyes stood there, looking back at them. He wore a fine suit and shiny black shoes. Cuff links sparkled from his wrists. A black cane with a silver crown warmed in the palm of his hand. To see such a man on the street, Finn would have thought him a banker or lawyer. But the feral eyes revealed a troubled soul within. He was a cave dweller, a man who lived so often in darkness that his eyes had lost the ability to adjust to light. Only black glass remained.

Philby, Willa, and Charlene stood frozen in place at his side. Something bad had happened to them.

"I think you'll need this, as it turns out. Two peas in a pod, the pen and the ink." Hollingsworth reached into his jacket and came out with Walt's pen. "You shouldn't have left that boy alone, you know? Never abandon your defenses."

"Pen and ink," Maybeck muttered to Finn. "No power without both."

"You give me that ink, and I'll give you your friends back. How does that sound?" His gang of four had recovered, save the boys Finn and Maybeck had tied up. Awaiting Hollingsworth's command, they held back from the Keepers—and the ink.

Finn wondered how the man could have possibly affected his friend's holograms. What powers did he have? For affected they were: unmoving and frozen in place.

"I don't think that's going to happen," Finn said.

"I'd be careful. I don't make offers twice."

Finn reached out and took the ink from Maybeck. He held it out as he walked forward, closing the distance to Hollingsworth. He unscrewed the bottle's small tin cap.

"I'll pour it out right here," Finn said.

"You wouldn't."

"Really?" Finn tipped the bottle. Ink splashed onto the concrete floor.

"NO!"

"Release them now."

"I will not!"

"You will." Finn poured out more of the dark, viscous ink. A few drops splattered onto Charlene's dress shoes. Color raced up her leg and spread through her as Hollingsworth, Maybeck, and Finn watched in astonishment. The flow of change in her looked like the change that pixie dust made when the animated Tinker Bell waved her wand.

Shaking herself like a sleeper emerging from a dream, Charlene suddenly stepped forward and flung herself at Maybeck.

"I heard it all," she said.

Maybeck squatted, colored his fingers with the ink, and flicked it at Philby and Willa. Like Charlene, color flowed through their bodies; in a flash, they came back into being.

Hollingsworth staggered backward toward the door, overcome by what he'd just witnessed.

The Kingdom Keepers rushed outside to stop him.

59

THE REAL DEAL

IT STRUCK FINN AS AN apparition: something remarkable this way comes. Hollingsworth and his gang of four stood in front of a tall man. At this hour, the rising sun pinned to the horizon backlit him, turned him into a faceless silhouette. The brightness of the sun enlarged his shape and burnished the edges of his form until he almost seemed to float.

When the man spoke, Finn recognized his familiar crackling voice.

"You're nothing but trouble, Amery."

A wave of goose bumps seemed to surge across Finn's body.

"You'll not stop me," Hollingsworth spat. "You may think you will, but you won't. I have destiny on my side. I have creatures you created."

The villains! Finn thought. The Overtakers.

The silhouetted man spoke. "I've just been informed by a reliable Cast Member—whether I believe him or not is another matter—that perhaps I won't stop you, but these five young people will. Finn? Amery will give you my pen now."

He knew Finn's name! Finn stepped forward.

But Hollingsworth didn't move. "Another step and I smash it."

Finn had been so focused on the man that he'd missed the four men in Disneyland security uniforms who'd appeared on either side. They stepped forward, but Walt Disney waved them back.

"Amery, please. Enough of this."

Hollingsworth clearly weighed the odds. "I'll smash it to the ground. Your choice . . . *sir*." He spoke each word venomously, as if the syllables were blows he was raining down. "Bad always overtakes good. Darkness consumes light. What you've built here is temporary."

He raised the pen higher, about to smash it to the ground.

"Hey," Finn called to Maybeck. He pinched his own throat.

Maybeck nodded. He stepped up behind Hollingsworth. Hollingsworth's boys made a move, but there was no Maybeck to grab—only a projection.

Maybeck reached his DHI arm *inside* of Hollingsworth from behind. Through the man's shoulder blades and up to his windpipe. He focused and squeezed.

Pain ripped through both men, Maybeck crying out, Hollingsworth gasping for air. The comingling of projection and corporeal human caused Maybeck intense pain. Hollingsworth reached for his own throat as if to pull away the hands choking him—a hand that the others couldn't see.

He let go of the pen.

Finn's DHI dove toward the pavement, rotating in midair to put his back to the asphalt. He looked up to see the pen falling toward him, tumbling end over end. He reached. Grabbed. And snagged it.

Maybeck released Hollingsworth, withdrew his arm, and staggered back. Charlene caught hold of him as he sagged, hissing in pain.

Hollingsworth gagged and coughed. As he staggered forward, the guards took hold of him and the four young men in his gang.

"Take them to the gate and show them out," Walt Disney said. "Amery, the next time I'll have you arrested."

"The next time," Hollingsworth said, "it will be my park, not yours."

"We'll see," Walt Disney said.

Finn handed the great man his pen. "I believe this is yours."

"You've worked so hard to find it," the man said. "Why don't we fill it up with ink and give it to you? There will still be plenty left over for me."

"How did you find us, sir?" Willa blurted.

"I was paying a surprise visit to the boy, Wayne. Great promise, that boy. He interests me very much. I found him in a dreadful state, and he told me quite a story. When he mentioned my Lilly Belle, I had to listen all the more carefully."

He stopped, scrutinizing the Keepers, and then stepped forward. "May I?"

Finn wasn't sure what he was asking, but who was going to turn down Walt Disney? "Yes, sir."

Walt waved his hand through each of their bodies. "Extraordinary! So impressive! I can see a big spooky house with people just like you gathered around a dining room table. The guests would love it! Are you dead?"

"No, sir. More like an illusion."

"Well, I understand illusion!"

"Yes, sir."

"I'm Willa!"

"Terry Maybeck."

"Charlene!"

"Philby!"

Finn hadn't realized the others had drawn so close.

"Pleased to meet you all. In the short time we had together, Wayne tried his best to explain who you are and what you need. I close my mind to nothing, you see. I admire Einstein greatly."

"Our having the pen is important to the future of the company," Philby said. "Let's put it that way."

"That I can understand. Thank you, son."

"If it isn't too much trouble, sir, could we put some ink in the pen as you suggested, enough so it won't dry out for a very long time?"

"This ink doesn't dry out, Finn. This ink isn't like any ink you've ever used."

"I believe that, sir! I've seen it in action. What we need . . . what the *future* needs . . . is for your pen, the one with your name engraved on it, and some of the special ink, to be placed in the cup holder in your office."

"My office? What do you know about my office?"

"On the sixtieth anniversary of Disneyland, sir, your office, your exact office, is going to be moved from a museum in Florida back to where it is now in the studios. People from all over the world will come to walk through it."

"You must be joking? Florida? How would my office get all the way to Florida?"

"You'll have to work that out yourself," Philby said. "I imagine Wayne might have something to do with it, sir."

"Well." Walt Disney rocked back on his heels and smiled. "With Wayne's help, I'll do as you ask."

Finn swelled with pride over being a Kingdom Keeper.

"You won't regret it," Philby said.

"I'm not sure I'll have a chance to admire or regret it, young man. But I'm inclined to believe the lot of you. And good grief, if Amery Hollingsworth's involved, I want to make sure I do nothing to help him in any way."

"You've got to protect the pen and the ink," Charlene said urgently. "None of us want to stop you from all the great things you're going to do, sir. But that ink, in the wrong hands . . . If you can keep Hollingsworth from getting hold of it, there's a good chance he never accomplishes what he's trying to accomplish."

"Which is?"

"It's a little unbelievable, honestly."

"Try me."

Charlene gathered her composure. "That man wants to divide your villains, to turn them against your good characters."

The sun lit up more of Walt Disney's famous face. The mustache, his pleasant smile, and his kind eyes came into view. For a moment, the Keepers just stared.

"The stolen celluloids . . ." Walt Disney said. It took him a moment to recover. "What you're telling me makes more sense than you know. Amery is not to be trusted. I will take better care because of you all."

"We're so glad you understand!" Philby said.

"Isn't it a shame that some people seem determined

to turn good experiences bad? To me, it seems we are in a promising new time, an era of imagination and following one's dreams. For people like Amery . . . Well, I pity their bitterness.

"Now," Walt Disney said, "how else can I help you?"

"Actually, sir, I think we'll be leaving soon."

60

JINGLES ALL THE WAY

THE FOLLOWING NIGHT, Jingles delivered a message to Jess and Amanda via the carousel.

You must be DHIs. Tomorrow, same time.

Convincing Joe to allow Jess and Amanda to cross over turned out to be easier than either of them would have guessed. He was surprisingly sympathetic and understanding.

"Security caught you on videotape when you took that note off Jingles's mane," Joe explained. "I saw first-hand how hard you worked, what an effort it took to get that note. I know how much this means to you. And I know the Keepers are somehow in a place the rest of us only dream of. I'm with Disney, girls. We're hired to dream. I've been a dreamer since I was five. I want to believe in time travel! Whether it exists or not, I want it to be real. I'm willing to play along because I *want* to play along."

His office was unusually quiet: he'd shut his door and switched off his phone.

"I think they're going to send something," Amanda said. "Philby must think it's important that we're DHIs when we receive it, or why ask for that detail?"

"Agreed," Jess said.

"Once we're DHIs," Amanda said, "Jess and I go through the same procedure the Keepers did: the music in Walt's apartment, King Arthur Carrousel, Jingles."

"How can you possibly know those details?" Joe asked angrily.

"We know," Amanda said.

"And do you have something for them?" Joe asked, raising an eyebrow.

"We do," Jess said. "I've dreamed something I need to share. It's supported, you might say, by a bunch of things we've learned in the past few days."

"Can you share it with me?"

"I can, and I will, but not if you laugh or criticize us, or try to stop us because of it. I know that's a lot, but we're convinced, and we won't allow you to talk us out of sharing our news."

"I see." Joe seemed to be fighting back a smile. "I can respect that."

"Are you sure?"

"Do you know how we get our best ideas?" Joe asked. "By having lots of bad ones. And it isn't enough to have an idea, you have to test it. You have to see if it will stand or fall. The Imagineers, the whole company lives by these rules. You've just become Imagineers, I think!"

"Amery Hollingsworth—"

"Junior, we call him," Amanda added.

"Junior," Jess continued, "picked up where his father left off. Barracks 14 is part of his new plan. He intends to use kids with extraordinary powers, kids like Mandy and me, kids he can influence, can brainwash, to help him destroy the parks. Disney itself, if possible. We were supposed to be part of that. Wayne found out about Barracks 14 somehow, and he got Amanda and me out. He helped us escape and brought us down to Orlando to help the Kingdom Keepers defeat the Overtakers. It was a plan. This whole thing was a plan from the very start. None of it was coincidence. Wayne knew exactly what he was doing."

Jess took a deep breath and interlaced her fingers. *You have the strength to continue,* she told herself.

"Hollingsworth Senior had a similar plan. Something to do with the pieces of animated movies he stole. Always of the villains. Amanda, Tim, Emily, and a friend of ours, Nick, believe that Hollingsworth intended to animate those cells himself, but in a more black-magic kind of way."

"A more Evil Queen kind of way," Amanda added.

"That way," Jess said, "he could create a team of his own special villains to rise up against the others. He'd make Ursula and Maleficent enemies. Such a divide would mean disagreement, divisiveness. Battles. Hollingsworth Senior intended to use the friction of villain against villain to strike a spark—the spark he needed to create the Overtakers. That friction, you might call it a legacy of secrets, would eventually strengthen the resolve of the villains. Once he had those Overtakers angry enough, he would direct that rage against the good Disney characters. That started the after-hours battles, the war, that's raged for decades."

"The war the Kingdom Keepers eventually won in Disneyland," Amanda said. "At least we think they have."

"But the Kingdom Keepers are back there now," Joe said, leaning forward on his elbows. He seemed to be listening very closely. "They can stop that divide. They can stop Hollingsworth's plans."

"With the pen. It won't be enough. Finding the pen is great, but that's just a solution to one of the earliest battles the Keepers were involved in."

"Hollingsworth hasn't released the Barracks 14-ers yet," Amanda said. "When he does, Disney will be up against children and kids like us. Maybe a hundred of them, all with skills and abilities that make magic look like child's play."

"Just like the Overtakers, the Barracks 14 kids never exist if the divide between the villains can be prevented," Joe said softly. "Am I actually saying this? Am I supposed to go along with what you're thinking?"

"That's the same question the Keepers face every time they cross over. The same question I ask myself when I move something without touching it. Or when Jess's dreams come true. 'How can this be happening?' But, what do you think, Mr. Garlington? Is any of this real?"

Amanda moved a penholder across Joe's desk. He watched in amazement.

"At some point, the Keepers are going to figure out how to return," Joe said. "They're smart that way."

"That's just the thing," Jess said. "You've put your finger on it!"

"We can't let them," Amanda said.

61

AROUND AND AROUND WE GO

At 2 a.m. Amanda turned on the music box in Walt's apartment. She marveled at the lack of blue outline around her body—a result of the DHI upgrade. To look at her, to look at Jess, you saw two young women. There was no sense whatsoever that what you were looking at was only projected light.

Jess carried the coded note they intended to tape to Jingles's neck. The girls hurried down the stairs and ran across an empty Disneyland, suddenly feeling gleeful and happy. They felt like princesses. They felt like heroines.

Arriving at the spinning King Arthur Carrousel, they saw Nick, Emily, and Tim, each positioned equidistant around the carousel's circle.

"Nothing yet," Tim said, "but it only started moving a few minutes ago."

"Very interesting," Nick called out in his dry way. In moments like these, he reminded Jess and Amanda of Philby.

Emily looked sleek and slim in her invisibility suit. They'd decided to have her wear it in case they faced any trouble from the associates of Jason Ewart.

After twelve minutes of anxious waiting, the carousel slowed and stopped. The group came together.

"It's going to be tonight," Amanda said. "I know it is."

"I'll restart it in case it won't do that on its own," Tim said. "Walt's apartment, right?"

"Better that I do it," Emily said. "In case it's a trap. Maybe the plan is to separate you two." Her eyes were on Amanda and Jess. "To kidnap one of you at Walt's apartment, then move in on the other."

"You'll have to be careful, then," Amanda said.

Emily reached down and switched on her suit. She disappeared. When she reappeared, she was grinning. "Won't be easy catching me! See you in a few minutes."

62

ARISE

An exhausted Tia Dalma, who had not slept for five nights, strained to reach out and take the hand of the looming figure swirling ephemerally before her. Part smoke, part colorful form, part human, part wraith, the green-skinned shape came and went.

"Stay," Tia Dalma whispered. "Rise, and remain in the land of the living."

The figure had grown to the size of a real woman, though she hid now within the smoke. Her fingers twitched as if desperate to grab hold.

Tia Dalma understood she had to come to her; there was no point in lunging out and trying to snag that glowing hand. All such efforts over the past twenty minutes had failed.

"We need you," Tia Dalma said. "We miss you, sister. You will be whole again. A dark fairy once more. You will be more powerful than ever before." She inhaled deeply and called, "Rise and remain!"

The figure's head moved as if she could hear. Not the words, exactly, but the voice. Or perhaps she sensed the presence of the living.

"Come to me. Remain with me. Your home is here."

Again, the long green fingers twitched, seeking purchase.

"They are here, the Children of Light. They are gaining great power. We . . . need . . . you. . . ."

A painful cry cracked the air. It might have been heard for miles around. It might not have left the station. The hand jutted out and found Tia Dalma's.

The two women held hands and slowly, carefully, Tia Dalma drew the other through the small slit in time that had opened, delicately pulling her through unscathed.

63

AN APPARITION

THE CAROUSEL STILL DIDN'T MOVE. Positioned at compass points around the carousel's circle, Amanda, Jess, Nick, and Tim waited for Emily to restart Walt's music box from Walt's apartment.

"What's keeping her?" Jess mumbled to herself.

"I hope she's all right," Tim called out, his voice thin and tense.

"Same," Amanda said.

A woman's high, painful scream split the air. It came from somewhere nearby.

"What the heck was that?" called Nick. He suddenly looked young, and very scared.

"No idea," answered Jess. "But I don't like the possibilities."

"Whatever happens," Amanda said, "you and Nick keep back, Tim. Jess and I can't be hurt as DHIs, and the software we're running allows us to do all sorts of amazing stuff."

"We're kind of superhuman," Jess said. "If there's trouble, let us handle it."

"I'm not real comfortable with that," Tim said.

"I am!" Nick said, winning a laugh from both girls.

The first wave of attackers came from Mr. Toad's Ride. The Three Little Pigs were not little. They looked like wild boars. They were followed moments later by a drooling wolf with intense, angry eyes.

Amanda *pushed*. The first of the pigs wiped out, but the next two continued charging. The new leader headed directly for Amanda. He lowered his head and rushed *through* her hologram, crashing into the carousel and knocking himself unconscious. Piggy number three backpedaled, fell, and did a convincing impression of a hockey puck before colliding into the brick wall outside the ride.

The carousel began moving. Quickly, it gained speed.

"It's moving faster this time," Tim shouted.

"Hopefully that's a good thing," Amanda said. They held their positions around the carousel, watching for any changes in Jingles, searching the dark for more Overtakers.

Three boys appeared—the same three thugs from the Cone Shack. No Jason Ewart.

"You're out past your bedtime," the lead boy said. An absurdly good-looking blond guy with a surprisingly gentle voice, he looked like a surfer.

"We're going to have to punish you for that," said

the boy at his side. A skinny, dark-haired kid, his face pained, he looked like a poster child for runaways. Jess took note of him—he was the one who'd hurt you big-time and apologize later for overdoing it.

"Go easy," Tim said. "Take a step back, pal." He couldn't help himself, Jess realized. He was going to make himself a part of this no matter what she and Amanda said.

"Tough boy?" Skinny taunted.

Jess kept her eye on the revolving carousel, mentally urging Jingles to deliver something.

Skinny went down hard, like a rug had been pulled out from under him.

Emily! Jess thought.

Though the surfer chuckled, he looked inwardly ter-rified. His arm was yanked invisibly up behind his back, his body forced to the asphalt. He cried out.

Skinny had eyes as wide as a five-year-old lost on Halloween night.

"You've seen our magic," Amanda called out. She was at Jess's side now. "Go, and we won't hurt you."

The third teen, younger and far more innocent looking with his kind blue eyes and boyish face, helped Skinny to his feet. Surfer dude tried to work the pain out of his shoulder as he joined them. The three boys put their backs together without any kind of signal, covering themselves from all directions. They waved their hands in the air, as if they *expected* to be battling something invisible.

A second later, the surfer connected, and Emily cried out. As she hit the asphalt, her right leg appeared—only her right leg, clad in a Mylar suit, the torn fiber-optic wires suddenly visible. Where the leg stood, alone, the invisibility suit began to spark and show flashes of Emily. The effect was chilling, like a specter or ghost.

"Run!" the surfer shouted. The other two needed no encouragement. The three scattered at full speed.

As they fled, two wraiths burst from Mr. Toad's Wild Ride and soared into the night sky like smoke. Jess cried out, pointing upward.

"I see them!" Amanda said, her voice quavering.

"What . . . are . . . those . . . things?" Tim called out.

"Overtakers!" Jess's limbs tingled. "Have to be!" She fought against the tug from her hologram's all clear. She would not allow fear to corrupt her.

"How is that possible?" Amanda groaned, straining to keep an eye on the wraiths.

Emily's suit failed completely, and she became fully visible again. At that moment, the two wraiths dove, skeletal arms at their sides, their bodies aimed directly for Amanda and Jess.

"Separate!" Amanda shouted. She needn't have—

Jess knew the danger of standing too close and making themselves an easy target. She was already moving away.

Amanda stood her ground as Jess hurried around the carousel counterclockwise. The wraiths fell, two rockets aimed right at her. Just as they split apart, Amanda *pushed* as hard as she could. The wraiths flipped over like they'd been hit by a hurricane wind, blown so high into the sky that they vanished in the dark.

"Guys!" Nick shouted. "Package delivered!"

Something rectangular was clinging to the neck of the Jingles carousel horse.

Tim bravely charged the one remaining pig. He kicked it in the snout. It squealed, turned, and ran. "Nick! I'll cover you! Go for it!"

Nick jumped the rail and jogged alongside the moving carousel until his pace matched its speed. He leaped onto the spinning platform and ran clockwise, shortening the distance to Jingles.

"More . . . of them!" Jess shouted.

Overtakers emerged from all sides: snakes, a warthog, a pair of skeletons from Haunted Mansion.

It didn't make sense, Jess thought. The Keepers had finished off the Overtakers. There had to be some explanation. But the wraiths . . . the Haunted Mansion skeletons . . . She strained for some kind of answer.

And there it was. There she was.

"Not . . . possible," Jess muttered. "Mandy, look!"

The dark vision before her wasn't like the villainess's former self. It was like she'd been put back together by a five-year-old. Her shoulders slanted drastically to one side like the Hunchback; one of her legs was shorter than the other. Her eyes were not level on her face; in fact her head looked as if it had been sat on and squished. But her green skin and black clothing, with its purple lining, identified her clearly. Unmistakably.

The crippled Maleficent limped toward the carousel, her longer leg dragging roughly against the ground, a black raven perched on her shoulder, a staff in her left hand supporting her. Behind her, stepping like a bridesmaid, came Tia Dalma, the Creole witch doctor.

The apparition glowed green. She looked as if every step hurt, and moved like a female Frankenstein—something incorrectly, improperly reassembled and resurrected.

The approach of the creatures continued, unrelentingly.

"Nick, make it quick!" Tim said, his voice breaking in terror.

Nick reached for the package attached to Jingles.

"WAIT!" Jess cried. "It has to be one of us!" She didn't know if she'd dreamed this, or if seeing Maleficent had caused it, but *she knew*. "Hologram to hologram!" she called out, already up on the moving carousel. "I've got it!"

She met up with Nick and pulled the device from the neck of Jingles. The package had been cross-taped and was difficult to dislodge, but soon Jess had it in her hologram hands. The carousel spun. She ran to the edge. Nick followed. They jumped.

"I don't think they want Tim or me," Nick called out for all to hear. "I think we can hold them off for you."

"Not how we roll!" Amanda called. "We go together. And now! We do *not* want to tangle with that thing."

Working fast, Jess unwrapped the package. "It's a phone and a note. From Philby!"

"We need to go now!" Amanda said. The wolf was slinking closer, nearing her hologram at a steady pace.

Maleficent continued her slow approach. She waved her staff; the wolf yipped and backed away from Amanda. *Interesting*, Amanda thought. The dark fairy wanted the girls for herself.

"Boys first!" Amanda called. "Then Jess and Emily. I'll *push* and buy us time to get through the castle. Go!"

From the Keepers, Jess had learned the importance of working as a team and the role of leadership. In situations like this, you didn't stop to argue. She ran toward the castle, Philby's package in hand. The two boys got ahead of her. Emily was at her side.

Amanda pushed, *hard*. Maleficent arched her back but did not stumble. The raven blew off her shoulder and tried to fly, but tumbled. Amanda felt her strength tapped. First the wraiths, now Maleficent. She didn't have it in her to run, to catch up with the others.

Jess looked desperately over her shoulder. An unsteady Maleficent fought to regain her balance. By the carousel, Amanda slouched. Jess stopped, the others halting with her, at the entrance to the castle tunnel.

"Mandy!"

The creatures closed in on Amanda.

"Mandy! RUN!!!!" Jess tearfully cried.

Amanda looked at her. Then at the creatures and Maleficent, drawing ever closer.

I love you, she mouthed silently to Jess. She struggled toward the spinning carousel, fell onto it, pulled herself up, and moved toward Jingles.

"MANDY!!!" Jess was on her knees. Maleficent was nearly to the carousel.

Amanda climbed onto Jingles. As the platform spun, she lost sight of her friends.

And they, of her.

When Jingles next appeared, the horse stood empty.

Amanda had vanished.

Into the past.

64

HELLO, GOOD-BYE

A FEW MINUTES PAST 2 A.M., Finn and Philby walked away from King Arthur Carrousel in a somber mood.

"We should have talked him out of keeping the ink around," Philby said.

"That wasn't going to happen. He's Walt Disney. He's not about to hand over a vial of magical ink to some kids he barely knows."

"But if it's here . . . if Hollingsworth has any shot at getting it—"

"I know!" Finn said. "Believe me, I know."

"If my phone doesn't reach them," Philby said. "If the Cryptos don't allow the girls to be DHIs, we're never going home."

"We've been over this. We can't be negative. We have to stay positive."

"I thought Charlene was the cheerleader."

"Ha-ha! Have you wondered why Walt didn't try to lock up Hollingsworth?"

"For what? Trespassing? I think he's had enough. I don't think he wants anything to do with him."

"Yeah, you're probably right." Finn tried to think of something positive to say. They were stuck, sixty years in the past. The only phone—Philby's—that could manually effect a Return had been surrendered to a carousel horse and had disappeared, maybe forever. Only a perfect string of events and permissions sixty years in the future would allow him and the other Keepers to see their families and friends again.

"You okay?" Philby asked.

"Not really."

"Willa and I are so . . . We're such good friends. Maybeck and Charlene, too. That must be tough on you. I realize that."

"It's okay. We're all friends. Charlene is acting weird toward me. I don't know what's going on."

"She's always liked you. You know that."

"It's not that. I'm just . . . confused. I miss Amanda."

Finn heard running feet behind them. His nerves spiked—had to be the hooligans! Philby heard it, too; he instinctively ducked and pivoted, preparing to defend himself.

Finn wondered about the power of thought. Like Jess, he had successfully envisioned the future on several occasions. And here he was, doing it again. He was missing Amanda so much, so deeply, that he'd painted a mental picture of her, looking more beautiful than ever, running toward him. His brain had gone so far as to hear her shoes slap the pavement. Imagination apparently had no bounds.

It wasn't Amanda but Philby's astonishment that told him he had it all wrong. "What . . . the . . . hel—?"

"Hello!" the girl called. Amanda's voice. Amanda's face. Amanda's run.

The figure threw herself into Finn's open arms. He caught her and spun her around, the two of them laughing loudly, spinning, the castle and star-filled sky spinning with them. They held one another, laughing and giggling. They could have been in Paris or Rome or Times Square. It was by far the most romantic moment of Finn's short life.

He never wanted to let go.

65

TEARS OF JOY, TEARS OF PAIN

JESS CRIED. At any other time, she would have been thrilled to be sitting in a living room chair in the Dream Suite. Not today.

When Amanda crossed over, Jess had fainted and hit her head. Tim, Emily, and Nick had carried her briefly before Joe's team caught up.

Through her tears, Jess reread Philby's instructions—he wanted them to use his phone to effect the Keepers' Return.

"The note says they, the Keepers, worked out everything with Walt's pen," Jess told Joe. "Philby thinks you guys won't help them, that Mandy and I are their only chance of returning, of getting back."

"He has that wrong," Joe said. "Of course we'll help, but the Legacy changes when we can do it."

"He doesn't know that. He wants me to return them tonight. They're expecting me to return them tonight using Philby's phone." The tears started again. She felt so embarrassed by the crying.

"Amanda will explain the Legacy to them."

"The first time Finn crossed over, he lost his memory."

"I'd forgotten that. But it was when he returned, wasn't it?" Joe said. "We don't know what state he was in when he arrived in the past."

"He didn't remember, so no one knows."

"That is problematic," Joe said. An associate leaned over to whisper in his ear. Joe sighed. "You'll all be signing new documents in the morning. Right now, I think it's best we get what's left of a night's sleep, and let tomorrow work itself out."

"And if it doesn't?" Jess asked, her voice stinging. "Work itself out?"

Joe placed a caring hand on Jess's shoulder. "This is Disneyland. It always does."

"I need you to promise me something," Jess said to him privately.

"Go ahead."

"If the others in the Tink Tank try to convince you not to mess with the past, to leave things the way they are, I want you to take this," she said, placing Philby's phone in his large hand. "Philby had a work-around to manually return them. You have to promise me you will bring them—bring us—back."

"'Us'? What's this 'us'?"

"What if Amanda didn't get the message to them? We can't risk it. You're going to write the message about the Legacy on my arms. Right now, before anyone stops us."

"Am I?"

"You are. And then you're going to create a diversion to allow me to get out of this suite." She waited for Joe to object. He did not. "I'm able to dream the future. Right now, that's much more important in the past."

"We both know how twisted this sounds, right?" Joe said. "I'm not alone in this."

"Promise me."

"I promise. But what if you do slip out of here? What do think you're going to do?"

"The sun isn't up yet," Jess said, a tiny smile of satisfaction playing across her lips. "And I have a date with a music box."

Don't miss the next adventure:

A KINGDOM KEEPERS NOVEL

THE RETURN

BOOK THREE

DISNEY AT LAST

KEEP READING FOR A SNEAK PEEK
AT THE NEXT BOOK IN THE SERIES

1

GRAY FINGERS OF DEAD TREES twisting toward the sky warned of just how far he was from civilization. The still water of the Mississippi swamp absorbed the tarry black of the night sky, creating a crater, a void in the earth's surface, bottomless and dangerous. It held secrets, whispered of curses and secret burials. Sticks rose like bones from its muddy surface. A slice of yellow moon, shrouded in wisps of rapidly moving cloud, proved too weak to throw shadows, yet strong enough to reveal the stark landscape.

The man riding in the black chauffeur-driven 1953 Buick Roadmaster's backseat looked away from the water, as if witnessing a secret act he had no business seeing. No business being here. Four hours from the airport, where his private plane had landed. Three hours of nothing but the occasional deserted gas station or dirt roads leading nowhere. He lit a cigarette and smoked it aggressively.

His driver consulted a large foldable map and then monitored the car's odometer, alert for an upcoming turn. It was 1955; handheld cell phones wouldn't be in use for thirty years; GPS wouldn't be in public use for another forty.

"When we arrive," he instructed the driver, "you are not to leave the car no matter what you may see."

"Yes, sir."

"Doors locked."

"Yes, sir."

"You know these parts?" he asked the man.

"I know *of* them, I guess you could say. Back a couple years—forty-eight, forty-nine it was—a young girl and her mamma went missing out this way. Canoe trip, I believe. God rest their souls."

"Are you scared?"

"I don't scare easily."

"Answer the question."

"I am. Yes, sir. Folks like us, like you and me, are not welcome here. These folks keep to themselves, to their ways. You might say they operate by their own laws. I've heard not even the po-lice travel out this far."

"No heroics."

"No, sir."

"You drop me. Come back in an hour. If you don't see me, leave as quickly as you can."

"Now that just goes against everything in my job description, Mr. Johnson."

The man in the backseat nearly chuckled at hearing

his alias spoken; he'd forgotten his personal secretary had hired the car anonymously for him. This was no typical business trip.

"You tell your dispatcher it was on my orders. My secretary will back you up."

"Yes, sir. I'll do as you say."

The car slowed; the driver flicked the turn signal, its dashboard indicator flashing red throughout the interior. It seemed as much a warning for those in the car as an alert for other vehicles. The car swung right down a potholed and puddled lane narrowed by encroaching vines and spiny brambles. A mile passed, the dirt track as tight as a throat, swallowing the car as it passed through.

"No one done come this way in a long, long time. You sure 'bout them directions?" The driver used the wipers to repel the tangles of spiderwebs and insect cocoons covering the windshield.

"The swamp water is what connects these people, not roads. It would have been faster for us in a boat."

"You wouldn't catch me dead in a boat out this way." The driver laughed. "I'm likely wrong 'bout that. Might be the only way you'd find me. Dead, I mean." He slowed the vehicle. The branches scraped the car's exterior, screeching like newborns. "I keep up like this, won't have no paint left."

"Another half mile."

"Won't be no road, another half mile."

"Just the same: another half mile." The man sat back patting the sweat off his brow with a neatly pressed handkerchief.

"Better be someplace to turn around. Ain't no way I can back up in this kind of dark. Feel like we've been eaten by a snake. Jonah and the whale. Know what I mean?"

Exactly half a mile farther they reached a spot where the vines and swamp grasses had been whacked short by a sharp blade. A long, rickety dock connected to a lazily erected tin-roofed shanty the size of a one-car garage. The smell of wood smoke hung in musty air thick with mosquitoes. The passenger calling himself Mr. Johnson walked the docks length as the car perfected a seven-point turn to reverse direction. The car waited, facing out.

The man walking out to the dock believed the smooth brown rocks, arranged like stepping stones alongside, to be a form of environmental decoration. When they moved, his breath caught. Humanoid figures stood up, men and women, silhouetted waist deep in the turbid lake. Their dark skin, yellowed by the light of the moon, looked sickly and grotesque. It took a moment to realize the figures were neither living nor dead, but in a suspended state between the two. Hypnotized, perhaps. Drugged? Or, more likely, long left for dead.

Together, the creatures strode toward the dock,

streaming wakes behind, blocking any chance of the man's return to shore. They pulled themselves up onto the squealing wood, dripping a dark goo too congealed to be water. The man quickened his pace, which only served to aggravate the twelve figures as they moved more urgently toward him.

A wizened, crippled thing appeared in the shanty's open doorway. He? She? It leaned upon a crooked hardwood cane, one shoulder higher than the other, knees buckled. Clumps of what had to be hair hung from its head, covering an animal-skin tunic. Hair beads clattered like dull bells.

The water-things advanced, now so close the passenger could feel cold breath on the back of his neck. A disgusting smell, like old hamburger left too long in the fridge, overcame him.

The beaded, bent creature waved its open palm. The water-things grunted and moaned—dogs denied a meal. They backed away and stepped off the dock, splashing into the water.

"Join me, if you will," said it with the cane. "Youse welcome to set a spell."

"I am—"

"Amery Hollingsworth."

"Close enough. Astonishing." Amery Hollingsworth had not supplied his name.

"Youse gots youself three young 'uns, all boys, and a missus."

"Impossible!"

It smiled crookedly. "I'm a boastful sort. You must forgive an old man his small pleasures." The broken and bent thing indicated a well-worn stump stool, its wood polished by decades of human contact. Firelight caught shadow images on the bare walls in a rapid-fire slide show. There were six such stumps arranged around a small open fire at the room's center. Nothing larger than twigs crackled as they burned.

Hollingsworth took a seat facing the . . . man. Yes, an old, old black man with slate-gray cataracts for eyes. His voice was rougher than the skin on his hands.

"Your buggy left youse behind, son."

"He'll return in an hour," said Hollingsworth. "It has taken me three years to find you."

"Me, or a man *like* me?" The crippled man chortled.

"What kind of man is that?"

"Youse the one comin' here, no invite. Youse best tell me."

Hollingsworth nodded. "A man with a certain . . . reputation."

"Such as?"

"Reanimation," Hollingsworth stated bluntly.

"That right there, a big word. This right here, a simple man."

"You've turned sticks into snakes."

"So did Moses. Don't youse make me into no Moses. 'Sides, I done rocks into frogs, never no sticks. Them sticks ain't living. That right there no easy thing, son. Leave that to thems above."

"A humble servant serving what master?"

"Ain't right to go asking no question you can't handle."

"I can handle more than you might think."

"I don't do much that there thinking, son. Me is more just a part of things. The nature of things. Ash and water. Blood and wine." He reached into a shallow pocket on the tunic, hesitated, and then withdrew a four-foot water moccasin, still dripping wet. It could not have fit into that pocket.

He threw it at Hollingsworth, who erupted off the stump and slapped the thing to the side. It clattered to the wooden planks. A leg bone of some kind, bare and bright, no longer a snake.

The old creature chuckled. "Yep. Figured as much." He shuffled over, picked up the bone, and threw it into the water; a snake swam away on the surface. "Why you here, son?"

Hollingsworth sat down and wiped his brow with

a starched handkerchief. "I propose a partnership," he said.

"Why on God's precious earth should I listen to such poppycock? Mine is not a gift to be bought or sold. That would be sinful."

"Bartered then, negotiated."

"A trade? I think not. Youse come a long way for nothing, Mr. Amery. It is no short walk back down that there road. Your man not coming. I seen it in his heart."

"I offer you your own . . ." Hollingsworth searched for the correct word. "Circle, I believe it's called."

"I's work lonesome. No need no circle."

"A traveler," Hollingsworth said, "can always use sorcerers and sorceresses."

"Words. A man comes into another man's abode, he must be right careful with his words. I's but a humble servant."

Hollingsworth tugged at his suit trousers, unbuttoned his collar, and loosened his tie. "I can provide you witches, warlocks, maids, and servants. Your own kingdom. I can elevate your *reputation* from a shrimp-eating swamp priest to dark lord of your own kingdom. We work together, you and I. We achieve a greatness both of us want. A kingdom, if you will, never before experienced on this earth since the Dark Ages."

The old man's eyes rolled into the back of his head

in an expression of pure pleasure. "Youse keeps on talking, son. A poet, youse is."

"Imagined, but never realized. Conceived of, but rarely demonstrated. I offer you a kingdom, a circle, comprised not of those dead-eyed stumbling zombies out there, but witches with power, real power. The kind of power it takes centuries to develop. I lack the ability to control such fiends, even if I could create them, reanimate them. You, on the other hand, can do both."

"I's done no man's bidding but me own."

Hollingsworth took a long, calculated breath. "I don't venture into such an arrangement lightly. We'll take a blood oath, me and you. I'm aware you could . . . terminate me and our relationship. You won't kill someone who shares your blood."

The strange, bent man examined Hollingsworth, head tilted, clouded eyes roaming. "Youse done exaggerated your powers of persuasiveness, son. If I done wants, I kills you here and now."

"I could have gone to she of the desert or the great beast of the snows. I came here."

The man shuddered. "A mouth like yours is trouble."

"I had a feeling about you," Hollingsworth said. He met eyes with the Traveler for the first time, well aware he risked a spell being cast. "We travel to the edge of the great sea, to the city of the Angels."

"I's hears of this place," the man said contemplatively. "'Course I do. Whys you think an old bent soul like mine would bother, son?"

"You've dreamed of it," Hollingsworth said. "You've *seen* it in your future."

"My future, unlike youse, stretches far."

"You can see my future?"

"Youse think these old eyes give me vision?" He chortled again. "Youse one ambitious man."

"The Lost Angels."

"I heard youse."

Hollingsworth dipped his hand into a pocket and removed a straight edge razor. He unfolded the blade and it glinted in orange firelight. "Shall we?"